It wouldn't be the first time the Executioner had been forced to rethink a mission

The chill draft caused by the train's motion buffeted him and pulled at his clothing. From the tracks the ground fell away in a long grassy slope. Some way ahead he could see clusters of lights, indicating some habitation. A town. That meant people and maybe the chance to gain some other kind of transportation.

The sudden shriek of the train's whistle alerted him. The train reduced its speed somewhat. He watched the ground some feet below. It still seemed to be moving by at a dangerous speed.

He figured it wasn't going to get better than this. He was about to take a calculated risk—one that might leave him injured. But if he decided to stay on the train he could find himself in the hands of the authorities and his freedom might become a thing of the past. Bolan swung around so he faced the way the train was moving, waited for the clearest patch of slope and went for it.

MACK BOLAN ®
The Executioner

The Executioner
Don Pendleton's®

DESPERATE CARGO

A GOLD EAGLE BOOK FROM
WORLDWIDE®

TORONTO • NEW YORK • LONDON
AMSTERDAM • PARIS • SYDNEY • HAMBURG
STOCKHOLM • ATHENS • TOKYO • MILAN
MADRID • WARSAW • BUDAPEST • AUCKLAND

Recycling programs
for this product may
not exist in your area.

First edition April 2010

ISBN-13: 978-0-373-64377-6

Special thanks and acknowledgment to
Mike Linaker for his contribution to this work.

DESPERATE CARGO

It is easy to be brave behind a castle wall.

—Welsh proverb

The men who hide behind their wealth and pretend to be brave will pay the ultimate price.

—Mack Bolan

THE
MACK BOLAN
LEGEND

Nothing less than a war could have fashioned the destiny of the man called Mack Bolan. Bolan earned the Executioner title in the jungle hell of Vietnam.

But this soldier also wore another name—Sergeant Mercy. He was so tagged because of the compassion he showed to wounded comrades-in-arms and Vietnamese civilians.

Mack Bolan's second tour of duty ended prematurely when he was given emergency leave to return home and bury his family, victims of the Mob. Then he declared a one-man war against the Mafia.

He confronted the Families head-on from coast to coast, and soon a hope of victory began to appear. But Bolan had broken society's every rule. That same society started gunning for this elusive warrior—to no avail.

So Bolan was offered amnesty to work within the system against terrorism. This time, as an employee of Uncle Sam, Bolan became Colonel John Phoenix. With a command center at Stony Man Farm in Virginia, he and his new allies—Able Team and Phoenix Force—waged relentless war on a new adversary: the KGB.

But when his one true love, April Rose, died at the hands of the Soviet terror machine, Bolan severed all ties with Establishment authority.

Now, after a lengthy lone-wolf struggle and much soul-searching, the Executioner has agreed to enter an "arm's-length" alliance with his government once more, reserving the right to pursue personal missions in his Everlasting War.

Prologue

During its long, slow voyage from Thailand, the *Orient Venturer* made a number of calls into friendly ports. Sometimes it was to take on more cargo, or to unload. It refueled and during those stays in port the captain played host to officials who marked his cargo as legitimate and departed the ship with considerably more cash in their pockets than they'd had when they boarded.

The *Orient Venturer's* voyage was one it had made a number of times. In its hold, or in the steel seagoing containers secured to its rusting and scarred deck plates, it carried the mixed cargo that marked it as a ship of all trades. The cargo—mainly clothing and electrical goods, manufactured in Asian sweatshops—would find its way into stores and retail outlets spread across Europe. Cheaply made, the goods would be sold at marked-up prices for Western consumers. These items brought a fair profit for the company that owned the ship.

One container, however, held cargo that would net an even greater profit for the men behind the *Orient Venturer.*

The special cargo was stowed in a special container. A close inspection would have shown that the container had been altered to facilitate its cargo.

In the roof were a number of vented grilles to allow air to travel in and out of the steel box. This was necessary in order to keep the cargo of young Thai women and children alive.

The eldest woman was twenty-two, the youngest twelve. They were all kidnap victims, intended for sale when they reached their destination. They had no choice in the matter because they were virtual slaves. They'd been stolen from their homes for induction into the twilight world of human trafficking. At journey's end they would be passed along to their new masters. Some would be forced into the garment industry where they would work endless hours for starvation wages. Others would be moved into prostitution, the sex industry, or they would go as personal playthings for wealthy clients. The younger and prettier a girl, the more likely she would be bought for sexual gratification.

Business was thriving. The *Orient Venturer* made regular trips delivering the cargo to mainland Europe and the United Kingdom. The men behind the business were based in Rotterdam and London. The organization conducted business globally, procuring assets for clients in the Middle East and the United States. It was well run, protected because of weak legislation and the inability of legal forces to act without absolute and watertight cases. One slip, one word or phrase, on a document, and the whole case could be thrown out of court. Proof positive was almost an impossibility, and although a dedicated effort was being made, no indictments had yet been achieved. Government task forces working together had their hands tied. They struggled for months to concentrate their investigations only to find that their superiors, sensitive to the demands of the courts, would shake their heads and demand even more proof.

The task forces looked for ways to gather their evidence and took the decision to insert undercover agents into the organization in an effort to obtain what they needed.

Dean Turner and Ron Bentley were seasoned agents, working for the joint task force. When they had been asked to take on a covert assignment to infiltrate the trafficking group in Rotterdam they didn't need to be asked twice. Once assigned they distanced themselves from the main group, setting themselves up to watch suspected members of the trafficking organization. Over a couple of months they concentrated on the Rotterdam group, looking for any members who seemed to be vulnerable to turning, and finally fixed on a single individual who expressed some vocal dissatisfaction with his position within the organization.

The initial contact went well. Their man seemed to have a grievance against his employers and a tendency to complain about them to the American undercover agents. They spent time with him, sympathizing with his complaints, and slowly reeled him into their confidence. In the end he agreed to provide them with evidence that would give the task force solid evidence into the workings of the trafficking group.

However, when the agents made the rendezvous to meet their contact they were ambushed, disarmed and taken to an isolated location.

They were told they were going to be made examples of—used to show the task force that further efforts to break the organization were useless. The traffickers wanted the international task force to know powerful forces ranged against them. The organization had high-profile protection. They could not be touched. No one could harm them. The agents would be used to make the task force realize they were simply wasting their time.

For three days the agents were savagely tortured, their naked bodies abused and broken. Photographs were taken to be sent to the task force and a final message stated where the bodies could be found.

The stark warning, showing the brazen contempt the traffickers had for the task force, had its effect. After the bodies had been located and removed, the task force was ordered to stand back and reassess its operational method. There was a need to regroup—by no means to admit defeat, but the clear message to the task force from the traffickers had got through, and it was realized that the enemy had the upper hand.

1

From the window of his hotel room Mack Bolan could see the distant configuration of Rotterdam Port, the night sky ablaze with lights. He saw a vast sprawl of warehouse units, cranes and endless rows of steel cargo containers. He was seeing the vista through the sheeting rain covering the city, blown in from the cold swells of the North Sea. Across the stretch of water was England, the secondary target of Bolan's mission.

The Executioner's presence in Rotterdam was down to intel he received during a briefing with Hal Brognola back in Washington. That clandestine meeting between the man from Justice and Bolan had kick-started the Executioner's journey to Europe. After touching down at Schiphol Airport, Bolan had ridden a local train to Rotterdam and his prebooked room. The weather had been rough for most of the flight and stayed the course while Bolan had transferred to his hotel. It was midevening, the sky already dark. Bolan had a rendezvous with a contact the next day, so he figured he would have an early meal and turn in. The turbulent weather during the flight had denied him sleep, so a solid night's rest was advisable.

Bolan turned from the window when he heard a tap on his door. He crossed the room and opened up. A trolley was wheeled inside carrying the meal he had ordered. Bolan handed the service girl a tip, then closed and locked the door after she left. Bolan was on alert. He wasn't the paranoid type who saw threats lurking in every corner. Even so, past experience had taught him never to leave anything to chance.

He took off the covers and checked the meal. It was exactly what he had ordered. A steak, potatoes, salad. He pulled up a chair and settled down to eat. The food was good. Only when he was done did he activate his tri-band cell phone and tap the speed-dial number that would connect him with Hal Brognola. The connection hummed and buzzed, then the big Fed's voice reached Bolan.

"So how is Rotterdam?"

"Cold. It's raining like it's in for the duration. I'm fine. You have any updates for me?"

"No. Status hasn't changed much since we talked and you flew out. The operation is stalled. The heads are talking. Trying to come up with a fresh way of moving on, but as of now it's a no-go. Those two agents getting killed has hit hard. You know why. Suspicions there was a mole inside the task force appear to have been proved. Turner and Bentley were betrayed and the fact we have someone operating inside the group and capable of passing along information makes everyone suspicious of the man next to him. No one is going to commit to anything."

"Let's hope my meeting in the morning throws up something useful," the Executioner said.

Brognola hesitated before he replied.

"Tread carefully with this man Bickell. Hasn't been proved he was the one who turned Turner and Bentley over to the opposition but he was the only man who had access to them. The more I think about it, the less I'm in favor of you using him."

"Right now we don't have anything else. I'm not about to go into this meet blind."

"Striker, these people are bad. You saw what they did to our two mans. They work a business that treats human beings like so much merchandise. Don't believe they won't do the same to you given the chance."

"Understood, pal, now quit worrying and give me some good news."

"Your Brit buddy," Brognola said, referring to David McCarter, the Phoenix Force commander, "has a contact for you in London. He can set you up with specialist equipment. I'm sending a photo over your phone for identification. And I'll text a name and phone number to set up your meet. This man is supposed to be good. He'll sort out anything you want. Anything else you need right now?"

"Just a good night's sleep," Bolan said. "I'll be in touch."

Bolan checked the information Brognola had sent to him. A half hour later he turned in, clicking off the light. He lay staring at the rain-flecked window, his mind still active as he reviewed the past couple of days and the events that had brought him to Rotterdam and his upcoming meeting with a man who might turn out to be a Judas.

Two Days Earlier, Washington

DRESSED IN CASUAL clothing he might have been just another tourist taking in the sights of the nation's capital.

But Mack Bolan was a world away from being just that. As he strolled around in the pale sunlight, observing the scene around him, Hal Brognola fell into step beside him.

"Looking good as ever," Brognola said lightly. "Your life-style must suit you."

"You didn't call me just to boost my confidence, Hal."

"Would you believe I need your help on a problem?"

"Go ahead."

"A joint US-UK-European task force has been compromised by the deaths of two of its undercover agents. Dean Turner and Ron Bentley. They had gotten close to the group the task force was investigating. Human trafficking on a big scale. Working out of Europe and serving the needs of clients in Europe and the U.S. Striker, this is as nasty as it gets. These people are running a virtual slave trade. Men, women and even kids." Brognola pointed at the slim briefcase he was carrying. "I have the whole dossier in here. Details the perps. Their locations. Right now the operation has stalled because there's some concern how deep infiltration might have gone. The whole thing is on hold. And while that happens the suspects are still operating. Evidence against them is all suspicion but no substance. Nowhere near enough to even haul anyone in. It's a big organization. Run by an influential head honcho with top-class protection. Hugo Canfield. British citizen. He has a hotshot lawyer with an impeccable record standing behind him. Dutch man called Ludwig van Ryden. And he uses that man every time one of his clients even gets a parking ticket."

"What do you need, Hal?"

"Someone without ties to any part of the task force. A clean slate. No allegiances. Nothing that connects." The big Fed paused. "And someone who can leave the book of rules at home."

Brognola opened his case and extracted a thick folder. He handed it to Bolan. "We can see the end result of this business, Striker. What those bastards do to people. I want to reach the head and cut it off. The task force has its hands tied right now and I'm damn tired of the restrictions holding us back. If I had my way I'd go in all guns blazing but I'd have to fight bureaucracy first and last. I need a lever. Something I can use to force the game into the open."

"Where would I start?"

"Our dead agents had an informant. Part of the organization but he convinced our mans he wanted to quit and was willing to cooperate. Name of Wilhelm Bickell. Based in Rotterdam, where the traffickers are said to have what Bickell called a distribution point. We don't know if that's true because our mans were killed before they got that information to us. All we have is a cell phone contact number for him."

"It's thin," Bolan said. "But I've started with less." He weighed the folder in his hand. "I'll need credentials. Anything else you can conjure up."

Brognola nodded. "No problem." He tapped the folder. "The phrase *read it and weep* applies pretty well here, Striker."

THE EXECUTIONER SPENT most of the day going through the contents of the explicit data. It covered suspects, the trafficking group known as Venturer Exports and its head, Hugo Canfield. Its grip on human trafficking was widespread and from the text of the reports Bolan became aware of the callous indifference of the people running the enterprise. The hub for Venturer Exports was mainland Europe and the U.K. Its market was worldwide and even Mack Bolan, well versed in the evil manifested through man's indifference to human suffering, was forced to sit back and take a moment's respite. It appeared that the practice of slavery was still thriving. From his reading it seemed that the majority of victims involved came from those ravaged parts of the world where recent conflicts had created rich hunting grounds for the traffickers. They scavenged through Asian and Eastern European countries, snatching people off the streets, collecting them from holding camps. The countless numbers of displaced people were seldom missed. Officials were paid off, heads turned and no questions asked. The victims were bundled into containers and taken by road, across borders where money replaced transit visas, and the human cargo was waved through without an inspection. The final destination of the converging containers appeared to be Rotterdam, and from there the merchandise was sent to whichever market placed its order.

The slaves provided cheap labor for sweatshops, for service industries, where the employers held the workers illegally.

They were in foreign countries without proper papers, earning little money and constantly under the threat of violence if they made any kind of protest. Young women, chosen for their good looks, were channeled into the many-tentacled sex industry, from making adult movies to working the streets. And there was the ever-present shadow of the drug business in the background. The data Brognola had provided included photographs that emphasized the ever-present dangers encroaching on the lives of the traffickers' victims. The sick, the dying and the dead. Drug affliction. The punishment meted out to a victim who had rebelled. Or those who simply succumbed to the pitiful life forced on them.

Read it and weep.

Brognola's words had not been far from the truth. Venturer Exports and the men profiting from it had to be stopped. The Executioner was onboard.

2

Wilhelm Bickell, average height, near-bald head glistening from the rain, hunched his shoulders beneath the long raincoat. Bolan recognized him from the photograph in the folder Brognola had provided. The image had been taken from a distance, but it was not difficult to identify the man. Bickell had an extraordinarily plain face. His outstanding feature was his large, crooked nose supporting a pair of heavy eyeglasses. According to the intelligence relating to the man, Bickell was a fixer for Venturer Exports. The detail provided by Turner and Bentley had him down as dissatisfied with his position. A disgruntled employee passed over by his superiors, tired of being treated as mere hired help. He was supposedly ready to turn against them for the simple emotion of revenge. The two agents had nurtured his feelings, fueling his resentment. They had been preparing Bickell as an aide in gaining possession of evidence that might have turned the task-force investigation to a positive outcome. That hope died after they had been lured into a meeting, taken captive and tortured savagely before being killed.

The Executioner kept those thoughts in mind as he stepped away from the café door and crossed the sidewalk to where Bickell was standing.

"Wilhelm Bickell? I'm Cooper."

Bickell nodded.

Bolan took his hand from his coat pocket and palmed the leather wallet holding the U.S. Justice Department badge

Brognola had supplied. Next to the badge, beneath a plastic cover was a laminated card with Bolan's picture and cover name on it.

Bickell's eyes, magnified by the lenses of his glasses, examined the big American's face. The only contact he had had with Bolan was over the phone, arranging the meet. He recognized the voice.

"This is not a very satisfactory way for us to meet, you understand. *Ja?*"

"Under the circumstances I was given little choice. Turner and Bentley didn't leave much in the way of contact details. You remember them, don't you?"

Bickell visibly stiffened. Red spots colored his pale cheeks.

"Of course I remember them. We were working together. Am I under suspicion concerning their deaths? Perhaps you are not aware of the risk I took even associating with them. My own life is in danger now."

"We're all in a risky position, Bickell. I came to Rotterdam to try and pick up where the others left off. Are you willing to continue cooperating?"

"Of course," Bickell said. "I am ready to help any way I can."

A little too quickly, Bolan thought. Slow down, Bickell, you're making yourself obvious.

"We should walk," Bickell suggested. "I really feel I am being watched. You understand? *Ja?*"

"Let's go," Bolan said.

Bickell led the way along the sidewalk. The rain and the early hour had reduced the number of pedestrians. They walked for a few hundred feet before Bickell paused at the mouth of a side street. His hesitation warned Bolan, but for the present he played along.

"There is a quiet coffee shop down here," Bickell said. "We can talk in private. *Ja?*"

Bolan fell in alongside the man and they walked along the

street. The tall buildings on either side reduced the rain to a slight mist. They also cut the intrusion of sound and it enabled Bolan to pick up the soft murmur of a car engine and the sound of wet tires rolling along the street. From the corner of his eye Bolan saw Bickell's shoulders hunch under his coat. The sound of his footsteps sharpened as he began to walk faster.

"We running out of time?" Bolan asked.

Bickell said something Bolan couldn't catch. But he understood the threat offered by the pistol that emerged from the right-hand pocket of the man's coat. The muzzle aimed at Bolan.

"Over there," Bickell snapped, gesturing with the pistol.

The Executioner saw they were at the entrance to an empty delivery yard, the gates standing open, the adjoining building deserted and quiet. Bickell's gun hand gestured again and Bolan walked ahead, the Dutchman following. As Bolan turned to face Bickell, the car he had heard turned in through the open gateway and rolled to a stop. A tall man climbed out and pushed the wooden gates shut, dropping a metal bar in place. He moved to stand a few feet behind Bickell, hands thrust deep in the pockets of his thick coat. A moment later he was joined by the man who had been behind the wheel of the car.

"Tell me, *Mijnheer* Cooper, are you so trusting it never occurred to you that something like this might happen? Or are you simply stupid?" Bickell asked.

"Look at it from where I'm standing. I only arrived last night and it appears I have already been betrayed by the man who set up Turner and Bentley for execution."

Bickell didn't like the inference, but shrugged it off.

"That was so easy it was almost embarrassing. Those two were so naive they deserved to die. Like so many Americans they believed in trust and loyalty. It was like shooting fish in a barrel."

Bickell said something in Dutch to his two companions. It drew a round of laughter.

"So, Cooper, they sent you in like the Lone Ranger to deal with the bad mans. *Ja?*"

Bickell raised his left hand to wipe at the rain spots on his glasses. It created a thin window of opportunity. It was enough for Bolan to bunch his right hand into a big fist that struck out at Bickell's face. Bolan hit him twice. The blows were powerfully brutal. They slammed into Bickell's mouth and nose, jerking his head around and toppling him against the side of the parked car. Bickell slid across the rain-slick surface, his legs going from under him. He hit the ground on his knees, head dropping. Blood spilled from his battered face.

"For Turner and Bentley," Bolan said softly. "Consider it a down payment."

The pair behind Bickell came alive, producing handguns. They covered Bolan, who had already stepped back, his hands raised in surrender. When they saw he was not going to do anything one of them moved to where Bickell knelt. He reached out a hand and dragged Bickell to his feet, pushing him against the side of the car. He also retrieved the pistol Bickell had dropped. Then he moved up to Bolan and expertly checked him for weapons. Satisfied the American was not armed he rejoined his partner.

Bickell, hands pressed to his bloody face, stared at Bolan. The left lens of his glasses had cracked when Bolan hit him and the single eye left visible blazed with undisguised anger.

"Bastaard." The invective was muffled but there was enough force for Bolan to understand the feeling behind it.

The man who had searched Bolan moved to open the passenger door and roughly hustled Bickell inside. He slammed the door and walked around to the driver's door. He barked a command to his partner, who moved to reopen the gate. Then he gestured at Bolan.

"In the back, Cooper."

Bolan did as he was told. With the gate open the second man

climbed in beside Bolan, covering him. The car started and reversed out onto the street. It was driven to the far end, then picked up a wider street that wound through the city. The thought struck Bolan that no one had made any move to prevent him seeing the way they were going. Their ultimate destination looked to be an intended one-way trip for Bolan. He sat back, taking in the scenery, his agile mind working on that fact. His captors wanted him alive for the present. His future was another matter. Once the opposition had decided how much— or how little—he knew about their operation, his usefulness would end. These people had already shown how little they cared when it came to disposing of unwanted baggage.

With that in mind Bolan prepared himself for what might come. He had no illusions. What waited for him at the end of this drive would be far from pleasant if he failed to make use of any opportunity presenting itself. He was not being driven to a barbecue. Pain and suffering were the only items liable to be on any menu put before Bolan.

He concentrated on his captors. The damage he had inflicted on Bickell would keep the man out of any hard action. His injuries would divert his attention away from Bolan. Not a great victory but at least it had cut the opposition by a third. Until they arrived at their destination Bolan wasn't going to know by how much that percentage might rise. He had assessed the two men accompanying Bickell as solid professionals. It appeared that their orders had been to bring Bolan in alive and unharmed, and they were doing that. Bickell had let his mouth run away with himself and had received the necessary chiding to shut him up temporarily. From the brief time he had been able to watch the others Bolan had seen they were strongly built, capable of handling themselves. And both were armed. Bickell was unarmed, his fallen pistol having been retrieved by the man behind the wheel.

The Executioner sank back in the soft leather seat,

watching the wet streets of Rotterdam slip by. As they eased
through the narrow streets Bolan caught glimpses of the river
that ran through the city. Cranes and warehouses began to
dominate the skyline. They were heading in the direction of
the port. The car made some sharp turns, moving along
narrower streets that edged the main port facility. There were
businesses along this section. Distribution warehouses.
Service industries. Private vehicles were replaced by vans
and trucks. The car made a sharp right turn that took it along
a narrow road that paralleled the water before swinging in
through open gates into a freight yard that had a large warehouse structure at the far end.

There didn't appear to be much activity around the yard.
Bolan noticed a number of large steel containers, some
stacked three high. There was a car parked near the warehouse. They drove over the yard's rutted surface and through
a high doorway into the warehouse. As the car came to a stop
inside Bolan heard the metallic rattle behind them as a metal
roller door was lowered.

Bolan's minder produced his pistol, gesturing. "Get out."

With the pair of minders flanking him Bolan was walked
across to an office block against one wall. The door was
opened and he was pushed inside. Bolan sized up the man
awaiting his arrival.

Well dressed. A sober suit and tie. Expensive. The cold expression on his face did nothing to endear him to Bolan. He had
a fine look to him. Almost delicate. His skin was silky, lips col-
orless, pale blond hair. Rimless glasses with lightly tinted lenses
shaded his gray eyes. He was observing Bolan with an intensity
that could have been intimidating to anyone with less confidence.

"Where's Bickell?" the man asked.

Bolan picked up the English accent.

The minder who had driven the car wagged a thumb in
Bolan's direction.

"There was some aggravation. Willi came off worse," he explained in his heavily accented English. "He's never learned to keep his mouth closed. He's in the car."

The blond Brit leaned forward a little, stroking the tip of his narrow chin.

"I was surprised when you contacted Bickell. Obviously the example of your dead friends failed as the deterrent it was intended to be."

"Did you expect us to ignore it?" Bolan said.

"Had it not occurred to your superiors that Bickell might have been the one who turned on your friends?" The man adjusted the hang of his jacket.

"We guessed. It was decided to draw him out. Give him a chance to repent his misdeeds."

"A sense of humor. I like that in a man. But it isn't going to save you."

"I wasn't expecting it to. I just wanted to get a look at the kind of people who would kill so readily."

"Look, Cooper…is that correct? *Cooper?* Turner and Bentley, or whatever their real names, were dealt with as part of a tactical maneuver." He smiled. "Sounds bloody pretentious, doesn't it? But they were getting a little too close to us at a busy time. Couldn't afford to have them snooping around like that."

Bolan stayed silent, watching the man. He was playing it light, but there was intelligence in those eyes.

"You can't avoid it," Bolan said. "Sooner or later your organization is going to come down. Killing Turner and Bentley shows you're getting scared because the investigation is closing in."

The Brit smiled. Not from bravado. It was clearly from the security that he felt.

"It will never happen, Cooper. Turner and Bentley were blundering around like a pair of blind men. They had no idea

what they were taking on. Just like your bloody task force."
He held up a single finger. "You can't touch us. Understand.
You cannot touch us. Keep sending your sad little agents and
we will get rid of them just like Turner and Bentley. And
you, *Cooper*."

He turned aside to speak to Bickell's heavies. The conversation was brief, words muffled. Then he glanced back at Bolan.

"Now?" asked the man who had driven the car.

"Yes. We get rid of him. No time to play games this time.
Just kill him and dispose of the body." The Brit barely glanced
at Bolan as he made for the door. "Your trip here was a waste
of time. Pity you won't even get to see the sights."

As he passed through the office door the driver attracted
his attention.

"What about Bickell, Mr. Chambers? He *is* becoming a li-
ability. Since we dealt with those Americans he's become
nervous. Scared. He could break. We don't think he should
be trusted any longer."

Chambers stopped in his tracks, turning to face the driver.
His pale face showed twin red blotches on his cheeks.

"What are my orders about using my name? Tell me."

"Never to mention it. I apologize for my error, sir."

The Brit glanced across at Bolan.

The big American shrugged.

"I'm not going to be telling anyone. Am I, Mr. Chambers?"

A thin smile curled Chambers's lips.

"Very true, Cooper. Very true." He turned to the driver.
"Make sure they are *both* taken care of. We can't afford any
more of Bickell's nerves."

Chambers stepped out of the office.

The driver perched on the edge of the office desk. His
partner moved for the first time since they had entered the
office. "Willi?" he asked.

"Bring him in here. Give Chambers a minute to get clear.

You know he prefers not to be around at times like these," the driver said.

"He has no stomach."

"It's what we are paid for."

As the partner left the office Bolan glanced at the driver. "Is the English for my benefit?" he asked.

The driver grinned, seeming to enjoy the question. "Rotterdam can be a very hospitable city. But not exactly so in your case."

"And there I was hoping you might show me around."

The sound of a car engine rose as Chambers drove away, the noise fading quickly. Bolan heard the scrape of shoe leather on the concrete outside the office. The door was pushed open to admit Bickell and the driver's partner. The lower part of Bickell's face was swollen and bloody. The moment he saw Bolan he erupted into a wild verbal assault.

The driver yelled at him. Bickell ignored him, still screaming. Without warning he launched himself at Bolan, arms flailing wildly.

The driver's partner reached out to grab Bickell. He had both hands free, having put his pistol away.

Bolan allowed Bickell to get within a foot or so, then launched himself into action. He caught hold of Bickell's coat, swinging the man off balance, and used him as a battering ram against the driver. Bolan's contained energy lifted Bickell off his feet and he was catapulted into the driver. Locked briefly together the pair tumbled back over the desk, sliding across the smooth surface and over the far edge.

The moment he released Bickell, Bolan swung about and met the driver's partner head-on. Before the man could put up any defense Bolan slammed into him, hitting him in the face with a crippling elbow smash. The man grunted, stunned, briefly stalled, blood gushing from his crushed nose. Bolan hit him again, then caught his shoulders and spun the man around, wrapping his arms around the man's neck. Bolan applied pressure, twisting, until he heard the crunch of crushed vertebrae. He felt the man shudder, body going into spasm, before it became dead weight. Bolan's right hand moved down and located the pistol in the deep pocket of the man's coat. He reached in and hauled the heavy automatic pistol clear. It was a SIG-Sauer P-226. The Executioner knew the weapon well. As he swung the gun up, turning, he let the dead man slip from his grasp. The weapon's muzzle lined up on the desk as the driver struggled upright, head and shoulders coming into view. Bolan's fingers stroked the trigger and released a trio of fast shots into the driver. The slugs cored in through the target's chest. The driver fell back and slammed against the wall, a stunned expression on his face.

As the driver slid sideways, blood smearing the wall, Bickell lurched upright, hands grabbing for the pistol still in the dead man's hand. He snatched it free and turned the muzzle toward Bolan, his finger jerking back on the trigger in a moment of frantic zeal.

The bullet hit the wall behind Bolan. The Executioner returned fire, his double shot blowing through Bickell's upper body and dumping him on the floor. Bickell hunched up in fetal curl.

"Not the way I wanted this to end," Bolan muttered.

3

The Executioner moved from body to body, checking pockets and placing the contents on the desk. He had three handguns and extra magazines. He took a cell phone from Bickell and one from the driver. Wallets offered banknotes and credit cards. The only one with identification was the driver. It gave his name as Rik Vandergelt. Bolan kept that. He also took the banknotes. Cash money was always useful. He pocketed the cell phones.

The Executioner searched the office. He wasn't expecting hard evidence to directly point the finger at the trafficking business. He was just hoping to find something to work with. The desk yielded little of interest. He moved on to the battered wooden filing cabinets standing against one wall. The first held not much more than office stationary. The second had three drawers. Two were empty. The top one had a couple of folders stuffed with invoices. They were all from a company in the U.K. The company, South East Containers, was based near a coastal town that served as a conduit for the container business with Europe. The invoices were dated as far back as a couple of years. Bolan was about to leave the invoices when his attention was caught by the name of the company's director, printed in a small box at the top of the invoice.

In itself the name wouldn't mean very much. A legitimate-sounding company. Legitimate-sounding director.

Except that he had just ordered Mack Bolan's death before walking out of the office.

The director was Paul Chambers.

Bolan folded one of the invoices and slid it into a pocket. As he placed the stack of papers back in the drawer a pale cream envelope he hadn't noticed slipped from the documents. He picked it up and took a look at the address. It was to the same one that the invoices had been sent. The postmark showed it was at least three months old and mailed from Amsterdam. The envelope held a single sheet of good-quality notepaper. The same color as the envelope, the paper was heavy and embossed. The heading showed it was from a law firm in Rotterdam. The brief text in a smart font was in Dutch. One line indicated a time and date a week earlier. Bolan stared at the note, his eyes checking out the printed name at the bottom of the text.

Ludwig van Ryden. The lawyer Brognola's information had named.

Small beginnings.

Bolan had long ago learned never to ignore any lead, no matter the initial insignificance. The letter went into his pocket next to the invoice.

Bolan took the SIG-Sauer and the extra magazines. Leaving the office he crossed to the car that had transported him to the warehouse. He made a quick search that netted him nothing. The car was clean. He debated whether to use the vehicle, making a quick decision to leave it where it was. The car might be fitted with a manufacturer's tracking chip, allowing the opposition pick him up once they realized the vehicle was missing. Bolan decided he would be better off hiring a vehicle himself.

He walked away. It was still raining, the morning overcast. The weather was the least of his concerns. It took him twenty minutes to retrace the route the car had taken. Back on a main thoroughfare he managed to catch a passing cab and asked to be returned to his hotel. Back in his room he stripped off his damp clothing and took a hot shower. Clad in a thick bathrobe he rang room service and ordered a pot of coffee. It arrived quickly and Bolan filled a cup. He had the company invoice and the letter from the man called van Ryden in front of him. He took the pair of cell phones and switched them on. Bickell's phone listed more than two dozen incoming calls, the majority from the same number. Vandergelt's phone showed a couple of calls from the same number. The number matched the one on van Ryden's letterhead.

Bolan activated his phone and called Brognola. His friend's voice was slurry from sleep when he answered. "You get a kick waking me up?"

"Hal, if you insist on going to bed every night, what can I do?"

The big Fed laughed. Bolan heard him moving around before he spoke again.

"How did the meeting with Bickell go?"

"Interesting. You can scratch him off the list. He *was* the one who drew your mans into a trap. Had me walk into a setup with a couple of his Dutch buddies. We went to a rendezvous with a Brit named Chambers. He wasn't too happy with me. Seems your task force was getting close to Venturer Exports. So the hit on your mans was ordered."

"You mentioned Bickell in the past tense."

"After Chambers ordered his local heavies to feed me to the fishes matters got a little heated. Venturer Exports is down three employees."

"Understood. Did you gain any intel?"

"Couple of things. I want you to check into a U.K. company called South East Containers. Director is Paul Chambers. Has to be the same one who wanted me dead. I also found a connection with your lawyer Ludwig van Ryden. Another name for you—Rik Vandergelt. He was one of Chambers's enforcers. See if there's anything on the database."

"Okay. I'll get right on to it. Striker, you need anything else?"

"Right now, no."

"Expect a call," Brognola said.

"I may be on the move."
"No surprise there."

BOLAN DRESSED in one of the suits he had brought with him. He tucked the SIG-Sauer in his belt and buttoned his jacket. From a leather case he took a couple of printed business cards Brognola had provided. They showed Bolan as an executive from a computer software company based in Maryland. It was a fictitious company located at a nonexistent address. The telephone and e-mail contacts would route any caller to an automatic response that would accept the call and promise a return response. Bolan placed the cards in his wallet. He called the front desk and asked for a cab to take him to the *Hofpoort* district of the city. It was in the business center of Rotterdam. Ludwig van Ryden's office was located there.

Bolan dropped his damp clothes into a plastic bag and took them down with him, asking for them to be cleaned and pressed. His cab was already waiting when he emerged from the hotel. The weather had brightened, the rain had stopped. The Executioner settled back for the journey, planning ahead for his anticipated rendezvous with Ludwig van Ryden.

THE OFFICE BLOCK was one of a number in the neat plaza. The notice board outside told him van Ryden occupied a suite on the sixth floor. Bolan made his way toward the entrance, pausing briefly to switch off his phone. Brognola had called during the cab ride to inform him that Ludwig van Ryden was one of the key names on the task-force database. His association with individuals within the trafficking business was known to the force, but they had nothing they could move on with certainty. The man was sharp. His reputation as a lawyer who worked very closely with human rights groups made it difficult to nail. The slightest hint of any possible move against him brought instant and vociferous agitation from influential members of the Dutch establishment. The big Fed provided information that van Ryden had made a number of visits to the U.K. where he had meetings with Paul Chambers and Hugo Canfield.

"Rik Vandergelt is known to Interpol. He served a couple of prison terms a few years back. Since his last incarceration he's managed to stay out of jail. Seems he got himself a hotshot lawyer. Name of van Ryden."

"Keeping it in the family," Bolan said.

The Executioner stepped through the glass doors of the office block, hearing them swish shut behind him. He crossed the art-deco lobby and smiled pleasantly at the young woman behind the expansive reception desk.

"Do I need to sign in?" he asked, placing his hands on the marble-topped counter. "My first visit to Rotterdam. I guess I'm still finding my way around."

The receptionist observed the tall, good-looking man, noting the intense blue eyes and the genuine smile. His voice was deep and a little unsettling. His steady gaze, appreciating her blond beauty, took her by surprise. She was not accustomed to such intimate scrutiny. The sensation was not unpleasant.

"Have you an appointment with anyone?"

Bolan shook his head. He took out one of his business cards and slid it across the counter for the young woman to read.

"I only got in last night. Haven't had the chance to make formal arrangements yet. Would have done it this morning but my meetings went on longer than I expected. Next thing I received a call from my CEO to catch the evening flight to Paris, but to call in and say hello to Mr. van Ryden. We're hoping to meet up with him soon to negotiate some long-term representation with our company." He increased his smile. "Help, please."

She returned his smile and picked up her phone, tapping

in a number. When it was answered she spoke quietly, her eyes never once leaving Bolan's face. When she was finished she replaced the receiver.

"Mr. van Ryden will see you immediately," she said. "He has a meeting in half an hour but says he can spare some time." She directed Bolan to the bank of elevators across the lobby. "Sixth floor. Suite thirty-two."

"If I wasn't leaving in a few hours I would invite you out for dinner."

"If you were not going away I would accept."

"Maybe next time."

"Yes. Maybe next time." She watched him walk to the elevator, giving a sigh before she returned to her duties.

Definitely next time.

BOLAN STEPPED OUT of the elevator, checking the wallboard for directions. Suite thirty-two was to his left. He pushed open the pale wood door and stepped inside. An outer office contained a desk and another attractive young woman. The Dutch seemed to have got it right, Bolan decided.

"Mr. Connor?" the woman asked, pushing to her feet. She was strikingly tall. She guided him to double doors and knocked, pushing open one of the doors to let him enter. It closed firmly behind Bolan.

Ludwig van Ryden's office was wide, spacious, furnished expensively. The man's desk looked large enough to host a dinner party. There was an open laptop computer in the center. The office was a mix of pale wood, glass, stainless steel. Hidden lights illuminated a collection of slender glass sculptures housed in wall cabinets. A half-open door showed a private washroom. Underfoot the carpet was thick and soft.

The lawyer rose from behind his desk to meet Bolan. He was in his forties. A tall, leanly fit man wearing a suit that had probably cost a small fortune. His thick brown hair fell to the collar of his jacket. He came around the desk to take Bolan's hand, his smile showing even white teeth.

"Please sit down, Mr. Connor. Would you like a drink?"

"Thanks, no." Bolan sat in one of the cream leather chairs, watching van Ryden fill a heavy tumbler with whiskey. "You might want to make that a double, van Ryden," he said quietly.

The lawyer half turned, an amused smile on his lips. Then he saw the pistol Bolan was pointing in his direction. For a moment he froze, glass in his hand.

"I don't understand. What is this?"

"*This* is a gun. Taken earlier from a friend of yours. Rik Vandergelt." Bolan saw the color drain from van Ryden's face. The name had meant something to him. "I see I have your attention now."

"I do not know what you mean. The name means nothing to me."

"Right. So you've forgotten that you represented him legally? I'm sure he could have done with your advice a couple of hours ago. Then we have Paul Chambers. And Wilhelm Bickell. I don't suppose you know them, either?"

"Of course not."

"So you'll be even more surprised if I tell you my name isn't Connor. It's Cooper."

The lawyer flinched at the mention of the name. He recovered enough to move the whiskey glass, raising it to his lips and swallowing the liquid in a single gulp. Bolan saw it as a simple ploy to allow van Ryden time to gather himself. When the man returned his gaze to Bolan he had composed himself.

"We could spend the next hour playing word games," van Ryden said. "But that would be a waste of your time and mine, *Mr. Cooper.* So, what is it you want?"

"American agents Turner and Bentley were both murdered

by your associates. Bickell arranged for the same to happen to me. It didn't happen as planned. Bickell is dead. So is Vandergelt," the Executioner said.

"If I knew these people, what am I supposed to understand from what you have told me?"

"It's simple enough. You and your associates are involved up to your necks in human trafficking. I'm here to serve notice. Nothing fancy wrapped up in legal terms. Time is up for all of you. I'm going to close you down. All the way. Mark it in your diary, van Ryden."

The lawyer took a moment to absorb Bolan's words. He looked like a man who couldn't decide whether he had heard the truth, or been fed a line. He ran a hand across his mouth, then wagged a finger in Bolan's direction.

"A joke. This is a bad joke. *Ja?*"

"Call your associate Chambers. Ask him about Cooper. We were face-to-face this morning. Maybe he'll see the funny side. And don't waste time denying any involvement with Chambers. It's on record you've had meetings with him in the U.K. And with Hugo Canfield."

The lawyer sobered up suddenly, accepting that the stranger in his office was deadly serious. He glanced at the black muzzle of the pistol. At Bolan's unflinching gaze. He realized he was in a risky position. He became a lawyer again, relying on his bargaining skills.

"You have virtually admitted killing Bickell and Vandergelt. You're an American in a foreign country. You represent the U.S. government. How do you think the Dutch police will view this? Add the fact you have walked into my office and threatened me with a gun?"

"I'm sure you're going to make it clear for me."

"Cooper, you cannot win. Everything is against you. So I admit I am working with Chambers. There are others. Far too powerful for you to influence. I am a respected member of the community. Who do think they will side with? *You?* I do not think so."

"Let me think about that. In the meantime I need to make sure you don't raise the alarm when I leave." Bolan pressed the muzzle of the pistol against van Ryden's forehead. "Take off your belt," he ordered.

"Why?"

Bolan waggled the pistol. "Humor me. I'm an American in a strange town and it's been difficult to say the least. So I'm allowed to act oddly. Now do it."

The lawyer did as he was told. Bolan made him face the desk, hands behind his back. He used the thin belt to strap the lawyer's wrists together, tightly. Pushing the man around the desk Bolan shoved him into his chair. He yanked out the telephone cable and circled van Ryden's neck, drawing it around the seat's headrest. Bolan pulled it tight enough to be uncomfortable.

"Don't struggle against it. The knot I've tied will pull tighter if you put pressure on it," the Executioner said.

Bolan was lying but van Ryden didn't know that. His face was shiny with sweat and his eyes showed real fear.

The big American crossed the office and stepped into the well-appointed washroom, grabbing a couple of towels. He used one to blindfold van Ryden. The other he partially stuffed into van Ryden's mouth, muffling any sound the man might make. Bolan spun the leather seat and pushed it away from the desk, leaving it facing the window.

Bolan checked the open laptop on the desk. The lawyer had been composing an e-mail. It was addressed to Paul Chambers. In English. It was advising the arrival of cargo that night at a place called *Noosen Hag* and told Chambers that distribution would take place within a few days. He was to expect his consignment then. Bolan memorized the location details. He would follow it up after he left van Ryden's office.

Unsure what was happening van Ryden began to use his

feet to turn his chair around. Bolan waited, then moved in close, bending to whisper in the man's ear.

"I said don't move. Try that again and I'll tighten that cord around your neck myself."

Bolan rolled the chair across the office and into the washroom. He flicked off the light and closed the door on van Ryden.

Bolan let himself out of the main office, pausing to say goodbye to van Ryden for the benefit of his secretary. He closed the door, turning to smile at the young woman.

"Mr. van Ryden said to tell you he's making a private call and doesn't want to be disturbed. He'll call when he's done."

The secretary nodded. "Thank you."

Bolan stepped into the corridor and made for the elevator. On the ground floor he walked calmly out of the building, raising a hand to the girl he'd spoken to earlier. Outside he walked along the street until he was around the corner from the building before he hailed a cab to take him back to his hotel and a call he needed to make to Washington.

4

Bolan's call to Brognola had resulted in the man coming back to him with details on the location. The big Fed had gone into the task-force database and it had provided Bolan with enough intel to hire a vehicle and drive along the coast to the isolated promontory where *Noosen Hag,* the former oil storage depot, stood. Brognola's check had revealed that the depot, closed down for three years, had been leased through a shell company fronting for a consortium proposing to regenerate the site. It turned out that the consortium had connections with businessmen allied, through shadowy links to South East Containers, in turn tied to Venturer Exports. The various connections were all carefully concealed by setups and financial maneuvering in attempts to hide who was really at the helm. But as Brognola had pointed out *all roads led to Rome.* In this instance Hugo Canfield's name kept popping up. Distanced from the everyday workings of the multilayered companies, his presence kept revealing itself. Still vague enough to prevent any interference by the legally bound task force, leaving them looking on, unable to act against him. Brognola offered the information to his loose cannon, knowing full well that Bolan would act on it.

The defunct oil refinery was having a busy night. From his vantage point Bolan could see a number of parked vehicles. Panel vans. Private cars. There was some activity on the concrete jetty built to serve vessels belonging to the oil company. Powerful spotlights, powered by a portable generator, illuminated the area.

Bolan had made his way to the site in the Toyota SUV he had rented earlier in the day. He'd covered the twenty-five miles in ample time and parked at a safe distance to go in on foot for the final distance. Crouching in shadow behind a scrap heap of rusting steel edging the jetty, only yards from the activity, Bolan watched as a crane hoisted a large steel container onto the trailer of a low-loader rig. He had watched the container being off-loaded from the small container ship that was now making its way back out to sea after delivering the container to the waiting handling crew. The turnaround time had been fast. No delays. The container ship would be back on its original course within a half hour.

He had counted six in the crew on the jetty. Only two were showing weapons—H&K MP-5s. That didn't mean the rest were unarmed. Bolan had the SIG-Sauer P-226. It held a full 15-round magazine and he had three more as backup. Unless he could pick up additional weaponry the pistol was going to have to earn its keep. Time was against Bolan, as well. It wouldn't be long before the container was opened and its cargo released. That was a relative term. The people inside the container would simply be exchanging one form of captivity for another. Steel container to panel truck. Not a great exchange, thinking ahead to where the unfortunate passengers might finally end up.

Someone on the jetty crew started to call out orders. Bolan saw figures move to the front of the container and begin to unseal the doors.

As the container doors swung open, the gunmen standing guard, one of the crew hauled himself into the opening. From where he crouched Bolan could hear his barked orders. Moments later shuffling figures appeared at the opening of the container. They reacted when they saw the weapons aimed at them, but there was nowhere for them to go. One by one they began to drop to the ground, huddling together out of instinct. Bolan saw mostly women and young girls. When one held back she was pushed forward, stumbling to her knees. The muzzle of a submachine gun was jammed into her spine. The gunman took hold of the girl's long dark hair and dragged her to her feet. He was yelling at her as he slapped her across the face. He raised his weapon and took aim.

He didn't get a chance to fire. Bolan tracked in with his weapon and put a single shot through the back of the man's skull. The gunman pitched forward onto his face, blood pooling around him.

The jetty crew panicked. The Executioner took advantage of the chaos. He targeted the men wielding weapons, the SIG-Sauer cracking steadily. The men carrying the guns were down on the jetty before they were able to pinpoint the hidden shooter. Bolan changed position, moving around the scrap metal and emerging near the container. He met one of the remaining three crewmen face-on. The man was dragging a pistol from beneath his jacket when Bolan slammed the SIG-Sauer across the side of the man's skull. The man grunted, stumbling, and Bolan helped him down with a bone-crunching second blow. The man hit the jetty facedown.

The Executioner crouched briefly to take charge of the man's pistol. He heard someone yelling in English. He ducked around the end of the container where the captives were scattering along the jetty. He caught a glimpse of others still inside the container, shrinking back from the chaos outside. The crewman who had climbed inside the container was still there. He had a gun in his hand as he leaned cautiously from the opening. He failed to see Bolan until it was too late. The SIG-Sauer cracked, driving two 9 mm slugs into the man's torso. He tumbled from the container onto the hard concrete. His skull bounced against the jetty.

As Bolan checked the far side of the container he saw the sixth man making a run for the parked cars. Bolan hit him with a few 9 mm slugs to the legs, taking him down in an uncoordinated sprawl.

"Anyone speak English?" Bolan asked the women in the container. Two of the young woman acknowledged his question.

"Get them to calm down. Tell them they are going to be freed."

Bolan walked to where the leg-shot man lay. The man had rolled onto his back, sitting up and staring at his shattered limbs. Bolan kept his pistol in clear sight as he approached the man. He spotted the man's dropped weapon and kicked it across the jetty and into the water.

"Must hurt like hell," Bolan said.

The man swore in English, his brittle British accent exaggerated by the pain from his wounds. He dragged himself to the container trailer and pushed his back against one of the rear wheels.

"I'll bet you're the bastard who took down Bickell and his minders. Right, am I? They told us to watch out in case you showed."

"Lucky for me you didn't pay too much attention," the Executioner said.

"Fuck you, Yank. My legs hurt, you bleeder."

"Can't you see the tears in my eyes?"

"What are you going to do to him?" A woman's voice came from behind Bolan.

He turned. It was the young woman he had spoken to. Her gaze was fixed on the wounded crewman. There was no pity in her eyes as she stared down at him. She was attractive, but right then her face was a hardened mask of sharp angles, pale and bloodless.

"What does he deserve?" Bolan asked.

She turned her gaze on Bolan, searching his face, seeing someone who would treat her respectfully. Despite her drawn, pale features the Executioner could see she was a determined young woman. He glanced beyond her to the rest of the "cargo" from the container. They were all exhibiting the ravages of their ordeal but they were far from being defeated.

"He deserves the worst we could do to him," the young woman said. Her soft voice bore traces of an Eastern European accent. "But if we did that, then we become as bad as they are."

The crewman glanced at her, unsure how to take the remark. He had the sense to stay silent, concentrating on his wounds.

Bolan drew the woman aside, looking over her shoulder so he could keep the wounded Brit in sight. "What do I call you?"

"Lucky?" She reached out to touch his arm, a simple gesture that expressed her feelings. "My mother was always telling me my humor would get me into trouble. My name is Majira."

"Where did they pick you all from?"

"Pristina. Off the streets. My own fault for walking home alone after dark. But what was I supposed to do? Never go out? Lose my job? I had heard about the traffickers. How they grab people and send them abroad. I never imagined I would be one of their victims. Nor would any of the others." She took a breath, her voice breaking slightly. "It is the children who would suffer worst. We all understand what would happen to them. Sold to...to soulless monsters who would abuse them."

"Not his time, Majira."

"You are American. Why are you doing this?"

"Long story. Let's say I'm trying to shut this group down."

"Are you a policeman? One of the good mans?"

Bolan nodded. "I'll go with that. The name is Cooper, by the way."

"So, Cooper, tell me, what happens now?"

Bolan looked at the huddled figures. He turned, checking out the darkened buildings at the landward end of the jetty.

"Take everyone to those buildings. At least you'll have shelter while I organize things. Do it now, Majira."

She nodded, turned quickly and spoke to the group. Her voice persuaded them to follow her. Bolan watched the uneven line moving away, the older women comforting the children. He waited until they had vanished inside one of the buildings before turning his attention to his captive.

"What's bloody well going on?" the Brit asked.

"I feel more comfortable without witnesses," Bolan said, standing over the downed man and staring at him.

The Brit watched him, short-lived defiance showing through his pain. He wasn't sure how to perceive the tall, black-clad American. One thing he did know. The man was serious. The way he had taken down the crew had been an eye-opener. Once he had his opening he had taken out the opposition with ruthless efficiency. Being the sole survivor might not turn out to be the greatest blessing.

"What?" the Brit asked. "Christ, if you're going to kill me get on with it. Standing there saying nothing. It's creepy." His remark was said more out of bravado than anything else. In truth he was scared.

"Tell me about the two Americans you killed."

"Now you wait a minute. I had nothing to do with that. It was down to Willi Bickell and the blokes who run things. No shit, mate, they did it. I'm just hired help."

Loyalty never flew the coop so fast, Bolan thought.

"Chambers is the head man around here?"

A frantic nod. The Brit looked eager to talk, hopeful it would go toward extending his life span. The man was no different to anyone else. His first thoughts were of his own survival.

Bolan made a show of ejecting the pistol's magazine and snapping in a fresh one. He dropped the ejected mag into his pocket, moving round the prone man on the ground.

"What the fuck are you doing?"

Bolan glanced at the man. "I can't afford loose ends."

"You can't. You people don't go round executing people."

"People like me?" Bolan said.

"You're a cop. And bloody cops don't—"

"I think we need to clear something up. I never said I was a cop. I don't have a rule book."

"Look, fuck this game. You can't just shoot me like this."

"No?"

"Can we deal?" the man pleaded.

"Maybe you don't have anything I want."

"Try me. But we make a deal first or I don't say a thing."

"My word good enough?"

"I have to trust you? Big risk for me."

"You're still alive."

The Brit considered his situation. He wasn't going to get a written guarantee, and he was in no shape to play hard to get.

"So what do you need to know?"

"Tell me about van Ryden?"

"He fixes things. Has connections here. Arranges for people to look the other way so we can get cargo in and out. He works with the top level in the U.K., as well. Yeah, well, Chambers does the hiring and firing here and at the U.K. base, but Hugo Canfield is the real man in charge. Chambers is second fiddle, really. He likes to throw his weight about. Canfield is the man. But you wouldn't want to tangle with him. He's too big. Can't be interfered with. The man has a cop in his pocket. An Interpol agent. Probably even customs officers. Hell, maybe even higher than that. He runs in serious circles. No shit, mate, Canfield is bad news. I'd sooner sit naked in a crate of fuckin' rattlesnakes than cross Canfield."

"What about a database? Names and locations?"

"Even if I told you, there isn't anything you can do."

"So what have you got to lose?"

"Only my balls. If they find out I gave them up what they did to your undercover men will be like a slap on the wrist."

"One way or another you're going to tell me. I can walk away and let you bleed to death, or end it with a bullet behind the ear. Believe me when I say I don't give a damn one way or another. It's your choice. Your buddies took the hard way. That can be arranged for you."

"What about protection? I've cooperated. You can get me protection."

Bolan took out his cell phone.

"I can make the call from right here if you give me what I need."

"I did hear van Ryden has a database on his computer. It's supposed to have details on everyone who works for Venturer. Means they can keep tabs on us all. Hold on to all our unsavory little secrets. Keeps it at his home outside the city. Place is watched over by armed security. Only other thing I can tell you about is the farm they use to house people while trade is done. I can give you a location for both places."

Bolan made his call minutes later. When Brognola came on Bolan briefed him on the status of the mission.

"If the task force wasn't wrapped up in protocols and red tape, maybe they could have gotten further," Brognola grumbled. "So tell me again about these people you found."

"Women and children. One I spoke to said she was snatched in Pristina so I'm guessing this group came from that area. Off-loaded from a container ship. I arrived in time to prevent them being moved off the dock and sent to God knows where. Hal, do you still have people on the ground hereabouts?"

"Part of the task force is cooling their heels in Amsterdam. You need their help?"

"The women and kids need looking after. Somewhere they'll be secure until a decision can be made about them. I also have a survivor from the crew who were going to ship them out. He's wounded. Needs medical assistance and protection. Your task force might be able to get more info out of him."

"I expect you've already got what you need?"

"We exchanged mutual considerations."

"I'm sure. Striker, let me talk to our people out there. I'll come back to you ASAP."

Bolan spent time collecting weapons from the dead crewmen. He placed his small arsenal just inside the open container. He kept one of the MP-5s and extra magazines for his own use. He checked out the cab of the big tractor-trailer unit and located a first-aid box under the passenger seat. Using the contents he bound up the Brit's legs, applying pressure pads to slow any further blood loss.

"First you shoot me, now you bandage me up. What next? A mug of hot sweet tea?"

"What do you think?"

"Sounds like I'm a dead man either way."

"Redemption can go a long way to keeping you alive."

"Meaning what exactly?"

"You gave me what I needed. So I'll keep my word. You'll be taken into protective custody."

"Don't I have a say about all this?"

The hardness that etched itself across the big American's face told the man he had said the wrong thing. The blue eyes were suddenly like chips of ice. He could almost feel the chill emanating from them.

"I'd be justified to shoot you right now after what I've seen tonight. You people are crawling in the gutter. You sleep well at night? Seeing those young kids and knowing the life you're sending them to? Have you looked at pictures showing how those perverts treat them?"

"Look, I just work on this part of the business. Collection and distribution. Never seen where they go."

"That clear your conscience?"

"Mate, I've been struggling for years to do that. Probably too late for me. I'm just trying to earn a living. Bloody hell, aren't we all?"

Bolan didn't answer. He had all too often heard the

excuses, the self-justification, the criminal element came up with to whitewash their activities. He didn't believe a word of it. He dismissed it as he always did, because if he digested it and analyzed the pathetic reasons he might have turned his gun on them out of sheer disgust.

Reasoning platitudes were the get-out clauses from the mouths of criminals through the decades. From mass murderers to raving dictators who slaughtered thousands, there was always an excuse. A smiling word that was supposed to wash away the bloodlust and the wanton elimination of entire cultures. The perpetrators never considered they had done anything wrong. It was always the rest of the world that was out of step. That did not understand why a particular horror had been committed. Some odd quirk lodged deep in the homicidal, deranged minds of the despots allowed them to excuse away what they had done. If they explained it they self-purged their conscience. They became heroes instead of maniacal villains. And in many instances they often convinced others to see the justification.

In Mack Bolan's eyes a bloody-handed butcher was just that. There was no redemption. No vainglorious explanation that wiped away the needless deaths of men, women and children. Evil was evil. It would never be reconciled as far as he was concerned. It was why the Executioner existed. Why he stood against the monsters.

Someone had to.

Because if he didn't, who would?

5

Hugo Canfield was having lunch at his London club when the maître d' brought him the telephone. He plugged it into one of the sockets, then placed the instrument on the table for Canfield.

"The caller said it was quite urgent, Mr. Canfield."

Canfield nodded. "Thank you, Enright." He waited until the man had withdrawn before picking up the receiver.

"Canfield."

"This is van Ryden. Is it convenient?"

Canfield allowed himself a slight smile. The club dining room was exceptionally quiet. Only two other diners were seated together on the far side of the opulent room. All Canfield could hear was the low murmur of their voices and the click of knives and forks as they ate.

"It will cease to be if my roast beef gets cold."

"There has been a problem with the latest cargo due for delivery. I thought you should know."

"Explain 'problem,' Ludwig."

There was a slight pause before van Ryden spoke. "The problem occurred at the delivery location and the cargo was lost."

"I'll be going back to my office after lunch. Use the jet. I want you in London before the end of the day."

"Of course, Hugo."

Canfield ended the call. He beckoned for Enright to remove the phone, then returned to his meal. He found his appetite a little soured at the news. Hugo Canfield did not enjoy being told that one of his shipments had been lost. He knew the details of the particular cargo that had been expected in Rotterdam. He had invested time and money, as he always did, and if it had been lost, then that meant he was going to be down a considerable sum. Not only that but he was going to have to disappoint important clients. They would not be pleased, which meant Canfield would not be pleased. Client satisfaction was something he prided himself on. It was one of the reasons his organization was the best. He allowed no slackening in standards. He would not tolerate failure.

He smiled suddenly at the thought of van Ryden sitting in the comfort of the Learjet as it crossed from Rotterdam to London. The man would not enjoy the flight. His churning stomach would not be put down to air sickness. He would be worrying. He would not realize that Canfield was not about to lay the blame on him. The lawyer was responsible for the legal part of the operation and logistics. He also dealt with finance. He was not a field operative.

Let the man worry, Canfield decided. It would not do him any harm. It paid to keep his people on their toes, to shoulder their responsibilities.

Canfield finished his meal, called for his car to be brought to the entrance and strolled to the reception desk where he collected his coat and hat. He made an imposing figure. Just over six feet tall, athletically built—he kept himself fit—and expensively dressed. Women found him excitingly attractive and he played on that. His aloof demeanor toward those he considered below him made others step back when confronted. He *was* powerful. He exercised immense control and had no hesitation when it came to using his influence.

When he stepped outside, shielded from the London rain by the doorman's umbrella, his year-old, top-of-the-range Bentley was already at the curb. The doorman opened the rear door and Canfield slid onto the soft leather seat.

"Back to the office, sir?" asked Gantley, his driver and minder. Gantley was a former British Army military policeman. A big man. Solid and tough. Above his hard face he wore his hair close-cropped. He had worked for Canfield for eight years, was loyal and had a fearsome reputation for brutal violence. "Bloody day, sir. Global warming obviously hasn't reached London yet."

"Always the pessimist, Sergeant Gantley."

"That's me, sir. So, the office?"

"The office. No rush now. Mr. van Ryden is flying in from Rotterdam so there's plenty of time."

"Way the traffic's building up he'll more than likely be there before us."

LUDWIG VAN RYDEN WAS shown into Canfield's spacious Canary Wharf office just before five o'clock. Watching from behind his executive desk Canfield was barely able to refrain from smiling at the concern on van Ryden's face.

"Sit down, Ludwig." Canfield caught the attention of his secretary, who had shown the Dutchman in. "Jane, please arrange some fresh coffee for us. Or would you like something stronger, Ludwig?"

"Coffee will be fine."

As the door closed behind the young woman, Canfield pushed to his feet and stood at the wide window that overlooked Canary Wharf. He never failed to enjoy the view. It excited him.

This was *his* pinnacle.

It had taken him a long time to build his organization—taking it from humble beginnings all the way to an empire that spanned the globe. On his way to the top Canfield had honed his skills on the backs of others. Weaker men failed to spot the quiet ambition of the younger man in their employ. Canfield had been a good pupil. Always watching and listening, gathering his strength by exploiting others. When he was ready he struck.

During his climb to absolute power he left behind a trail of dead bodies. Literally. But Canfield always covered his tracks. There were rumors about the way he worked, but Canfield was sharp enough never to leave evidence that might point the finger his way. Each time he took out rivals he absorbed the operations they had been running, slowly and carefully creating his own. Now he controlled a powerful criminal network that had its hand in a number of illegal operations, the most lucrative was his human trafficking.

It had not taken Canfield long to realize the potential of the trade in people. From the very young to adults, the slave business was thriving.

The suite of offices at Canary Wharf, the prestigious docklands business complex, housed Canfield Enterprises. Day to day it carried on the legitimate side of the business. Finance and development. It acted as a cover for Canfield's murkier business dealings. The majority of the people working there knew nothing of Canfield's other enterprises. The legitimate business earned him a lot of money and contacts he made from that part of his empire were icing on the cake.

His illicit enterprise had recently brought Canfield's organization under the close scrutiny of a multination task force. The goal of the task force was to gather enough evidence to allow the law to close him down. That was the plain and simple fact. The intent was there but the task force, though it had its suspicions, was unable to garner the hard evidence that would lead to Canfield's conviction. The task force worked within the constrictions of lawful intent. They had to follow the rules. Canfield was under no such regulation. He worked by his own set of rules. There were no limits in his world of business. As long as he made his money and increased his power, then he was satisfied. He was already ultrawealthy and making more money by the day. He was a well-known businessman. He had, over the years, cultivated many relationships with respectable people in positions of power. Some of those individuals were also under his patronage because Canfield had something on them. He disliked the word *blackmail,* preferring to see the associations as a mutual understanding between friends. He protected them by keeping their guilty secrets hidden away, suggesting that reciprocating gestures from them would retain the status quo. Within his circle of friends Canfield had government ministers, cops, wealthy individuals who moved in high circles.

Hugo Canfield felt very secure in his world.

The recent events in Rotterdam, namely the disposal of the two American agents who had managed to penetrate his organization, had been a means of announcing to the task force that they were ineffective. That nothing they could do would ever touch him. It showed that he, Hugo Canfield, had the power to do such a thing without fear of reprisal. The task force knew what had happened, but there had not been a thing they could do about it. Proof positive did not exist. If they had arrested Canfield, or any of his people, it would have ended up with them all walking free because there was not the slightest shred of evidence against him. Or the people who had carried out the torture and murder. His legal team would refute any and all charges against him as being without basis. The task force would have one chance to take Canfield down and one chance only. They needed proof absolute. To the last detail. Evidence both documentary and verbal. Witnesses. They would need enough backup to fill a courtroom. The task force knew that and so did Canfield. Despite the international members of the task force they had nothing they could use against Hugo Canfield. With his contacts he would be able to buy, destroy or wipe out anything the task force threatened him with.

"Wait until the coffee arrives, then we can talk," he said over his shoulder to van Ryden.

The lawyer was in no hurry to get to the reason he was in London. He had been debating the matter with himself during the flight in Canfield's jet. Whenever he had flown before he had always immersed himself in the luxury of the executive aircraft. Canfield had ordered many custom additions to the airplane during its construction. It was equipped with the most comfortable seats van Ryden had ever sat in. It had a communications system that would have cast a shadow over Air Force One. Onboard entertainment played to perfection and the cabin crew were able to serve up practically anything a passenger wanted. On this particular flight van Ryden had found he couldn't face anything except for a couple of glasses of whiskey. Even they failed to quell the queasy sensation growing stronger in his stomach the closer he got to London.

The office door opened and the young secretary wheeled in a burnished steel trolley. It held the coffee Canfield had ordered.

"Would you like me to pour, sir?" Jane asked.

"We'll be fine," Canfield said. "And, Jane, no interruptions until I say. No exceptions."

She nodded and withdrew, quietly closing the double doors.

Canfield moved to the trolley and poured two cups of coffee. He handed one to van Ryden, then resumed his seat behind his desk.

"Bring me up-to-date, Ludwig. I have some details but I need clarification."

The lawyer explained the occurrences from the meeting between Wilhelm Bickell and the American, Cooper, to the strike against the freshly delivered cargo at the former oil dock. His delivery was detailed and precise. He felt as if he was in a courtroom at that moment, though for once it felt as if he was on the witness stand himself.

Canfield listened without comment, drinking his coffee, his

eyes fixed on van Ryden throughout. When the lawyer finished and took a long swallow from his own cup, Canfield waited for a few moments before he responded.

"Do we assume that it was this man, Cooper, who carried out the attack at the dock?"

"Who else would it be? He dealt with Bickell and his men. He is obviously a man who believes in direct action. As the strike at the dock showed."

"What do we know about this man? Apart from the obvious fact he knows his job."

"All searches have failed to bring up anything about him. His initial contact with Bickell suggested he was involved with the task force. He isn't on any databases I had our people check. It's as if he doesn't exist."

"His actions are certainly real, Ludwig. The bullets he used killed my people, his ability to have the cargo taken into care was certainly real. I'll have my sources look into who this bastard is. Someone, somewhere, must know about him."

"He fooled Bickell into believing he was genuine."

"Bickell was an incompetent idiot. He should have contacted me before he went ahead and arranged that meeting. What the bloody hell did he think he was doing? Did he imagine that every time he was confronted by someone from the task force all he had to do was kill them? The removal of Turner and Bentley was a single, clearly defined warning to the task force that they were on dangerous ground. I was not advocating open season."

When van Ryden appeared reluctant to say any more Canfield realized he hadn't been told the whole story. He refilled his coffee cup, sat again and asked the lawyer outright what else he had to say.

"He came to my office, Hugo," van Ryden said. "Tricked his way in as a potential client, then made it clear his intentions are to bring us down."

He detailed what had happened from the moment the man named Cooper had entered his office.

Canfield laughed. "If nothing else he has a bloody nerve. Whoever he is, this man doesn't sound like your everyday task-force agent. He must be some specialist. I don't suppose he gave anything away we could use?"

"Hugo, I was scared. He tied me up, blindfolded and gagged me and shut me in my own washroom. I'm no hero. The man terrified me. I admit that. He was serious. He proved that by the attack at the dock. For all I knew he had come to my office to kill me. And before you ask, I did not divulge any information. He already knew of my association with you."

"Now that is interesting," Canfield said. "The man has background details on our operation. Has information about us. What does that suggest?"

"That he does have some kind of contact with the task force."

"They haven't advertised their investigations to the media. Cooper must have been fed intel to get him on track."

"But he is only one man."

"He's shown us that one man can do a lot of damage. He doesn't follow any kind of rule book. Works instinctively and just goes for his targets." Canfield sat back, considering the options open to him. "Time for some of our resources to earn their retainers. The problem with a wild card like Cooper is not knowing where he's going to show up next."

He reached out and tapped a button on the office intercom. "Jane, get me Paul Chambers. Tell him to drop everything and get here immediately. ASAP. Any objections just put him directly through to me. I'll deal with him."

"Yes, Mr. Canfield. Does that mean you'll be staying over?"

"I won't be going anywhere until I've spoken to him."

"I'll arrange for a meal to be delivered later. What would you prefer this evening?"

"I leave that in your capable hands, Jane. And make the meal enough for two. Mr. van Ryden will be joining me."

"Will you need me to stay?"

"That won't be necessary, my dear. You just make the arrangements, then you can go home as normal."

Canfield spent the next hour discussing with van Ryden the need for damage control over the missing cargo. Client satisfaction meant a great deal to Hugo Canfield. He had a good record and the thought of that record becoming tarnished did not sit well.

"We need to arrange with Timor to gather another cargo to be ready to ship out when I give the word. I'll have to smooth things over with our clients about the delay. I think a discounted rate should make them happy. Everybody likes a price drop."

"I am sure *they* won't lower the charges when they move the merchandise on."

Canfield shrugged. "What they do with the cargo once they have bought and paid for it is their business. As long as we receive our fee I don't give a damn."

"What can I do to help?" van Ryden asked, eager to please his employer.

"In the morning you get back to Rotterdam. Speak to De-Chambre first, then arrange for him to contact me. He's been damned quiet since he fingered those American agents. Perhaps I'm being too soft with him. Then you go home and lay low for a few days. Relax. Stay away from your office. Keep your security crew on hand."

"I will contact DeChambre as soon as I get back."

"Make sure he is aware I am not happy. My God, the man is an Interpol inspector. Wouldn't you expect him to have at least a suspicion the Americans had sent someone else over after the deaths of Turner and Bentley? Tell DeChambre I want some answers, or his monthly retainer might suddenly dry up. That should kick-start his French arse. Now, loosen your tie, Ludwig, and don't stay so uptight." A wide grin crossed Canfield's face and he leaned forward to clap van Ryden on the shoulder. "God, I would have given a fortune to have seen your expression when Cooper walked into your office and poked a gun in your face."

The lawyer still paled when he recalled the incident. He failed to see what was even faintly amusing about it. "Hugo, I think I will take that drink now, please."

Canfield poured him a large whiskey.

"Here, get that down, then we can go over the details of this Russian drug deal. We need to work on our distribution list."

6

Harass the enemy. If there's no opportunity to confront him in a full-on attack because he has an overwhelming force, the next best thing is to hit and run. Strike here, then fall back, move on and hit somewhere else. Keep the enemy guessing. Don't allow him to take a breath before you strike somewhere else. Take him down piece by piece.

It was a strategy the Executioner had employed many times before. He worked more often than not as a single entity without the privilege of a large supporting team behind him. His lonely war gave him no other option. Bolan had adapted to this over the years and he felt no disadvantage in having to operate without backup. On the reverse side of the card, working alone meant he could concentrate fully during an attack without having the burden of allies on his mind—no worries whether they were safe, whether they had been compromised. He only had to concentrate on himself. Responsibility came with its own shackles. When the need arose Bolan shouldered responsibility without thought, but when he was moving into a lone combat situation his mind could focus on the mission full-time.

He had liaised with Stony Man Farm. Aaron "the Bear" Kurtzman had assigned his cyber team to run a detailed check on Ludwig van Ryden's background. Especially his home. By the time Bolan was in full receipt of the information he knew enough about the lawyer's house to walk around it in the dark. He wasn't even surprised that Kurtzman had come up with detailed architect's drawing for the place.

When Bolan had staked out the property initially it quickly became evident that van Ryden was not at home. The house stood empty, no vehicle evident on the paved driveway. A call back to the Farm to run a check on van Ryden's whereabouts gave Bolan the answer to his query. An innocent telephone call to his office came back with the information that Mr. van Ryden was out of the country on business for a couple of days. So the Executioner had to wait. He did it by taking in the sights of Rotterdam he had almost missed on his arrival. He rested up for the battle to come.

When Bolan took up his surveillance again he still spent a fruitless stakeout. But on the second morning circumstances changed for the better.

The van Ryden residence stood in well-landscaped tranquility. The low-rise house was at least a quarter of a mile from the road, fronted by the curving driveway lined by slender trees and cultivated bushes. At the rear sweeping lawns reached to a high fence that encircled the acreage. A paved patio jutting out from the back of the house had a large swimming pool and a stepped terrace that allowed observers to look down on the pool.

Bolan had climbed the fence during the early morning hours and was concealed in the dense foliage of the garden that occupied the northeast corner of the property. From his vantage point he was able to watch the back of the house without being seen himself. He used the powerful binoculars he had purchased to maintain a solid watch over the house, and during the couple of hours he had been in position he had spotted the appearance of van Ryden's security team. It consisted of a pair of armed men, dressed in suits and ties, who made regular patrols around the property. Bringing them into detailed closeup Bolan saw the sentries wore lightweight headsets that allowed them to communicate with each other,

and maybe an internal control, as they patrolled the grounds.
The paved driveway now held three expensive cars.

At 7:30 a.m. van Ryden, dressed in bathing shorts,
stepped out through French doors. He hit the water and for
the next twenty minutes swam up and down the length of the
pool. He finally emerged and picked up the towel he had
brought out with him.

Bolan watched him walk back inside the house, picked up
the MP-5 he had brought with him from the dock mission and
began to work his way through the foliage in the direction of
the house. He reached the north corner, staying in the cover
provided by the heavily bushed garden and waited until the
sentry appeared. The man had an MP-5 hanging by a strap
from his left shoulder, his hand resting lightly on the weapon.
He walked past Bolan's hiding place with feet to spare. Once
he had his back to him Bolan rose silently, stepped up behind
the man and took him in a blood choke hold, applying instant
pressure to carotid and jugular.

Starved of blood the sentry had little chance to fight back.
As soon as he felt the man's legs weaken Bolan followed him
down, keeping up the pressure until the sentry lost conscious-
ness. With the sentry on the ground Bolan disabled the comset
and stripped it clear. He threw it aside, into the tangle of
bushes. From his back pocket Bolan pulled out a couple of the
plastic ties. He looped one around the sentry's ankles, another
to bind his hands behind him. Aware that the man could
recover quickly Bolan took off the guard's tie, balled it up and
stuffed it into the man's mouth. He took the magazine out of
the man's MP-5 and threw both items deep into the undergrowth. He located a handgun, holstered under the man's
coat. Bolan disassembled the weapon and scattered the parts.

The Executioner had studied the routes the pair of sentries
had taken. He fell in behind the second man, trailing silently
in his shadow until he was walking the paved path that ran

down the side of the house's double garage. It was the ideal spot to deal with the man. Bolan moved up, ready to strike.

The sentry stopped suddenly, reaching up to check his comset, speaking into the microphone. Bolan didn't understand the words, but he picked up the urgent tone when the man failed to get a response from his partner. The sentry turned about, ready to retrace his steps. The first thing he saw was Bolan, poised only feet away. The sentry responded swiftly, snatching at his shoulder-hung weapon. Bolan closed in quickly, his left hand grasping the barrel of the submachine gun, forcing it skyward. His right hand snapped forward, closing around the sentry's throat, pushing him hard against the garage wall. The back of the man's skull slammed against the brickwork, the impact stunning him briefly and allowing Bolan the opportunity to lean in closer, turning and dragging the man's gun arm down across his shoulder. The sentry's resistance lasted only for as long as it took for his arm to snap. The MP-5 slipped from splayed fingers.

Bolan spun, braced himself and launched a full-on right fist that connected with the sentry's jaw. The impact threw the man to his knees, spitting blood. Bolan slammed his foot between his shoulders and hammered him to the ground, the man's face crunching against the concrete. As he bent to relieve the man of his handgun Bolan picked up radio chatter. He pulled off the guard's headset and listened closely. Someone was demanding a response in Dutch. Even though he couldn't understand the language Bolan recognized the urgency in the challenge.

Had his recon been spotted?

Whatever the reason for the agitation Bolan wasn't about to back off. He was too close to his target now.

He checked the handgun. It held a full magazine. He slung his MP-5 across his back. Turning he made his way around to the back of the house again, heading for the French doors van Ryden had used. The glass doors opened at his touch and Bolan slipped inside, pausing to check out the well-appointed room. Even his cursory examination told Bolan that everything in the room spoke of expensive taste. Recalling the detail Kurtzman had supplied this was the main living area. He knew van Ryden's study was directly through the arch ahead of him and to the right.

From somewhere beyond the room he heard a murmur of voices and footsteps on hardwood floors. Bolan moved to the far side of the room. If anyone came in they would be forced to take time to locate him. Maybe only for brief seconds but that would allow him the advantage.

Bolan spotted movement on the far side of the arch.

A tall, dark-haired man edged into the room. He carried the obligatory MP-5, the muzzle arcing back and forth as he surveyed what seemed to be an empty room. When he saw Bolan's dark figure against the end wall he tracked his weapon around, finger pulling back on the trigger. Slugs chunked into the wall, filling the air with plaster chips and dust.

Bolan's acquired auto pistol rapped out a fast trio of shots that hit the man in the chest. He stumbled back, a sharp cry bursting from his lips, and banged against the wall. As he did his finger held its trigger pull, sending 9 mm slugs into the wall above Bolan's head. More plaster dust erupted in white spouts. The shot man slipped to the floor, face contorted into a snarl of anger and he attempted to pull his submachine gun back on line. A fourth shot from Bolan caught him above the left eye, blowing a chunk of bone out of the back of his skull, spattering bloody debris on the door behind him.

Moving quickly Bolan crossed the room and stepped over the body, turning to scan the open hall and the doors beyond. He caught a flicker of movement ahead. He saw a figure emerge from an open door, pistol in hand. The man opened fire the moment he saw Bolan, then ran in a semicrouch across the open space, still triggering shots. Bolan heard the slugs thud into the wall. He stepped forward, dropping, holding the pistol double-handed as he picked up on the moving gunner. The Executioner fired off half the magazine, spent casings hitting the floor around him. The moving figure paused, lost coordination and crashed to the polished floor, skidding across the surface. The man rolled on his side, hauling his pistol around and fired again, not allowing himself time to lock on his target.

Bolan centered his weapon and returned fire, his slugs catching the gunman in the torso. The man let out a long gasp as he rolled slowly on his back and lay still. Bolan pushed to his feet and loped across to where the man lay. He kicked the dropped gun across the hall, threw aside the pistol that had locked on an empty chamber and drew the SIG-Sauer.

The house had fallen silent around him.

Four down.

Was that van Ryden's complete security complement?

Bolan figured that two on the outside, two more inside, would have been adequate under normal circumstances. Unless van Ryden recently felt he needed more. Bolan remained on full alert. Assumption could never replace caution. Complacency invited trouble. And Mack Bolan had never accepted complacency as a companion.

He picked up sounds from behind a closed door on the far side of the wide hall. He knew that was the study. Someone was speaking. Bolan flattened against the wall and picked up a voice he recognized.

It was van Ryden.

The conversation sounded one-sided. Bolan figured van Ryden was on the phone.

Calling in help?

The Executioner eased the door handle, pushing the door

open. The room was large and airy. He saw book-lined shelves, a large desk, a picture window showing the grounds.

He spotted the hunched figure of the lawyer with a phone to his ear, free hand waving to emphasize his conversation. He had his back to Bolan. He did not hear him enter. Or close the door and engage the lock. He made a final plea, then slammed the phone down. As he straightened up his senses warned him he was not alone. There was a handgun on the desk next to the phone and van Ryden's hand made a tentative move toward it.

"Not advisable," Bolan cautioned.

The lawyer turned to face him. His face had lost its color. Right then he looked far from his smart public image. His hair, still damp from his swim, hung limply across his scalp and he needed a shave. He was dressed in a gray tracksuit and running shoes. And he was visibly distressed.

"You cannot do this," he said. "Invade my home. Attack my house staff."

Bolan shrugged.

"Are all domestics in Holland expected to walk around carrying machine guns and pistols? Hell of a way to greet visitors."

A burst of defiance flared. "You are not a guest in my house. You are an invader. Have you forgotten who I am? A respected member of the legal profession. My name is known in high circles. I can have you arrested for breaching my human rights."

"Words, van Ryden. Coming from a scum who trades in human lives. I haven't forgotten what you are. You forfeited your rights when you took up your business. Remember what I told you in your office? I'm going to bring you and rest of your associates down. No hiding behind your *respectable* name."

The lawyer snapped. Eyes widening with a reckless gleam, a scream of rage burst from his lips as he snatched up a heavy paperweight from the desk and swung it at Bolan, ignoring the gun pointing at him. Bolan leaned back, feeling the disturbed air stroke his face as the paperweight curved past. The lunge pulled van Ryden closer to Bolan and before he could regain his balance the Executioner hit him across the jaw with the P-226, putting every ounce of strength into the blow. As bone crunched and blood flew from his open mouth van Ryden slammed down across the desk, scattering papers. The paperweight slipped from his grasp. His face thumped against the hard surface of the desk. As he struggled to push himself upright Bolan stepped in closer and slammed the pistol down hard against the back of van Ryden's skull. The lawyer groaned, his body becoming limp. Bolan stepped back as the lawyer slithered to the floor, sprawling on his back. His jaw was raw and bloody.

Putting the pistol away Bolan moved around the desk and sat down. He removed van Ryden's handgun. The computer sat in front of him. Bolan figured the lawyer would have data stored somewhere within the machine detailing the trafficking operation. In his capacity as the organization's facilitator he would need information. The problem was that the screen text Bolan was looking at was in Dutch. A language Bolan was unfamiliar with. Bolan took out his phone and keyed in the number to connect with Stony Man Farm.

"Striker," Aaron Kurtzman acknowledged when he came on.

"I need you to hack into a computer and download everything on it, then get the data translated into English."

"'Hacking,' as you put it, is for geeky amateurs. But I will electronically intrude into the hard drive and extract whatever is hidden there."

"Okay. Tell me what to do."

Bolan followed the concise instructions. With Kurtzman's program installed on van Ryden's computer it took less than ten minutes before the contents were transferred.

"I'll get everyone working on this. You need anything else?" Kurtzman asked.

"How about emptying this system? Wiping the memory? Give these bastards more to worry about."

"Sounds like someone has upset you, Striker."

"And some."

"A thought here. There could be backup to this data. Flash drives. I'll clear the hard drive and leave a little visitor. If they try to reinstall the data my little buddy will pick it up and fritz that, as well. How's that?"

"Pretty sneaky for a high-tech *hacker.*"

Kurtzman's booming laughter rumbled through Bolan's cell phone before he ended the call.

As the Executioner moved away from the desk the monitor screen began to flash with lines of rapidly scrolling codes. Kurtzman's wipeout program had started, methodically eating its way through the data embedded in the computer's hard drive.

The Executioner had reached the center of the room when he heard a rush of sound behind him. Bolan spun on his heel. He saw van Ryden halfway across the room, coming at him full-on. The lawyer's face was wet with blood, more of it making dark streaks down the front of his track suit, his mouth open as he let out a long, harsh scream of anger. Bolan saw the slim-bladed letter opener the man had snatched up off the desk. It was aimed in Bolan's direction. But van Ryden was no combat veteran. It was unlikely he had ever been in a violent situation in his life.

Bolan let the man get in close before he sidestepped, slamming a hard-edged hand across the knife wrist. As the blade spun from his nerveless fingers van Ryden squealed. In desperation he lashed out. Bolan caught the arm, turning it. He spun van Ryden in a half circle, then released his arm. The man's own weight carried him across the room. Out of control he crashed head-on into a glass-fronted display cabinet. His shout of fright was lost in the sound of shattering glass. Scattered porcelain figurines suddenly spattered with blood as van Ryden's severely gashed throat began to spurt. He fell to the floor, body going into spasm as his lifeblood began to spread in a wide, glistening pool from beneath his body.

"No more human rights for you to abuse, Mr. van Ryden," Bolan said as he left the room.

The phone call van Ryden had been making to his associates was more than likely to bring reinforcements. It was on Bolan's mind as he retraced his steps from the house, through the grounds and out to where he had parked his rented SUV. He slid the unused MP-5 beneath the seat. Climbing behind the wheel he started the engine and followed the narrow back road until he joined up with the main route.

7

Inspector Marcel DeChambre, Interpol, and joint task-force member, parked across the street from the hotel where the man known as Cooper was staying. He had made a telephone call a half hour earlier to be informed that Cooper was not at the hotel, and no, he had not checked out.

So where was he?

DeChambre's long fingers tapped impatiently against the steering wheel. He needed a result. The explicit order from Hugo Canfield had explained things very clearly. He expected DeChambre to come up with something that would identify Cooper. Canfield's message held a direct threat. He had not been paying DeChambre large amounts of money for the fun of it. He expected the Frenchman to earn his keep. If he didn't… There was no need for the sentence to be completed.

DeChambre understood. He had been associated with the Englishman long enough to have witnessed how Canfield dealt with those who let him down. Or betrayed him. De-Chambre had been present when the two American under-cover agents had been eliminated. The men DeChambre had betrayed when he informed on them to Canfield.

The extreme torture before the men were killed had convinced DeChambre that the man meant every word. Now he was under the spotlight. And there was no avoiding it. He served up Cooper, or paid the price for his own incompetence in not knowing the man had been sent to check out what had happened to Turner and Bentley.

Informing Canfield about the agents had been a good moment in his relationship with the man. It hadn't been a lasting moment. Canfield didn't concern himself about former successes. He lived in the moment and this particular moment was not boding too well for the trafficking group. The man named Cooper had already created enough problems. Apart from killing Bickell and his team, Cooper had brazenly walked into van Ryden's office and had presented the lawyer with his intentions to take down Venturer Exports. It had been a direct challenge, given by a man who plainly did not work within official rules. Cooper had then moved on to intercept a freshly arrived shipment, taking out the crew, freeing the cargo and getting them into the hands of the task force.

Canfield had been angry at this deliberately provocative act and it had been made crystal clear to DeChambre that he had to identify, locate and terminate Cooper.

No excuses.

No delays.

DeChambre's problems began when he made casual inquiries into the identity of the man who had handed the task-force information in the form of live evidence. No one had any idea who the man was. None of the agents working the case appeared to be worried about that. They were more concerned with what they could get from the freed people and the wounded crew member from the dock. DeChambre had not been able to discover where the man had been taken. The agents within the task force were staying silent on that matter and DeChambre stopped asking questions after a while, not wanting to make himself conspicuous.

Cooper had presented himself to Bickell as being from the same American department as Turner and Bentley. He had advertised his arrival time in Rotterdam and the hotel where he was staying. When DeChambre made a computer check of his own the search for Cooper came up blank. It was as if the man did not exist. That puzzled the Interpol agent even more. He made a deeper check, opening his search even wider. And still came up with nothing.

So he went looking for Cooper using old-fashioned policing methods. Sitting in his car across the street from the hotel, staring out through the rain-speckled windshield, he found his mind wandering away from Cooper to the subject of his own mortality. He had no doubt in his mind that if he failed to satisfy Hugo Canfield's demands, his life would end very quickly. He accepted the fact. Marcel DeChambre was a realist. No one had forced his hand when Canfield made him the offer to join his organization. If he had a weakness it was for money. His position within Interpol was never going to make him a rich man. By contrast his association with Venturer Exports had created opportunities DeChambre had never dreamed of. Canfield's extended influence brought DeChambre into contact with a number of the man's powerful friends in Rotterdam and throughout France. DeChambre's position within Interpol allowed him to work favors for these people. In return he received substantial financial rewards. DeChambre's nest egg had grown accordingly. He had hidden accounts, each holding extremely healthy balances. DeChambre wanted to be able to enjoy his money. That might not happen if he didn't locate and eliminate Cooper.

DeChambre felt the need for a cigarette. He thrust a hand into the pocket of his dark raincoat and pulled out a packet of *Gitanes*. The dark, extremely strong French cigarettes had been his favorite since his teenage years. His taste had never changed. With the current war on smoking—something DeChambre detested with a vengeance—*Gitanes* had ceased to be made in France. Ironically they were now manufactured in the Netherlands and DeChambre always kept a good supply in his apartment, bought from a small importer he knew. He lit one now, using a wooden match. He refused to pander to the trend for disposable gas lighters, convinced they ruined the flavor. Sitting back he drew deeply, inhaling the rich aroma. Wreaths of blue smoke drifted through the interior of the car. As he smoked he felt his mood ease a little. It was the effect of the tobacco, he knew. He was on his second cigarette when he recognized Cooper as the man alighted from a dark SUV. Cooper carried a bag with him as he went into the hotel.

DeChambre took out his cell phone, deciding he needed some of Canfield's backup crew. He saw that the phone was still switched off from the previous night. Still smarting from Canfield's demands he had forgotten to turn the damn thing on before leaving his Rotterdam apartment. As it powered up DeChambre saw a number of missed calls up and he recognized the caller's number.

Canfield.

He hit redial and sat waiting for his call to be picked up.

"Where the bloody hell have you been? What's the fucking point of a cell phone if you don't switch it on? What the hell am I paying you for, DeChambre?" Canfield shouted.

"Wait. I've spotted Cooper. He just walked back into his hotel. I've been sitting across the road for a few hours, but he's here now."

"Am I supposed to happy about that?" Canfield's voice rose an octave. "While you've been perched on your Gallic derriere Cooper has been busy. He turned up at van Ryden's house first thing this morning. Disabled the security crew—three of them are dead. And so is van Ryden. The bastard wiped the memory from his computer. Now I'm bloody certain he downloaded all the data on van Ryden's hard drive first. So understand why I'm not exactly wild with joy just because you've actually seen the bugger."

"I need some local backup and van Ryden should have given me a number to call—"

"He isn't exactly in any condition to give out numbers. And you don't have time to wait around for help. Christ, Marcel, you're a cop. Go into that hotel and arrest him. Drive to a deserted spot and put a bullet through him. The man is acting like a vigilante. No jurisdiction. Taking the law into his own hands. You arrested him and he tried to make a break. Make something up."

"Yes. I suppose I could do that."

"We can protect you. All I need to do is make a couple of calls. But I need that man out of the way. He's only been in the country five minutes and he's creating chaos. Just get it done." Canfield paused, then said, "I'll see what I can do with backup."

The call ended, leaving DeChambre holding a dead cell phone.

He stared at the hotel. The rain had increased again, dropping heavily from the leaden sky. The gloom only added to DeChambre's sullen mood. He lit another cigarette, drawing on it so hard the smoke stung the back of his throat. DeChambre decided he could have used a large tumbler of cognac to take away the taste.

He couldn't believe van Ryden was dead.

That was a shock. It was obvious that Cooper took no prisoners. Well, he wasn't going to find DeChambre so easy to dispose of.

He reached under his coat and eased out his pistol. A Glock 21.45 ACP. DeChambre checked the weapon and returned the 13-round magazine. He returned it to his shoulder rig, making sure the weapon hung right, then opened the car door and stepped out. He locked the vehicle and made a quick run across the road, depositing his cigarette in the gutter. In the lobby he shook the rain off his coat and crossed to the reception desk. Before the clerk could speak DeChambre showed his Interpol badge, leaning forward to speak quietly.

"It is important I check out a guest. May I see your register?"

The computer screen was turned so DeChambre could view the guest list. He located the name he was looking for and the room number.

"Thank you."

The clerk fingered his collar nervously. "Is there a problem?"

DeChambre shook his head. "Purely a routine check on a possible visa irregularity. Everything is fine."

As he walked away from the desk DeChambre glanced at the clerk. The man watched him for a few moments, then turned away, distracted by another inquiry. The moment the clerk's head was turned DeChambre turned and crossed the lobby, taking the stairs. Cooper was on the third floor. He took out his cell and this time deliberately turned it off. The last thing he needed was the phone ringing at the wrong moment.

As he climbed the stairs DeChambre prepared himself. The Glock was drawn, thrust into the deep right-hand pocket of his topcoat. He kept his fingers curled around the grip of the pistol. DeChambre reached the third floor and paced along the carpeted corridor, counting off the room numbers until he reached Cooper's. The Frenchman paused. A slight sheen of sweat covered the palm of his hand holding the gun. It was not the first time DeChambre had needed to do something like this on his own. He breathed deeply, calming himself.

Damn Canfield.

The man could have made this easier by sending along some local backup. But Hugo Canfield was not in the business of making things easy for those in his employ. It was a part of the man's makeup. A need to show his authority. His utter strength and power. And no matter what DeChambre thought personally he would do what Canfield instructed, because the man owned him.

DeChambre raised his left hand and knocked on the door.

MACK BOLAN TURNED at the sound. The last thing he expected was a visitor. Though it might be a hotel employee with fresh towels or something of that nature he would never assume anything.

He picked up his pistol, pushing it into the waistband of his pants, against his spine. Crossing to the door he stood to one side.

"Yes?"

"Mr. Cooper, my name is DeChambre. Inspector Marcel DeChambre. Interpol. Liaison with the task force. I need to speak with you urgently."

Bolan's mind worked swiftly. As far as he knew, his location in Rotterdam had not been broadcast to anyone outside of Brognola's area of responsibility. No communication had been sent to any European agency, even though the task force had some interdepartmental links. His thoughts covered the facts even as he opened the door and faced DeChambre.

The man was tall, lean, his head of thick dark hair still damp from the rain. He had a strong beak of a nose above a wide mouth. He raised his left hand after dipping it into his coat pocket, showing Bolan the ID wallet with his Interpol credentials. A shadow of a friendly smile edged his lips. Bolan ignored that. His gaze settled on DeChambre's gray-blue eyes. There was no friendliness there. The eyes mirrored the cold enmity the Frenchman held.

"May I come in?" the man asked.

Polite. Exhibiting a professional courtesy that was intended to relax Bolan.

"Sure," the Executioner said.

Bolan kept himself to one side as DeChambre stepped into the room. The man's right hand remained inside his coat pocket. Bolan followed the contours of the cloth, the shape of DeChambre's hand. It was a hand that was gripping something solid, fingers curled around the object. Bolan pushed the door shut, then watched as DeChambre made a slow turn to face him.

"I was hoping I might get a chance to rest up," Bolan remarked, keeping his voice conversational. "One of the problems of having a superior like Dillon. That man is so on the fast-track for promotion he keeps us on the go 24/7."

Bolan gave DeChambre points for a quick reaction. His moment of blankness was smoothed over by a Gallic shrug. "It is the same with my own superiors."

In that moment he was thinking about Hugo Canfield. But only as a superior in control, certainly not in intellect. Canfield was nothing but a thug in expensive clothing. Wealthy and powerful, but basically a peasant.

"You must have heard the man at briefings. Holds the floor and won't shut up," Bolan said.

DeChambre hesitated, slightly thrown off stride. He had no knowledge of a man named Dillon. Had not heard him speak. Had never seen him. He had been hoping to deal with Cooper without any difficulty. The American faced him, hands at his sides, apparently comfortable with the way the conversation was going.

"I am not—" he began.

"Familiar with Dillon?"

Now the American's tone had altered, his words taking on a harder edge. And the way he was staring at him made De-Chambre nervous.

"I understand that," Bolan said. "Seeing how Dillon doesn't exist."

Bolan saw the material of DeChambre's coat pocket move. Watched his arm draw back as the Frenchman began to take his hand out.

Bolan saw the dark metal of the pistol as it started to emerge from the pocket. He stepped forward, hands reaching out to catch hold of DeChambre's gun arm. DeChambre tensed, resisting, which was just how Bolan had expected him to react. The Executioner turned in, slamming into DeChambre as he executed a fast hip throw that launched the Frenchman across the room.

DeChambre crashed down on the bed. The recoil from the thick mattress threw him onto the floor, breath gusting from his lungs as he hit. Bolan didn't allow him any chance. He saw DeChambre's right hand, fully clear of the pocket, still gripping the Glock. Bolan stamped down hard on DeChambre's hand. He heard bones crunch a split second before DeChambre squealed in pain. Blood oozed from between the shattered fingers and Bolan kicked the pistol across the room. He bent and caught hold of DeChambre's coat lapels, hauling the man to his feet. DeChambre's face had turned ashen, thick hair falling over his eyes.

"You're the worst kind of man. A cop who betrays his own kind."

"They were American agents. I owed them nothing," DeChambre said.

The Frenchman threw up his left arm, jamming his hand beneath Bolan's chin, forcing his head back. Ignoring his pain he used his right arm to hammer at Bolan's face. DeChambre was no weakling. Bolan could feel the strength in his hard body as they briefly struggled for advantage. He felt the slam of DeChambre's knee against his thigh, absorbed the impact and retaliated with a savage head butt that rocked the Frenchman back on his heels. The stunning blow distracted DeChambre long enough for Bolan to circle his neck with one arm and twist the man off balance. As DeChambre turned, Bolan punched him hard under his ribs, delivering a number of crippling blows that left the Frenchman choking for breath. Weakened, DeChambre offered no resistance when Bolan pushed him upright and slammed a fist into the French cop's jaw. DeChambre backpedaled, coming up short against the wall, and hit the floor in a bloody heap.

He was too stunned to offer any further resistance as Bolan bent over him and emptied his coat pockets while checking for additional weapons. He tossed the items onto the bed.

"Nothing worse than a crooked cop. And especially one who turns on his own kind and allows them to be killed."

"Turner and Bentley knew what they were doing. You carry the badge, you stand the risk. What should I do? Cry for them?"

For a cold, heart-shrinking moment DeChambre thought the big American was about to turn on him. His cocky attitude became a greasy lurch in the pit of his stomach. The expression on his opponent's face was truly frightening. Then the moment passed.

"Get on your feet. We're leaving soon," Bolan said.

"Where are we going?" DeChambre demanded.

"You're going to be delivered to some of your friends in the task force. The American contingent. They'll be really pleased to meet one of the men involved in the deaths of their buddies."

"You cannot do that."

"Give you odds I can," Bolan said.

He took out his cell and made contact with Brognola. He explained briefly that he had a gift for the U.S. agents on the task force. When he told Brognola who he had and what the man was involved with, the big Fed said he would make contact about a handover location.

"If I was you, DeChambre, I would wave goodbye to my Interpol pension," Bolan said.

The Frenchman made no reply. He seemed more concerned with nursing his damaged hand.

Brognola called back within ten minutes, offering Bolan a location where he could meet up with members of the U.S. task-force contingent.

"No questions asked," Brognola said. "Lead man is Neil

Youngman. Just deliver DeChambre and get on your way. Okay?"

"Thanks."

Bolan ended the call. He pulled on his jacket and gestured for DeChambre to move. He showed him the SIG-Sauer before he slid it just inside the jacket. DeChambre slid his damaged hand into his coat pocket.

"Out the door. Turn right. Left at the junction. We can go down the emergency stairs. No games, DeChambre. The jury is out on you at the moment, so don't play clever."

They negotiated the concrete steps to the ground floor, emerging through the fire door into the alley next to the hotel. Bolan stayed just behind DeChambre. The alley brought them to the main street. The sidewalk was close to being deserted. The rain was keeping people inside.

"My car is just beyond the main entrance. Straight to it and get in."

Bolan indicated the SUV and they moved in the direction of the vehicle. They had almost reached it when three men stepped out from the hotel entrance. One ranged in close behind and Bolan felt the hard press of a pistol muzzle against his spine. A second stood on Bolan's right, his own weapon visible under his coat. The third man confronted DeChambre, a thin smile on his lips.

"Good of you to bring him out to us," he said in English.

"Bertran, he has a gun under his jacket," DeChambre said, turning to face Bolan. DeChambre wagged a finger at the SUV. "We won't be riding in your vehicle, after all," he said. "We can go across the street and get into my friends' car. Is that going to be a problem, Mr. Cooper?"

"Not for me," Bolan said calmly.

The man facing Bolan took the SIG-Sauer from his hand. Bolan's pockets were searched and his cell phone was removed and it vanished inside the man's coat.

Bertran took out his own phone and dialed a number. He moved aside from the group as they began to cross the street, so his conversation couldn't be heard by the American.

"Valk, we have him. Where are you? On your way? Okay. Listen, we're taking Cooper to the site as arranged. Why don't you and Lucien wait outside the hotel. We'll handle this end. When we are done we'll join you and DeChambre can get us into Cooper's room. We need to check it for anything he might have about the organization. You may want to keep an eye on his vehicle too. Dark blue Toyota SUV. Parked at the curb outside the hotel." He quoted the license plate number. "Okay? We will see you later."

Bertran finished the call and nodded to DeChambre as he rejoined them.

"Time to go, then." DeChambre said.

8

"You're not as clever as you believed you were," DeChambre said. He nodded curtly at the men covering Bolan. "Your task-force friends are going to have a disappointing wait." He gestured impatiently. "Get him in the car. Let's get away from here before anyone becomes curious."

Bolan was pushed into the back of the elderly Citroën waiting by the opposite curb and flanked by a man on either side. De-Chambre climbed in beside the driver. The car moved off with a brief squeal of rubber against the road surface, taking the first corner fast. The man beside Bolan rolled with the sway of the car and the Executioner felt the hard outline of the pistol holstered against the man's right hip. He filed away the knowledge.

"You have upset too many people, Cooper. Cost us a great deal of money and caused much damage. Naturally you are not very popular with my employer," DeChambre said.

"That would be Hugo Canfield," Bolan replied. "Knowing that makes my day worthwhile."

DeChambre turned to face Bolan. The Frenchman's face was flushed with anger. Self-consciously he reached up to finger the bruises that spread across his face. He exposed his battered hand, staring at the livid, bloody flesh. He reached inside his coat and drew out a handkerchief. DeChambre wrapped it around his injured hand, wincing against the pain.

"Make all the clever jokes you want. Just be aware that you have very little time left. In fact, only for as long as this ride lasts.

When we reach our destination you are going to die. Simple as that. Dead simple. You see, even I can make clever remarks."

"They say the French have no sense of humor. I think you just proved it."

DeChambre's expression hardened. His good hand gripped the top of the seat, knuckles growing pale.

"Can't this thing go any faster?" he snapped at the driver.

The man shrugged, but responded by jamming his foot down hard on the pedal and the Citroën increased speed.

Bolan could see they were passing through an industrial area. Warehouses and buildings flashed by, the majority of them empty. Over to one side Bolan saw the tall cranes and machinery of construction sites. A redevelopment area. He understood why DeChambre had chosen this place for his intended disposal of his problem.

It was time, then, the Executioner decided, to make his play, because the window of opportunity was closing fast.

Without warning he slammed the point of his elbow into the throat of the man on his immediate left, hearing the soft crunch of cartilage. The man clutched at his throat, gagging nosily. The moment he struck, Bolan leaned forward and wrapped both arms around the driver's neck, applying severe pressure and wrenching the man's neck with enough force to snap the vertebra. The driver uttered a startled gasp, his body rising from his seat, control of the speeding car lost in an instant. The Citroën began to swerve back and forth across the road.

Bolan felt his second minder lunge at him, hands scrabbling for contact. With the driver incapacitated the Executioner swiveled to meet his attacker, slamming an open palm full into the man's face, the heel of his hand connecting with the nose. The man's head snapped back, blood starting to blossom and pour down over his mouth and chin. Bolan's follow-up punch failed to land as the driverless Citroën was still veering wildly from side to side, throwing the occupants around like loose sacks of grain. Bolan gained a handhold, grabbing one of the trailing seat belts and wrapping it around his wrist. He held on hard as the car hit the rough edge of the road, wheels climbing up the turned-earth bank. The car's weight and speed carried it along the bank for several yards, the vehicle tilted at an angle.

Suddenly the wild ride came to an abrupt end. The nose of the Citroën smashed into a large concrete block partially sunk into the edge of the road. It was a section of construction fabrication waiting for removal. The block was solid, reinforced with steel rods, and it barely moved under the impact. The effect on the car was extreme. The hood collapsed as the engine was pushed back into the passenger compartment. Steel buckled and glass showered the interior. Neither De-Chambre nor the driver were wearing seatbelts and the driver was thrown forward into the steering wheel, then partway out through the windshield. DeChambre, with nothing to restrain him, was propelled out through the gap, his upper body slamming into the concrete block with enough force to crush his head to a bloody pulp and shatter bones.

If Bolan had not had the presence of mind to grab the nylon belt strap he might have ended up in the front of the car himself. He was thrown against the front seats, breath driven from his body. The two men with him, already immobilized, were battered by the effects of the crash. As the Citroën rocked to a halt Bolan had to push the limp forms off him before he could kick open a door and half tumble from the wrecked car. He hit the wet ground with a thump and lay sucking in harsh breaths. His chest hurt and his ribs ached. He lay still for a while until his breathing settled, then pushed to his feet, slumping against the side of the car.

Canfield's organization was persistent if little else. The man was fighting hard to preserve his business empire, and violent action appeared to be his hallmark. If that was what he wanted Bolan was happy to respond. He was determined to close down Canfield's sleazy operation. And he would battle his way through Canfield's entire crew, if necessary.

The Executioner glanced around. The area still appeared deserted and no one had come forward to check out the site of the crash. It would be better for Bolan if he distanced himself from the area before anyone did show up. He remembered that one of DeChambre's men had taken his gun. Bolan pushed away from the side of the car and leaned in to locate his weapon.

A slight movement warned him too late. The toe of a shoe slammed across the side of his face. The blow shoved Bolan back a couple of steps, pain flaring over his cheekbone. Bolan saw a figure push out of the open door, blood covering the lower half of his face.

The man whose nose he had broken.

The thug exited the car in a rush that carried him into Bolan, slamming the tall American off balance. The man wrapped both arms around Bolan's body, digging in his heels as he increased the pressure. Bolan felt his ribs move. The man was no weakling. He snuffled harshly through his shattered nose, spraying blood. Bolan jammed both hands under the man's chin and pushed hard, forcing the head back.

There was a momentary standoff, each man going for gold until Bolan slammed one knee up between his opponent's thighs. The man gave a screech of pain, his encircling arms slackening off. Bolan gave a final push and the startled minder was left open. A sledging fist slammed against the man's jaw, flinging his head to the side, giving Bolan the chance to grab a handful of thick hair. He swung hard, whacking the man's skull against the edge of the Citroën's roof a couple of times. The man went down without another sound.

Bolan searched the pockets of the man's coat and located his cell phone, the SIG-Sauer and the spare magazines.

Jamming the gun back into his waistband Bolan pocketed everything else, then turned away from the scene, retracing the route to the main road.

It took him close to a half hour and it was getting near dusk by the time Bolan found himself walking back toward the city. For once the rain had reduced to a fine drizzle. It was a small thing but he was getting tired of Rotterdam's wet season. It was a couple of miles before he hit the outer city and found he had a signal again on his phone. He punched in Brognola's number and let it ring until his friend's voice came through.

"Call off the meet. I won't be delivering DeChambre. I had a little confrontation with him and some of his buddies. They wanted to take *me* for a one-way ride. It ended badly."

"I'll have the team advised. What's going on over there, Striker?"

"Everyone I meet wants me dead, Hal. These are seriously terminally minded jokers."

"You're upsetting their paradise. On the bright side I spoke to my task-force contact. They have all those women in secure placements. And some detail has been forthcoming. The women have identified photographs, picking out some of the people involved in snatching them off the streets. All that is going to help build up the files on Venturer Exports. But still not enough to move on it. That lawyer of Canfield's would be hopping all over the scene before we moved a stick of furniture."

"Canfield's favorite lawyer won't be serving any more writs. The man is dead."

"Score one for us? So what are you thinking now, Striker?"

"That the world has forgotten the difference between doing the right thing and standing by watching."

"Striker, we've had this conversation before. If the task force went in now and arrested everyone on Canfield's payroll

who would benefit? His second-team lawyers would scream
abuse of human rights, quoting every law on the books, and
without every charge sheet being one-hundred-and-one-
percent absolutely correct down to the last full stop, the whole
crew would walk. Justice, here and in Europe would be
slapped with writs, false-arrest accusations and claims for
defamation. We'd have compensation claims being stuffed
into every orifice. And Hugo Canfield would be sitting in his
plush offices having a glass of champagne while he set up his
next trafficking deal."

"You know how to cheer a man up, Hal."

"They are lousy, lower-than-low scumbags, Striker. Safe
because they're having the last laugh at us. They know it.
We know it."

"They may be laughing, Hal, but it won't be for long. Right
now they're hurting and I aim to make them hurt even more.
One more strike here in Rotterdam, then I'm going after
Canfield and his U.K. setup."

"McCarter's man in London will have what you need. I'll
look out for smoke rising over Big Ben."

After he ended the call Bolan looked around for a cruising
taxi. He had had enough of walking around Rotterdam's
rainy streets.

"IT'S BEEN TOO LONG," Valk said again, glancing at his watch.
"They should be back by now."

"So where are they?" his partner asked.

"Try Bertran's cell again," Valk suggested.

Lucien nodded and dialed the number. He waited as the cell
rang out, shaking his head.

Valk banged his fist on the steering wheel. "Why don't
they answer?"

"You think maybe something went wrong?"

"Actually, yes."

"So what do we do?"

"One thing we don't do is call Canfield and admit our suspicions. You know what they do to the messenger with bad news."

Lucien managed a weak smile. Their employer's volatile moods were legend. No one ever wanted to get on Hugo Canfield's bad side. Or incur a visit from the man called Sergeant Gantley. He found himself reaching inside his coat for the pistol nestling in its shoulder holster. When his fingers touched the smooth steel it gave Lucien a sliver of comfort.

"This man. Cooper. He's no fool. Look what he did to van Ryden and his team. And at the landing dock. Valk, we should cover ourselves. Maybe he got away from Bertran and the others. Maybe we…"

Valk wasn't listening. He was staring out through the car window, past the rain spatter and the gloom. He was watching a tall figure emerging from a taxi that had just pulled up outside the hotel.

Tall.

Black hair.

An athletically built man dressed in black.

He paid the driver and moved down the sidewalk to an SUV parked at the curb. It was the vehicle that Bertran had identified as belonging to Cooper.

"I think that's him," Valk said. "Damn, it has to be him."

Lucien saw the man in question checking the SUV before turning and going into the hotel. He was about to ask what they should do, but when he saw that Valk had taken his own pistol from its holster, screwing on the threaded sound-suppressor, he knew he didn't need to ask.

"Let him get to his room," Valk said. "No fucking about, Lucien. I don't want this bastard playing any of his fancy tricks with us. We go in hard and shoot him. Plain and simple. It's past time for being polite."

"If that is Cooper—where are Bertran and the others?"

"If that *is* Cooper," Valk answered, "I think we already know where they are."

Lucien attached his own sound-suppressor. He slid the pistol back inside the holster, then ran the back of his hand across dry lips. He glanced at his partner and saw that Valk was wearing that expression he always displayed when he had worked himself into a killing mood.

"Let's do it," Valk said.

He was out of the car, striding across the street before Lucien could say a word. All he could do was step out himself and follow Valk to the hotel entrance.

They crossed the lobby and went to the desk where Valk caught the attention of the clerk.

"Hey, wasn't that the American, Cooper? The guy who just came in?" Valk had a wide grin on his face.

He turned to Lucien. "I said it was Cooper. Didn't he say he was staying here?" He turned back to the clerk. "I'm right? Cooper? We've been tracking him all day. Supposed to be going to a company celebration tonight, but he vanished earlier."

Valk lowered his voice to a conspiratorial whisper. "Sly guy—I think he met one of the saleswomen at the party last night and when we looked around he was gone." He glanced at his watch. "Only a couple of hours and he's supposed to be giving the big speech tonight. We don't get him there on time we'll be sweeping the streets tomorrow."

Lucien nodded, caught up in his partner's enthusiastic charade. "That's right. Help us out, friend. We need to get him all tidied up and daisy fresh. What's his room number?"

Valk had his cell phone out, tapping in a number. "Got to call our boss. Tell him everything's okay. Then see if we can drag Cooper back on form."

He went through the pantomime of talking to someone on the other end of the line. In fact, he had dialed his own home number and was speaking to his own phone, making up the dialog as he went along.

"We have him getting ready now, sir. What? No problem. We'll have him there on time. Yes, sir. My word, sir."

He closed the phone, glanced at his watch again. "Cooper? Room number? Please…"

The young clerk, looking from one man to the other, caught up in the excitement of the moment, blurted out the room number.

"Thanks, friend. You have saved our sanity and probably our jobs." Valk slapped Lucien on the shoulder. "Come on, let's go and get Cooper ready."

As the two headed for the elevator bank, Valk waved at the clerk. "Thanks, friend, you did us a real favor there."

The clerk watched the elevator doors close, frowning as the rush calmed down. He reached for the house phone and called the room occupied by the American named Cooper.

"*Mijnheer* Cooper? Reception. You have two visitors on their way up to you. They say they should be picking you up for a company social evening. Was I right in sending them up, sir? I hope I haven't disturbed you, only you did say you wanted a meal sent up because you were not going out again…"

The phone cut off abruptly and the clerk was left feeling that he had indeed disturbed the hotel guest.

BOLAN DROPPED THE PHONE back on its cradle and turned toward the door. He opened it and checked the deserted corridor. The elevator bank was to his left. He stepped out of the room and pulled the door closed behind him. He walked quickly and quietly to the far end of the corridor, reaching the junction a few doors along where the corridor made a right-angle turn in the direction of the emergency exit, the same one he had used to get DeChambre out of the hotel. He pressed against the wall, leaning slightly forward so he could watch the empty corridor.

Seconds later the elevator pinged and the doors slid open with a subdued hiss.

Bolan saw two men step out, checking the corridor before they walked briskly to his door. The way they moved told him they were anything but hotel guests, and when they each produced an automatic pistol, both fitted with sound-suppressors, he needed no more convincing. They stopped at his door, one turning to stand watch while the other reached to knock.

When there was no response the pair exchanged glances. The man who had knocked said something that Bolan was unable to pick up, then stepped back to give himself space. Bolan realized what the man was about to do even before he raised his right foot prior to launching a kick at the closed door.

Bolan slid around the corner and drew down on the man standing watch. He spotted Bolan the moment he stepped into view and called a warning to his partner. The man then extended his gun arm, the muzzle of his pistol sliding across his buddy's shoulder. The SIG-Sauer in Bolan's hand cracked twice. The first slug took a chunk out of the target's right shoulder, blowing a spray of blood and flesh from his jacket. The force of the slug twisted the man half around so that Bolan's second shot hit him in the throat and knocked him off his feet, gagging for air.

As the crack of the shots echoed in the second man's ears he spun on one foot, exceptionally fast, his pistol tracking in quickly. He fired on the move, his slug chugging from the muzzle and tearing a gouge of plaster from the corner of the wall an inch over Bolan's head.

The first man had barely hit the carpet when Bolan retuned fire from his one-knee position on the floor. He saw the gunman react to the slug that powered into his chest, knocking him back against the wall. As he rebounded from the impact the man took two more slugs from Bolan's weapon. They hit with tremendous force, shattering his spine. He faltered, surprise etched across his face as he fell face down on the carpet.

Bolan moved quickly, holstering his pistol, stepping over the bodies, and used his key card to open his door. In his room he picked up his bag. He always kept his belongings packed ready for a fast exit and right now that was what he wanted.

The thought crossed his mind that Canfield seemed determined to continue his attempts to get rid of him. How many more of his crew was he going to throw at Bolan?

Back in the corridor the Executioner turned and went for the emergency exit as he had done before, only this time he wouldn't be returning to his room. As he turned the corner of the corridor he realized that no one had come out of any of the rooms to check the disturbance. Either they hadn't heard the brief encounter because TV sets were playing, or the modern-day malady of minding their own business had struck once again. In a way he couldn't blame them. It was unfortunate that butting into the affairs of others often got the responsible individual into serious trouble, so people chose to stay behind their own closed doors.

As he descended the stairs Bolan knew that his luck would not hold for long. Sooner or later someone was going to find the bodies, and when they did, the missing Cooper was going to find himself the center of the Rotterdam police's attention.

He needed to distance himself from them quickly.

At street level he moved along the alley, reached the sidewalk and walked calmly to his waiting SUV. Bolan unlocked the vehicle and slid inside. He fired up the engine and eased away from the curb, merging with the traffic. He had no idea how long he might have before the cops picked up on his rental. In the time he did have he needed to lose the vehicle and get himself a fresh set of wheels.

HAL BROGNOLA WORKED his influence with the task force and arranged for Bolan to get his SUV off the streets. He parked in the basement garage of a derelict office block and left it for the task force to pick up. They had left a black BMW SUV for Bolan to take over. It had legitimate plates and no history that would attract attention from the local cops. The Toyota would be lifted by a recovery truck, concealed under a tarp and driven to a task-force safe house.

"You understand, buddy, that the task force will deny any association with you and your activities if questions are asked?" Brognola had told him.

Bolan had smiled at that.

"Hal, those words are like an old, familiar song."

"Off the record the team mans are high-fiving every time you hit Canfield's organization. On a secondary note the two mans at the hotel turned out to be a couple of local hitters allied to Canfield's group. Same as the ones who hijacked you along with DeChambre."

"Hal, stayed tuned. 'Radio Rotterdam' hasn't finished broadcasting yet."

9

The following day found Mack Bolan preparing for his planned hit on Canfield's main distribution site in Holland. The farm and the processing plant occupied a large area off the main route out of Rotterdam. The information the man at the dock had given him proved to be extremely accurate.

It took Bolan more than an hour to reach the location. He noticed that the area he had driven through was taken up by similar industry. This part of the country grew vast quantities of agricultural produce that was distributed all across Europe and into the U.K. There were constant streams of vehicles towing large containers that held fresh supplies of vegetables and dairy products heading for distribution points. A large percentage of these vehicles were on their way to Rotterdam. Bolan saw a number of South East Containers trucks arriving and leaving the Knookreising Farm.

He sat at the side of the road studying the layout of the farm. There was a wide turn leading off the road onto a paved strip that terminated in the large freight yard fronting the farm. There was an office block and, behind that, the sprawl of large greenhouses and open strips of planted fields. To one side were the processing and packing sheds. It was an impressive setup.

Bolan moved his powerful binoculars to the far distance where, his research had informed him, the original farm still remained. He spotted a large house built in the 1950s. Next to it were traditional Dutch barns and outhouses. Bolan saw a couple of South East Containers trucks parked nearby. According to the maps he had studied there was a minor road that ran along the back of the property, close to the original farm setup. It seemed to offer the best opportunity for him to check out the place.

He glanced at his watch. Midafternoon. Overhead the sky was heavy with dark clouds. It looked as if he really had chosen Holland's rainy season to make his visit. Bolan started the SUV and pulled back onto the road. He drove a couple of miles before he spotted the narrow road that skirted the eastern perimeter of the farmland. It took him almost twenty minutes before he found himself paralleling the main route. In that time he had encountered no traffic. The road he was on may have been the principal one when the original farm had been built, but the wider, faster main route had taken all the traffic. For Bolan's purpose that was ideal.

He pulled off the road, turning the BMW around before taking it down a rutted strip into the cover of tangled undergrowth. Out of sight Bolan was able to take his gear from the SUV's back and ready himself.

His intention was to dismantle Venturer Export's distribution base. Given the right equipment that would have been straightforward. But his access to specialist ordnance was virtually nil. Coming into the country unarmed and with no recourse to hardware meant the Executioner was winging his mission. Bolan didn't let that hold him back. He was just going to have to be a tad more creative. In the SUV he had the handguns confiscated from the opposition, plus the MP-5. The shoulder rig he had taken from one of the gunmen housed the SIG-Sauer. His second pistol was tucked behind his belt.

Before leaving Rotterdam Bolan had used some of the money taken from Canfield's people to outfit himself. A visit to a sporting goods store had offered him close substitutes for his combat gear. Combat-style pants, a thin sweater and a pair of sturdy walking boots—all in black. The photographer's jacket he had purchased at a store farther along the street provided pockets for his extra ammo clips. He slung the MP-5 across his back by the webbing sling and pulled on the dark cap he'd bought.

Exiting the vehicle Bolan eased along the bottom of the ditch and peered over the rim. A few lights were on in the farmhouse and buildings against the gloom of the afternoon and the overcast sky. He studied the layout. There would be adequate cover. He spotted parked farm machinery, stacks of crates and barrels. And he saw a few more people about than he might have expected on an old-fashioned farm. Bolan had a feeling they might be there because of him and the problems he had been creating for the traffickers. His appearance and interference had stirred them into defensive mode. Hit-and-run tactics had the effect of making the enemy nervous because they had no idea where or when he might strike again.

Look out, guys, I'm closer than you think.

The first drops of rain warned Bolan of the downpour about to come. He welcomed it. Rain would work more on his behalf than the opposition's. It would cover his approach. Deaden any sound. The rainfall began in earnest, heavy drops bouncing off the road. Bolan used the rain as his cue, pushing up to the road, crouching low as he went across it and through the tall grass to the perimeter fence. The outer fence was no more than a couple of feet high, a simple three-bar structure. From there Bolan wound his way across a hard packed-earth strip and dropped to a kneeling position behind an ancient, rusting trailer. Its tires were flat and cracked, the paintwork long faded and flaking. Bolan dropped flat and crawled beneath the chassis, working his way along the trailer until he was able to look out across the main yard.

The first man he saw might have been a farmhand. His clothes were nondescript, made for heavy work, and so were

the thick boots on his feet. But the squat submachine gun he
carried close to his body had no place on a working farm. The
next figure moving into Bolan's line of vision, clad in a similar
fashion to the first man, also had an automatic weapon. The
two men came together, shoulders hunched against the rain,
sharing their patrolling misery and the cigarettes they lit. Their
collars were pulled up and caps pulled down against the rain.

Watching them convinced Bolan they were protecting
something with a much higher value than the tomatoes being
produced across the way.

Human cargo.

Somewhere in the distance thunder rumbled, low and deep.
The intensity of the rainfall increased. The armed guards
parted company, each moving in a different direction. As one
man moved out of sight the other one moved in Bolan's
general direction, flicking his cigarette butt to the ground as
he tramped past the old trailer, cutting across the rear of the
farm property. Bolan watched where he went and waited patiently until he returned minutes later. There was no military
precision in the patrolling. The man simply wandered, the
submachine gun pressed close to his side as if he was afraid
getting it wet might render it inoperative. He walked past
Bolan again, moving down the side of the farm building, then
pausing to presumably check out his area of responsibility. He
kept looking skyward, displeased at the weather, shaking his
head a couple of times as he turned and resumed his restless
patrolling. When the Executioner saw the man moving into a
shadowed area, he slid out from beneath the trailer and fell in
behind him.

Typical of old, long-established farms, there were tumble-
down sheds and more abandoned machinery scattered around
the property. The grass grew randomly, sprouting in defiant
clumps between the rusting metal parts and cast-aside tires.

Bolan stalked his man until they were well to the back of

the old house. He moved up without warning, catching his un-suspecting quarry in a powerful neck lock. He dragged the man to the wet ground, ignoring the man's frantic struggle for his weapon, the hoarse gasp from a restricted throat. Slamming one knee into the guard's lower spine Bolan hauled back until he felt vertebrae snap. The man went soft in his grasp. Bolan released him and pushed to his feet, stepping back, catching a final shuddering spasm before the guard became still. The Executioner took the man's weapon and threw it into an untidy stack of old machinery. He slid the body out of sight under a trailer.

One less gunman to worry about.

Bolan wanted no surprises from guards coming in behind his back. No probe, whether hard or soft, guaranteed total security. Reducing that probability was Bolan's only safe-guard, though even he knew it wasn't going to shield him fully.

Flat against the end wall of the barnlike building, Bolan peered around the corner. The downed guard's partner was trudging up the slight incline, pulling up his coat collar and no doubt cursing the inclement weather. He slowed as he neared Bolan's position, looking around for his missing buddy, then continued on toward the corner of the barn.

Was he thinking his partner had stopped under cover for another cigarette? Maybe taking shelter from the downpour?

His casual movement gave the impression he was not alerted by any possible trouble.

Bolan let the man round the end of the barn, then used his right forearm to deliver a brutal throat strike. The guard's strangled cry was cut off before he could generate any warning sound. Trying to suck air through his crushed pas-sages the man offered little resistance to Bolan's follow-up maneuver. He caught hold of the guard's coat collar and pulled down, driving his knee up into the vulnerable face. The solid impact drove the guard up and back. He slammed against the wood wall of the barn, splintering a couple of the weathered slats, then pitched facedown on the rain-sodden ground. Bolan relieved him of his weapons, hurling them into the shadowed piles of machinery.

He was turning away from the barn when something caught his eye. A gleam of metal showing through the gap created by the broken wood slats. Bolan checked it out. Pulling away a length of wood he saw an inner lining of steel sheeting. Something was constructed within the wooden shell of the old barn. He didn't waste time speculating, though he didn't expect to find anything good.

He heard a rumbling sound. The rainfall was increasing. The ground under Bolan's feet was quickly becoming waterlogged, the disturbed earth sluicing down the gradual slope in brown rivulets. He crept around the side of the barn. Some twenty feet away the raw earth gave way to a concrete apron that provided hard standing for the vehicles that would draw up to the barn access. From his position Bolan could see that the sliding door had been rolled back. One of the South East Containers trucks had reversed up to the door and Bolan watched as the container doors at the back of the truck were opened. Figures clustered around the opening. One of them was gesturing, his raised voice reaching Bolan. Hesitant figures appeared at the edge of the container. One of the men reached up and caught an arm, dragging a young woman down out of the container. She stumbled as she landed on the concrete. Other hands reached out to steady her balance before pushing her roughly inside the barn. Bolan counted six more women being removed from the truck. The container doors were closed and secured. Someone banged on the side of the truck and it pulled away, moving down toward the main farm buildings.

The Executioner had his confirmation.

He pulled the MP-5's sling over his head, running a quick check to confirm the weapon was set for use.

There was one man lingering near the barn door. He was leaning against the frame as he spoke into a cell phone, his head nodding as he talked. He wore a long dark coat and a baseball cap.

Bolan edged along the wall of the barn, his eyes fixed on the man. The downpour muffled any sound he might have made and Bolan was standing directly behind the man by the time he completed his call and pushed his phone into a pocket. The webbing sling flipped over the man's head and Bolan twisted it, pulling it tight against flesh. He pulled the man back and down, jamming a knee into the spine as the squirming, panicked man struggled to reach for his gun. The powerful muscles in Bolan's arms were taut under the pressure he was applying. The frantic struggles weakened; the boot heels drumming against the concrete slowed, jerked into stillness. Bolan held his position for a few more seconds, then loosened his grip and drew the webbing strap over the man's head, dislodging the cap. He lowered the man to the wet concrete, caught hold of his collar and slid him away from the access door to the base of the barn wall.

With his MP-5 set for triple bursts Bolan edged around the access door, sparing a few seconds to assimilate the image.

The steel construction he had partially glimpsed through the broken barn slats was a twenty-foot-square lockbox, the front wall facing him, constructed of close-spaced bars with an inset door. Inside the box Bolan saw the group of young women from the container, some standing in listless poses, others sitting on the low cots that were bunched together at the far end of the box. Bolan's fingers tightened around the MP-5 as the image of the captive females registered. Herded into the steel box like so much cattle. Trapped, without hope, awaiting the next stage of their forced captivity.

On the far side of the barn were stored metal canisters and

Get FREE BOOKS and a FREE GIFT when you play the...

LAS VEGAS GAME

Just scratch off the gold box with a coin. Then check below to see the gifts you get!

YES! I have scratched off the gold box. Please send me my **2 FREE BOOKS** and gift for which I qualify. I understand that I am under no obligation to purchase any books as explained on the back of this card.

366 ADL E4CE   166 ADL E4CE

FIRST NAME   LAST NAME

ADDRESS

APT.#   CITY

STATE/PROV.   ZIP/POSTAL CODE

7	7	7	Worth TWO FREE BOOKS plus a BONUS Mystery Gift!
🍒	🍒	🍒	Worth TWO FREE BOOKS!
🔔	🔔	♣	TRY AGAIN!

Offer limited to one per household and not valid to current subscribers of Gold Eagle® books. All orders subject to approval. Please allow 4 to 6 weeks for delivery.

The Reader Service — Here's how it works:

Accepting your 2 free books and free gift (gift valued at approximately $5.00) places you under no obligation to buy anything. You may keep the books and gift and return the shipping statement marked "cancel." If you do not cancel, about a month later we'll send you 6 additional books and bill you just $31.94* — that's a savings of 24% off the cover price of all 6 books! And there's no extra charge for shipping! You may cancel at any time, but if you choose to continue, every other month we'll send you 6 more books, which you may either purchase at the discount price or return to us and cancel your subscription.

If offer card is missing write to: The Reader Service, P.O. Box 1867, Buffalo NY 14240-1867

BUSINESS REPLY MAIL
FIRST-CLASS MAIL   PERMIT NO. 717   BUFFALO, NY

POSTAGE WILL BE PAID BY ADDRESSEE

THE READER SERVICE
PO BOX 1867
BUFFALO NY 14240-9952

NO POSTAGE
NECESSARY
IF MAILED
IN THE
UNITED STATES

crates, some standing five high. There were also racks of wooden pallets and filled sacks.

In front of the stored goods were the men who currently dominated the frightening world the women had been forced into. The traffickers. Bolan had nothing but contempt for them as they talked and laughed, clustered around one of a number of desks holding a computer, the large monitor displaying pornographic images. Bolan counted five of them. They were intent on studying the screen images, oblivious to the Executioner's presence until one of them straightened to light a cigarette. He moved back from the main group, touching his lighter flame to the cigarette, casually glancing across the barn.

He saw Bolan.

His reaction was fast but not enough to allow himself and his partners clear space. The man shouted a warning, snatching at the handgun tucked behind his belt. He was still yelling when Bolan hit him with a 3-round burst that thudded into his chest, shoving him back against the edge of the desk. As the man arched back across the desk Bolan fed him three more slugs that shattered ribs and chewed at flesh.

The man's four colleagues scattered in a panic, reaching for weapons. A couple wore them in body holsters, the others grabbed at MP-5s on nearby desks.

By this time Bolan was on the move, angling in across the barn, his weapon up and firing, seeking targets. His mobility proved an asset. Bolan weaved about, laying down deadly fire that cut into the unprepared traffickers. His slugs punctured flesh, broke bone and caused bloody gouts and spurts. Only one of the crew got off retaliatory fire, yanking his own MP-5 around in a panicky sweep that sent gunfire ripping through the barn's timber walls. His action only lasted brief seconds before Bolan's strike continued. He stitched the man with a pair of triple bursts that slammed the trafficker back across the desk, dislodging the computer monitor and sending it crashing to the floor. The man rolled across the desk, arms thrown wide, his weapon spilling from his limp grasp.

Before he moved again Bolan exchanged the MP-5's magazine for a fresh one. It was time, mainly the lack of it, that dictated Bolan's actions. He crossed to the lockbox. The inset door was secured by a modern lock mechanism. He studied it, then heard a quiet voice. It came from one of the young women. He didn't understand the language and looked at her through the bars.

"English?" he asked.

She turned and gestured at one of the other girls, speaking to her.

"I understand a little," the young woman said. "There are…keys in drawer. I saw them put in there."

Bolan tracked her pointing finger and crossed to the desk she indicated.

"Yes. There."

He found a set of keys, took them back to the door and found the right one on the third attempt.

"Tell them to come out. We have to move quickly. Make them understand. Others may be coming because of the shooting," he said.

The woman nodded. She began to instruct the others and they responded without argument. They gathered at the barn door.

"That way," Bolan said. "You'll find a fence. A narrow road on the other side. Best I can do right now. Take them. *Go*."

"What will you do?" the woman asked.

"Whatever needs doing. Now get out of here."

The young woman nodded. Before she followed the others she bent to retrieve one of the abandoned handguns. "They will not touch us again," she said.

Bolan followed her to the door and watched the small group as they moved up the slope, away from the barn. He picked up sound coming from below his position. Turning Bolan saw an open-backed 4x4 swinging into view and racing in his direction. His presence on the farm was well and truly acknowledged now.

Bolan stepped out from cover to take the battle to the enemy.

10

The driver of the 4x4 raised a warning as the tall, dark-clad figure stepped out of the barn, the submachine gun in his hands raised. Beyond him the women from the lockbox were running free and clear. At the driver's shout one of the men standing in the exposed rear of the vehicle swung his weapon on-line and opened fire. The slight bounce of the 4x4 took his aim off-line and the stream of 9 mm slugs chewed wood from the barn wall, spitting splinters into the air.

The shooter's partner, less reckless, called him an idiot. He told him to hold back until they were closer. It might have been sound advice but in this case it did little to gain them any advantage.

The Executioner broke into a hard run, weaving slightly as he approached them, then brought himself to a stop. The MP-5 in his steady hands settled on the 4x4. Flame winked at the muzzle. Glass shattered as the windshield blew apart. The driver screamed as he caught a face full of razor fragments and 9 mm slugs. He twisted away from the windshield, losing control of the 4x4. It lurched to the right, jerking as the lack of control brought about a stall.

The pair of shooters were thrown off balance for seconds that cost them dearly.

Bolan raised the MP-5 as he stepped to the side, clearing the cab as the vehicle came to a dead stop. The shooters in the back reached out to steady themselves by grabbing the rail

at the rear of the cab. It was Bolan's opening. He took it
without pause, his weapon spitting triple bursts as he closed
in on the vehicle. The closest shooter jerked and twitched as
he caught a triple tap, the force of the slugs turning him
sideways, so that Bolan's second burst hit him in the ribs,
splintering bone and coring through to his heart. His partner
scrambled to the far side of the truck and jumped to the
ground, hauling his own submachine gun into position for a
fast response once he saw his target. He failed to see Bolan
drop to the concrete and angle his MP-5 beneath the 4x4. The
Executioner tracked the shooter as he moved the length of the
truck, then triggered two 3-round bursts that shattered the
man's ankles, dumping him screaming on the ground, blood
squirting from his torn flesh and shattered bone. The shooter
caught a quick glimpse of Bolan before the MP-5 crackled
again and the shooter's head snapped back under the force of
the 9 mm slugs.

Bolan yanked open the driver's door and hauled the body
from the seat and climbed in. He dropped the MP-5 and
dipped the clutch, turning the key to restart the stalled 4x4.
As the engine burst into life Bolan put the vehicle into gear
and slammed down on the gas pedal, sending the 4x4 into a
rubber-scorching lurch forward. He spun the steering wheel
and took the truck inside the barn, bringing it to a hard stop.
Out of the cab he grabbed his weapon and some spare magazines, then stepped around to the side of the 4x4, crouched
and raked the underside, puncturing the gas tank. Streams of
gasoline began to spurt from the ragged holes. Bolan kept
firing the MP-5 until the magazine was empty. The gas was
spreading in a wide pool across the concrete floor of the barn.

Crossing to the desks Bolan searched the floor and found
the lighter dropped by the first man he had shot. He scooped
it up and ignited it. The lighter flared as Bolan turned up the
butane. Bolan snatched up a discarded newspaper and formed

it into a loose tube. He lit the paper and let it burn, then tossed the flaming torch into the spreading gasoline. Vapor caught the fire, sucking at it hungrily. It engulfed the 4x4 in a frantic surge, flame swelling up in a ravenous ball. Bolan retreated, snapping in a fresh magazine for the MP-5. He had just reached the door as the truck blew, the force of the blast slamming between his shoulders and almost knocking him off balance as he stumbled out into the cool of the rain.

Raised voices made him turn. Three armed figures were running in his direction. They opened fire the moment Bolan appeared, slugs hammering at the concrete. Bolan pulled back, flat against the wall of the barn, feeling the heat from the fire starting to penetrate the wood. He raised the MP-5 and tracked the closest of the approaching hostiles. He stroked the trigger and saw his target stumble. The man went down all the way when Bolan hit him with a second triple burst. The sight of their partner falling made the other two fall back, hesitating as they realized their own vulnerable positions. Bolan didn't hesitate. He put a burst into one of the men, the slugs tearing through his shoulder and spraying bloody bits of flesh and bone from the wound. The man dropped his weapon, clutching at his shoulder. In his haste to get away he lost his footing and crashed headlong to the concrete. Bolan heard the crackle of automatic fire from the remaining man, felt the snap of slugs as they burned the air around him. He felt the shock of a hit as a bullet clipped his right side, just above the hip. The force knocked him off balance. Bolan forced himself to absorb the pain as he swung his MP-5 toward the shooter. He saw the man go down hard, his weapon discharging into the sky.

Clamping a hand over his bleeding hip Bolan straightened, turning to head back up the slope to his waiting car.

Behind him flames were flaring from between the wooden slats as the barn fire expanded. Bolan heard soft explosions from within the blazing structure and remembered the stored

canisters and packed sacks. He had no idea what they might
have held but they seemed to be reacting to the intense heat.
He had almost reached the low fence when a powerful explosion rocked the ground under his feet. When he looked back
over his shoulder he witnessed a series of blasts that threw spi-
raling geysers of flame into the sky, tearing out the barn roof.
He maintained his retreat from the farm as the explosions continued, the fireballs arcing across the farm grounds, raining
down on the main buildings and parked vehicles. Whatever
had been stored in the barn was proving to be highly flam-
mable and was creating chaos on the traffickers' base.

Bolan stumbled over the fence, going to his knees on the
rain-sodden ground, a sudden weakness starting to spread
over him. Reaction to the bullet wound. The hand over the
flesh gouge in his side was leaking blood between his fingers.
He felt the ground shudder as one of the arcing fireballs hit
the earth just yards away, spreading a burning mass of liquid
flame. *Too close,* Bolan decided. He struggled to his feet and
made for the road.

A rain-soaked figure appeared, hands reaching out to support
him. Bolan blinked his watery eyes and recognized the young
woman from the barn. The one who spoke some English.

"I can help. Come."

She let him lean against her. She was stronger than she
looked. One arm around his body she led Bolan across the
road and down the slope to his parked SUV. The rest of the
women were crouching down behind the vehicle. They
watched Bolan with wary expressions, faces lit by the rising
flames in the gray afternoon.

"We need to move away from here," Bolan said, using his
key to unlock the BMW. "Tell them to get in the vehicle. Now."

Before the woman had time to answer something caught
her eye and she gripped Bolan's shoulder. "They come."

Bolan swung around. Saw the approaching bulk of a big

SUV. It was speeding up from the farm, bouncing over the rutted ground. It hit the concrete strip, swinging out from its direct path as it powered past the blazing barn.

"In the car," he yelled, bringing the MP-5 on-line.

Bolan fought back the rising pain from the bullet gouge, ignored the blood still seeping from the wound, as he pushed up to road level, facing the oncoming bulk of the SUV. He saw a dark figure lean out from the side window and level a weapon. The muzzle flared briefly as the weapon crackled. The ill-judged volley went wide. Bolan stood his ground and returned fire from his static position, and as the heavy vehicle smashed through the flimsy perimeter fence, his burst clattered in through the grille and into the radiator. Raising his weapon Bolan hit the hood and the windshield. The glass failed to break, the slugs ricocheting off, leaving starred cracks. The effect made the driver haul on the wheel, the big tires squealing as they ground into the paved surface of the road. The SUV slid sideways, swinging dangerously close to Bolan as it came around. He threw himself out of harm's way, the bulk of the vehicle missing him by inches before it righted itself and powered along the strip of the road.

Bolan tucked and rolled, biting back the flare of pain from his wounded hip as he slid across the rain-soaked ground. He scrambled to his knees, bringing the MP-5 back on track as the SUV jerked to a sliding stop, rear doors swinging open. Armed figures disgorged from the vehicle. Bolan opened fire before they had the chance to set themselves and caught one with a couple of tri-bursts that slammed him back against the open door. The man on Bolan's blind side made it to the rear of the SUV, searching for a target. He walked into Bolan's steady fire and went down with a harsh gurgle.

Bolan heard the roar of the SUV's motor as the driver decided to gain some distance. He ran forward, raising the MP-5 to shoulder height, angling the muzzle, firing into the vehicle at window level. The side glass shattered as repeated bursts riddled the interior. The SUV made a brief forward jerk, then stalled, the motor dying. Bolan cleared the magazine, ejected it and felt in a pocket for a fresh load. He clicked it in place. He jerked the weapon around as the driver's door clicked open. The driver slid sideways, pushing the door wide as he dropped from the seat onto the road, blood gleaming on his torn neck and from ragged wounds in his face and skull.

Bolan stood in the middle of the road, soaked from the heavy rain, hand clutched over his bloody side. The MP-5 dropped in his right hand. He didn't hear the woman step alongside. Only glanced around when she touched his arm.

"Now we go," she suggested.

Bolan stared at her.

"Before others come. Please."

He followed her back to the SUV. The other women were already crowded inside the vehicle. The woman slid onto the passenger seat and waited until Bolan climbed behind the wheel. He started the motor and got the SUV moving up out of the hollow and onto the road. He hit the wiper switch and the blades swept back and forth, clearing the rain from the windshield. As he followed the road on its curving path back to the main highway the farm came into view on their right. The blazing barn was in plain sight, other fires raging from the fallout created by the explosion of the material stored inside the building.

Beside Bolan the young woman, still clutching the pistol she had picked up, nodded to herself as she stared at the blaze.

Bolan kept the BMW rolling, slowing only when he reached the junction where the side road rejoined the main route. He swung the wheel and drove past the jam of vehicles starting to crowd the highway. Once he was clear Bolan increased his speed. Twice they saw emergency vehicles heading for the blaze site. Hugo Canfield's people were going to have to answer some serious questions once the police became involved. Bolan's hope was that the disruption to the trafficking operation would simply add more pressure to his actions. He was also aware that Canfield's involvement would be well camouflaged and any connection between himself and the operation would be hard to prove on a legal level.

Bolan's past experience had educated him in the complexities of the criminal mind-set. Men like Hugo Canfield operated on a different level. Distanced from the everyday exposure of his criminal activities by legal manipulation, the use of cover titles and companies operating under him but run by underlings. Canfield was far beyond the grasp of law enforcement. He was able to make his profits by proxy. He allowed others to take the risks and the falls from grace. That was why the task force had not been able to reach him. Canfield simply sidestepped all their efforts, using the law and its complex infrastructure to protect him, while at the same time giving it the finger.

Now he had a different hunter on his trail. One who moved outside the restrictions of such laws. Mack Bolan used a simple logic. He saw the crimes. He identified the perpetrators. He did not stand idly by and do nothing.

Bolan considered the huddled group of young women in the SUV. They were the victims. Taken by force from the streets they called home. Transported to a strange place by men who saw them as nothing more than merchandise. Objects with a price over their heads, to be bartered for and sold into lives of deprivation and humiliation. The traffickers dealt in human souls, without any thought for the innocents they preyed upon. Human trafficking, in Bolan's eyes, was one of the most despicable crimes man had ever devised. There was something especially evil when men could take others of their kind and sell them like so much cattle, indifferent to the suffering they caused.

Hugo Canfield made vast amounts of money via this sickening business. He collected his payments from the people he sold to, enriching his already privileged life with increasing amounts. While he lounged in comfort the nameless victims were forced into degrading occupations, where any kind of resistance would be rewarded with violence. Their new masters looked upon their purchases as simply that—*purchases*—objects they could treat how they wished. The objects had no rights. No redress against the treatment they received, and there was nowhere for them to escape. Owned body and soul by their masters they found that the only relief they could expect came through obedience. Total, unquestioning obedience.

Venturer Exports existed because of the protective umbrella spread over it. A formation of powerful individuals who used their positions to hide the activities of the traffickers beneath complex covers. Favors and money fueled the actions of these protectors. Canfield knew his people and he lavished his bounty on them, sucking them into his circle. It was a self-perpetuating monster. One that demanded more from everyone involved. Any threat against the safety of the collective would bring powerful responses because there was too much to lose. Money aside, there were reputations and careers to protect. The higher the profile the more they had to lose. Bolan had already witnessed the willingness of his enemies to hit back. As far as he was concerned the responses he was getting indicated his strikes were starting to bite.

He had no option but to maintain his offensive.

"I think we have company," the young woman at his side said, her body twisted around in the seat as she peered through the BMW's rear window.

Bolan checked his side mirror and spotted a big silver Mercedes barreling along behind them. It wasn't so much the car but the aggressive way it was being driven that was alarming.

Bolan saw the vehicle accelerate. Silver spray misted behind it from the rain-slick road. It drew closer to the SUV. The driver was pushing to the limit. The thought of engaging on this busy strip of highway didn't sit well with Bolan. He always did his best to avoid involving those he considered innocents. It was looking as if his opponents had no such scruples.

A figure leaned out from one of the car's windows, a pistol in his hand. The shooter held his position for a while but was unable to gain a solid shot and finally pulled back inside the car.

"We can't avoid them out here," Bolan said to the woman. "Tell everyone to hang on."

These mans don't give up, he thought. Well, neither do I.

He jammed his foot hard down on the gas, sending the SUV surging forward. Peering through the streaked windshield he saw a sign ahead, indicating a right turn onto what appeared to be a construction site. Bolan hauled the wheel at the last moment, feeling the heavy SUV rock on its suspension as it fought gravity in the sudden turn. For a moment the rear wheels felt as if they were about to lose traction. They held and the SUV bumped over the edge of the paved highway onto a wide strip of hard packed earth made slippery by the falling rain.

Bolan checked out the way ahead. The muddy track opened out on a wide expanse of graded terrain. There were scattered items of heavy earth-moving vehicles. All of them sat motionless at the moment. To their left steel girders thrust up from concrete bases. Stacks of buildings materials dotted the site. All that was missing were the construction workers. They had quit for the day, or had been forced to quit because of the weather. Bolan didn't fail to notice the pools of brown water that had gathered in the ground hollows. Even with its high suspension and deep-treaded tires the SUV was finding the loose surface hard work. Glancing in his rearview mirror Bolan saw the Mercedes still in sight, but making its way over the muddy terrain.

Okay, Bolan decided, let's do it the hard way.

He gunned the engine, swinging the wheel around and faced back the way he had come.

Beside him the young woman gasped. "What are you doing? This is crazy."

"You could be right," Bolan said. "But it's been that way the past few days."

He aimed the big SUV directly at the Mercedes, arcs of mud spraying up from beneath his wheels. He saw the car slide to a stop, then start to flounder as it sank in brown mud, the driver giving in to panic as he tried to apply full power to the wheels. All he did was dig the car in deeper.

"You will hit them," the woman said.

"Maybe, but not with this," Bolan said, taking his foot off the gas pedal and pressing the brake.

The SUV slowed, sliding sideways as Bolan let go of the wheel. He grabbed the MP-5, shoved open his door and jumped out. The ground was soft, slippery, underfoot. He leaned against the side of the stalled SUV and worked his way to the front.

The driver of the Mercedes shouted something to his partners as he saw the black-clad figure emerge from the SUV. One of the back doors opened and Bolan saw a raised weapon. He shouldered the MP-5, tracked the shooter and hit him with a burst that shattered the door window before reaching the target. The man stumbled back, clutching at his punctured chest.

Bolan half turned and jacked out more bursts, this time aimed at the driver behind the windshield. It took a couple of assaults before the glass starred and imploded. The driver's hand flew off the wheel, a reflex action as he caught slugs and glass that tore the flesh of his throat and face. The car jerked to a sudden stop as the engine stalled. Bolan moved out from cover, closing in on the Mercedes. He had seen movement at the rear of the vehicle. The far-side rear door being pushed open. He flicked the selector to full auto and riddled the car with 9 mm death. He maintained his forward motion, pausing only once to feed in a fresh magazine before continuing his attack. He took it to the logical conclusion.

The Executioner checked the interior of the car. The driver and the two men in the rear lay in bloody sprawls. The one man who had stepped out lay facedown in the mud.

Bolan turned back to the BMW, seeing the white, shocked faces of the young women pressed against the window glass. They watched him without saying a word as he climbed back inside, dropping the spent MP-5 on the floor. He started the engine and slowly drove back the way they had come until they reached the road again. He wasn't in a talkative mood himself. The wound in his hip was still hurting. He could feel warm blood drawing the blacksuit against his flesh. He should have done something about it but his main concern was getting the women as far away from the farm as possible. The authorities were going to have a great deal to sort out. It would keep them occupied for some time and he wanted to use that time to get well clear. At the earliest opportunity he needed to call Brognola again to have him liaise with the task force so the women could be taken care of.

Bolan needed to take some time for himself to deal with his wound, get some rest and prepare for the next phase of his operation.

It was time to leave Rotterdam and relocate to the U.K.

Hugo Canfield had his secondary operation there and that was the Executioner's next target.

He had a final request for Brognola. Bolan needed a flight out of Holland. One that would not involve him having to negotiate official channels. Bolan's Matt Cooper identity had been involved in too much action within Holland's borders. He wanted to get out quickly and quietly, and enter the U.K. in the same way.

11

Len Watts waited for the Executioner in a quiet pub in Pinner, a suburb of London. His appearance did not hint at his profession. Watts, a tall, athletically built man in his early forties, had the look of an academic. He wore beige corduroy slacks and a tweedy sports coat, an open-neck shirt and tan loafers. His dark hair was collar length. Yet his easy manner concealed the sharp mind of a man with his finger on the pulse of the covert world he worked in.

McCarter had given little away when he had sent along the details to Bolan concerning Watts. Reading between the lines Bolan's guess was that Len Watts not only provided ordnance, but knew how to use it, and most likely *had* used it.

Bolan showed up on time, parked the car he had rented and went into the pub. He spotted his man seated in a booth near the oak-beamed fireplace, identifying him from the photograph McCarter had sent over. Watts raised his pint glass in acknowledgment and Bolan joined him. There was a full pint of beer waiting for him.

Watts offered a hand as Bolan sat down. "I ordered a couple of ploughmen's," he said

"Thanks," Bolan said. He took the glass and checked the beer. It was nicely chilled.

"So how is the old reprobate? Still a smart-arse?" Watts asked.

"You know him well, then?"

Watts chuckled. He took a swallow from his pint.

"Our relationship goes back a long way. Sometimes I think too long. But he and I have shared some hairy moments together." Watts paused as a server came with their food. Cheese, salad and pickle, with chunks of crusty fresh bread and rich butter. "Couple more pints, love."

They ate quietly for a while until Watts said, "I have what you asked for. It's outside in the boot of my car. When we leave I'll hand it over and we can go on our merry ways. I imagine with what you asked for your way isn't about to be all that merry."

"Something that needs to be done," was all Bolan said.

Watts nodded. He studied Bolan's face, picking up on a couple of healing marks in evidence.

"Fell over my skis," Bolan said.

"I understand they can be pretty aggressive at times," Watts said straight-faced.

As they stood to leave Bolan hesitated as the bullet gouge in his hip reminded him it was still there. He noticed Watts had seen the pause.

"Skiing again? Maybe you should think of quitting."

"Problem is it becomes an addiction. Hard to give it up."

Watts went to the bar to pay the tab, then led Bolan out of the pub. He pointed to a gleaming maroon Jaguar parked at the far corner of the parking lot. Bolan went to his car and reversed out of his spot, then drove across to stop behind the Jaguar. Watts opened the trunk and took out a heavy black bag. He opened the rear door of Bolan's vehicle and placed it on the floor behind the driver's seat.

"Everything you asked for," he said. "The explosive packs are already fitted with timed detonators. Just set them where you need and the handheld unit will do the rest."

Bolan shook the man's hand. "Thanks."

"You watch your back. And next time you see my buddy tell him not to stay away too long. He's a pain but he's a good friend. And there aren't many of those left these days."

Bolan raised a hand as he drove away, turning the car along the quiet road. He circled the outer road system that bypassed London and made for the coast. He had a room booked in a hotel that was no more than an hour's drive from the South East Containers offices.

South East Containers was the company Paul Chambers ran. The same company he had seen delivering human cargo to the farm outside Rotterdam. The Executioner had an appointment with the freight company. Initially it would be to reconnoiter the setup so he knew what he was up against when he made his full strike.

12

South East Containers occupied a large site ten miles inland from the ferry port where its vehicles maintained their schedules to and from Rotterdam Port. The freight business sat in near isolation, the closest village some eight miles along the road that ran west to east along the coastal area. The area around the site was timbered grassland, with some wide-spaced farms in the distance.

The location was ideal for Bolan's initial observation of the setup. He parked off the road, deep in a stand of trees and heavy bush. Dressed in casual clothing, with binoculars and a camera around his neck, he was prepared to check out the freight business and pass himself off as an enthusiastic photographer if anyone asked.

He had parked a half mile from the site, making his way through the greenery until he was able to scan South East Containers from concealment.

The frontage comprised of an expansive spread of concrete that allowed the large rigs to pull safely off the road. Large metal gates gave access to the freight yard itself and the whole property was enclosed behind sturdy metal fencing. Bolan could see cameras mounted strategically along the top of the fencing. Next to the access gates was a front office that housed security men. Bolan spent long hours watching the activity as South East Containers vehicles came and went, each checked when they arrived and again when they left.

At the far end of the freight yard was a long warehouse building with loading ramps and a number of roller-shutter doors at the rear of each bay. A concrete island in the yard held a number of fuel pumps where the drivers could fill up their diesel tanks.

Over the two days and nights Bolan observed the activity, he saw that South East Containers closed for trading by eight every night. Rigs were parked in the yard, the drivers taking their own cars and driving away, leaving the security team to watch over the site. As darkness fell powerful lights came into operation, covering the freight yard and the frontage. The cameras set on the metal fences rotated to cover both.

Bolan decided that if he was going to get into the freight yard and the warehouse the security facilities needed neutralizing first. And from what he had seen, the front office would be the place to start.

Day three was Saturday, and South East Containers closed for the weekend just after midday. Bolan watched the drivers park and leave in their own vehicles. He also saw the two security men hand over to a single man who arrived in a Land Rover. He parked inside the yard and they drove out. The gates were closed and the lone guard made his way into the site office.

Bolan saw the situation as his chance to make a closer inspection. It was necessary if he was going to carry out his planned strike.

He returned to his concealed car and drove back to his hotel, where he changed from his casual gear into a suit, complete with shirt, tie and polished shoes. Back in his car he returned to the South East Containers site, only this time he rolled his car off the road and across the concrete apron, parking. As Bolan stepped out of the car he could see the lone security man staring at him.

RAY KEPPLE FINISHED rolling his cigarette as he watched the tall, expensively dressed man climb out of the gleaming sedan and make his way across to the office. There was something about the man that aroused a nervous sensation in Kepple's stomach. He quickly stuck the thin cigarette between his lips and lit it, sucking smoke deep into his lungs.

The newcomer spotted him through the streaked office window and angled across to the door. He pushed it open, pausing in the frame. Kepple got an impression of a big man, physically fit under the suit. He had thick dark hair, his face tanned but showing some recent bruising. The eyes fixed on Kepple were of a startling blue, expressionless and cold. They unnerved Kepple.

"What can I do for you?" he asked.

Bolan had seen the name badge pinned to the man's shirt. "Ray Kepple. The man I came to see."

Kepple realized the man was plainly an American, his tone firm without being aggressive.

"Yes. Who are you?"

"I'm the man about to get you out of trouble."

"Eh?"

"You've heard about the problems in Rotterdam? Someone making a lot of noise? Upsetting business? It's making Mr. Canfield nervous."

Kepple rubbed the back of his neck, shifting uneasily from one foot to the other. "Well, I don't get involved in the operation over there. All I do is supervise things here."

"From what the boss man told me you're the main man here. Run this depot like clockwork. Keep the trucks moving on time and the merchandise turned around pretty fast."

"Canfield said that?" Kepple gave a nervous grin. "I like to think I do my job efficiently."

He didn't have that much authority around the place but someone seemed to believe he had, so why spoil their illusions.

"It hasn't gone unnoticed, Mr. Kepple. All the way to the top."

It was not very often Kepple received any praise for his work.

"Hey, you want a cup of tea? Coffee? I know you Yanks... Americans...prefer coffee."

"Yeah, why not, and the name's Ryan."

Kepple turned to the unit in the corner of the office where he kept the makings, switching on a plastic kettle. "Be a couple of minutes."

Bolan had settled himself by the desk, leaning against it. He appeared relaxed, studying the layout of the office. "Quiet around here."

"Oh, yeah," Kepple said. "Weekend, see. We don't operate weekends. Old traditions die hard in this part of the country. Half day Saturday. Sunday all day. Day of rest and all that stuff. We have to keep a low profile. Look suspicious to the locals if we didn't. And we don't want that, do we?"

"Hey, good thinking, Ray."

Kepple handed the visitor a mug of black coffee. The American took it, sampling the strong brew.

"Sorry it's instant. Don't run to fresh roast hereabouts. Yes, I keep my eye on the place. I mean, there's a lot of expensive vehicles back there in the yard. Mr. Chambers gets twitchy. Especially after all that bloody stuff in Holland. You understand."

"One of the reasons I've been sent over. No disrespect, Mr. Kepple, but there's a lot riding on keeping the operations running smooth. That's my job. Overseeing security. So I can report back to the man at the top and let him know he ain't got anything to worry about. If he's kept happy we can *all* be happy."

"Chambers said they're letting things cool for a while. No more shipments until we get the word again. Keep the place looking normal. No unnecessary activity."

"That's good," Bolan said. He placed his mug on the desk. "I need to let that cool. Now, you want to give me the guided tour? I can't see any problems here but we'd better do this right. You run a tight ship, Ray, I can see that." Kepple nodded. "Between you and me I just want to do my job and get back to London. Young lady waiting for me there and I wouldn't want to leave her standing, if you know what I mean."

"I understand."

"Look, just take me on a quick walk around the freight yard. I'll take a few pictures with my digital camera and report back when I get back to the city. Give you a good write-up."

Kepple stubbed out his cigarette, nodding enthusiastically. "Where do you want to start?"

"The yard is monitored? Cameras and stuff?"

"That's right."

Kepple led him through to the office, to another room where the security setup was housed. It was an air-conditioned control center where a bank of monitors relayed images from the freight yard. It was an expensive assembly.

"Digital cameras," Kepple explained. "Recorded so we can check back if we spot anything suspicious. Cameras are infrared so they can see in the dark. Bloody clever stuff."

"You said it, buddy. And you're the man in charge of all this? Impressive stuff, Ray."

"The freight yard is fenced all around. Steel embedded in concrete. There are even motion sensors on the gates and fences, so anyone trying to break in will set the alarms off. Now, in most cases the security system would be linked to the local cops. But it could prove embarrassing if they turned up and found *merchandise* on the premises. Chambers would go crazy if that happened. So would Canfield. We keep security in-house. If it's broken it's linked to the main office in London."

"Wise move, Ray."

Kepple led the way through a solid door at the back of the control center that opened on to the freight yard. The wide concrete area held a dozen of the distinctive South East Container rigs. All were locked. As they walked down the line of vehicles Bolan nodded his approval. He spent some time taking photographs with the compact camera he had produced from his suit jacket.

At the edge of the yard was the long, low-rise warehouse. "Your hospitality suite in there?" Bolan asked, grinning.

"Only ones who know are those involved in the business. Rest of the work staff are involved in packing and loading. We run a produce setup. Bring in stuff from Europe and ship throughout the U.K. The routine business, if you know what I mean. We have a five-star setup. Soundproof. Isolated. There's a false wall so that the day employees know nothing about it. The special deliveries are off-loaded at night when the day shift has gone."

He was warming to his subject now. Pleased to have someone around who seemed to appreciate what he did.

"Hell of a lot more fun than lugging crates of food around," the big American said.

"Well, I like to think of the merchandise as vegetables on legs," Kepple said, grinning expansively. "Expensive, but still bloody vegetables."

He wasn't looking at Bolan as he spoke, which was a good thing. If he had seen the ice-chip expression in the American's eyes he would have had doubts concerning his own life expectancy.

As they returned to the control room, Bolan walked beside Kepple.

"Great job you're doing here, Ray. When the big man gets my report he's liable to send you a bonus. I'm going to recommend that. I were you, though, I wouldn't let on to Chambers I said so. Don't want him grabbing all the glory when you're the man holding all this together. In fact Canfield said not to mention this visit to him at all. After what happened in Holland Chambers isn't what you'd call flavor of the month. You understand?"

"I know what you mean," Kepple said, inwardly pleased that Chambers was out of favor.

Bolan took a final look around, pretending to be suitably impressed. "If anyone did get in here could they disable the security system?" he asked.

"There's a master override that shuts the whole thing down, but it's in that box on the wall and it won't open unless I use my key."

"I hope you look after that key, Ray, my man."

"Always have it with me."

"So, you man the ship all night?"

"Today and Sunday. Never get any visitors over the weekend. Not even Chambers. He likes to live it up in London."

"Doesn't it get lonely?"

"I'm okay with that. I have my radio. That's all I need. My shift ends at 6:00 a.m. Monday Day crew comes on then. Drivers arrive at seven. Then I get to go home. Nice long break."

Back in the office Bolan picked up his mug and drank the rest of his coffee. He turned to Kepple and shook his hand. The American's big hand swamped Kepple's.

"Good job, Ray. I can tell the boss man things are running real smooth here. It's important right now. Lot of money at stake so it's reassuring to know the man in charge has it all tied down. You take it easy."

Kepple watched the American return to his car and drive away. As the vehicle coasted along the straight, flat road he rolled himself another cigarette, lit it and sat back behind his desk.

He wondered if the man had been telling the truth about a bonus. It would be nice if he did get something. He would keep that to himself. If Chambers learned about it he would moan and bitch. The man was a mean bastard. Liked to believe he was the smart one. Maybe this time it wouldn't be so.

Maybe this time it would be Ray Kepple who got the surprise.

13

Ray Kepple received his surprise far sooner than expected. And it was not in the form he had anticipated.

It came dressed in black. Armed. Carrying a heavy nylon bag, and made an appearance just after midnight.

Kepple, in the front office, had just fixed himself another mug of tea. From the control room behind him the plaintive wail of a female singer drifted through the open door. The lyrics told of her disappointment with her boyfriend who had run off with another woman, leaving her brokenhearted.

Give me ten minutes with you, love, and I'd change your mind, Kepple thought.

He chuckled at his own thoughts, picked up his steaming mug and crossed to the office door, unlocking it to step outside for a breath of fresh air. There was a full moon, casting pale light, and it was warm, surprisingly so for the late hour. Kepple knew he didn't make it any easier on himself with his constant smoking. The office reeked of stale tobacco. He had smoked since his fourteenth birthday, couldn't quit if he wanted to, but even he had to admit his habit did little to enhance the confined area in the office. He never smoked in the control room. He kept the place clean because Chambers would lose it if his precious, cutting-edge security system became tainted. And Kepple didn't like the chill, conditioned air. He had spent the past hour in the place, staring at monitors that never changed, and he decided he needed a mug of tea, a sandwich from his lunch box and a smoke.

He placed his mug on the office windowsill, pulled the makings from his pocket and proceeded to make a cigarette. As he wet the strip of paper something moved on his extreme left. It was only a fleeting shadow on the periphery of his vision. Kepple glanced in that direction and saw nothing but the sway of tall grass at the edge of the concrete apron near the road. He shrugged and returned to his cigarette. About to light it Kepple felt certain he saw something again.

"Bloody hell, son, you're jumping at shadows," he said out loud.

He lit the cigarette and took a deep pull on it. A moment later the smoke caught in his throat and he almost choked, coughing harshly. The cold press of hard metal against the side of his head was the cause. Kepple didn't need to be told what it was.

The muzzle of a gun was pressing hard enough to cause some discomfort.

"Ray, those cigarettes are not doing you any good," a soft voice said. "Are you carrying a weapon?"

"A what? A gun? No."

"Let's go back inside."

Kepple sucked frantically on the cigarette. He turned to walk back into the office. He stood just inside the office when he heard the door close and the lock click shut.

"Go sit down."

Before he turned around Kepple's suspicions were confirmed. He knew the voice.

Ryan.

The American who had visited him earlier. Supposedly one of Canfield's people. The man was a fraud. Nothing to do with the company and he had checked out the set up simply for a return visit.

The suit was gone. Now the big American was dressed all in black. He had a large black nylon bag dangling from his left hand.

"You bastard," Kepple said.

The American hefted the bag and dropped it on Kepple's desk.

"We were getting on well last time I was here, Ray. I thought we had something going on."

"I don't like being made to look a bloody fool. Jesus, Chambers will tear my bloody heart out if I let you—"

The big man gestured with the pistol. "Empty your pockets. Everything on the desk."

The Executioner watched Kepple turn out his pockets. He picked up the bunch of keys, weighing them in his hand.

"Sit down, Kepple." All friendliness was gone. "I want you to pass along a message to Chambers and Canfield. It's for both of them. Tell them their time is running out. Tell them it might be easier of they took the quick way out, because when I'm done there isn't going to be a damn thing left."

Slumped in his chair Kepple wondered what the American had planned for him. He understood now what the earlier visit had been for. The man had been checking the place out prior to this return visit. Learning how the security system worked, finding out how long Kepple would be on his own. And he, fooled by the man, had shown him around the control center, telling him exactly how to immobilize the system.

Kepple knew something else. This man was Cooper, the one who had been wreaking havoc around Rotterdam.

Bolan pressed the muzzle of the pistol against the side of Kepple's skull. With his free hand he produced plastic ties from a pocket of his blacksuit.

"Hands behind you," he said.

Bolan made sure Kepple's hands were threaded through the wooden slats in the chair, looped one of the ties over his wrists and pulled it tight. Then he secured Kepple's ankles to the chair legs.

"Hey, my wrists hurt," Kepple protested.

Bolan stood back, holstering his pistol. When he looked down at Kepple his face was impassive.

"If you were one of your 'vegetables on legs' you wouldn't feel a thing. Isn't that what you tell yourself?"

Kepple stayed silent this time. He had decided his survival was in his own hands. Antagonizing this man would not be a wise move. There was nothing he could do, so he kept his mouth shut.

The Executioner picked up the bag and moved into the control room. He checked the bunch of keys and selected one. It didn't fit the wall box. Bolan tried two more before the lock turned. He opened the door and checked the internal panel. Simple enough. He threw the cancel switch. When he turned to check the monitor bank the screens were blank. He moved to the telephone connections and pulled the lines from the wall sockets.

Kepple had said that the security system was linked to the London office. It wouldn't take long for someone to realize the link had gone down. Once that was certified, action would be taken. Before that happened Bolan would be long gone.

He pushed open the control-center door leading into the freight yard. His targets were the parked rigs and the warehouse behind. Bolan wasted little time. He moved along the line of vehicles, attaching a Semtex block to the underside of each of the trucks.

As Len Watts had told him the Semtex blocks were fitted with electronic detonators that would respond to the handheld activation unit he carried. As each block was fixed Bolan pressed the small button that primed the detonator, a red light winking to show it was ready.

From the trucks Bolan made his way to the warehouse building. One of the keys from Kepple's bunch opened the small side door. It didn't take Bolan long to find the "hospitality suite" at the far end of the building, concealed behind its false wall. Inside he found primitive living quarters equipped with basic wooden cots. The front wall was built from steel bars with a single door set in it. The place hadn't been cleaned for some time and Bolan could only imagine how the captive occupants must have felt. He placed one of his blocks through the bars, sliding it across the floor, then as he worked his way back to the exit he laid down his remaining explosive blocks. The final pack was placed near the fuel pumps. Dropping the nylon bag Bolan returned to where he had started, across the freight yard and through to the office where Kepple was making halfhearted attempts to free himself.

"You can't fucking do this," Kepple yelled. "Don't you realize how big Canfield is? The man will—"

"If he's half as smart as everyone keeps telling me, he'll cut and run. But I don't think he is all that smart," Bolan said.

"You really think you can get away with this?"

"Let's see," Bolan said. He walked out of the office.

At the point where the concrete apron met the road Bolan took the handheld unit from his pocket. The first key he pressed powered the unit. The second activated the detonation units fixed to the Semtex blocks, and the third started the timers. Bolan had set them for four minutes. Enough for him to get well clear.

He'd parked his rental car a hundred yards down the road. The Executioner pulled on the jacket he had dropped on the seat, fired up the engine and swung the car around, starting his drive back toward his hotel. The roads were quiet. Bolan saw no other vehicles as he cruised steadily away from South East Containers.

The explosions rocked the countryside. They detonated almost in unison, some after a microsecond delay. Overall it was like a single, massive blast that rippled and echoed. Bright fireballs rose into the night sky, expanding and shooting fire and smoke into the sky. Bolan slowed, leaning out of his window to look back as the destruction of Canfield's fleet took place. He felt the aftershock of the explosions rock his vehicle. Seconds later he heard the patter of debris fall to earth. The rumble of the blasts went on for some time, fading as Bolan drove on.

He settled back in the seat, his mind already locked on to the next phase in his systematic takedown of Venturer Exports.

14

"Tell me something positive," Hugo Canfield raged, facing the men sitting across the conference table. "I do not want an itemized list of the vehicles that were destroyed. Or an estimate of the damned cost."

No one spoke because they had no positive input to deliver.

"One man. One fucking man. And he is making fools of us all. The operation in Holland has been severely compromised. Now our transport was blown to hell while we were sitting back doing nothing."

From the end of the conference table someone spoke up. "Ray Kepple wasn't injured…"

The speaker's voice trailed off into an embarrassed silence as he realized the ineffectual content of his remark, and it became very quiet in the room.

"The fact that Kepple wasn't injured tends to make me think he wasn't doing his job properly. Think back to the fact that he took Cooper on a guided tour of the freight yard only hours before the bastard came back and blew it up." Canfield slammed his hand down on the table. "How did that happen? Cooper just walks in and presents himself as part of our operation and Kepple falls for it. Someone please tell me where we get these people?"

"Chambers hired him," one of Canfield's lieutenants, a lean, eager-faced young man named Travis said. "Kepple oversaw the site on weekends."

"Why is it every time I hear that name just lately I get a

queasy feeling. It was Chambers who screwed up trying to take care of Cooper in Rotterdam. Now his operation here goes up in smoke. Tell me where that walking disaster is right now."

"We, er, well, we can't seem to locate him, sir," Travis admitted. "He's somewhere in the city."

Canfield didn't speak for a while, leaving the gathering in uncomfortable silence until Travis spoke up again.

"I'll get some people on that right away, Mr. Canfield."

Canfield cleared his throat. "Do that. When you get your hands on him I want him here. I want it done discreetly. Make him realize this isn't a request, it's a fucking order. And I also want Kepple taken care of. He is superfluous to requirements and stupidity of the degree he's shown requires stamping on. The thought crossed my mind that the local police may be conducting a detailed investigation and they might be liaising with that bloody task force. If Kepple sees an opportunity to make a deal he might decide to cooperate to save his own bloody skin." Canfield let the words sink in. "Are we clear on this? It only takes a small stone to create ever-widening ripples."

"Are we still going to slow operations down?" Travis asked.

"I'm debating that. This Cooper seems to be concentrating his attention on Europe and now the U.K. Until we sort out this mess I'm considering stopping our trade here. The U.S. and Asia haven't been targeted yet so let's maintain those areas."

In Canfield's mind he was hearing the message Cooper had instructed Kepple to pass along.

Tell Canfield his time is running low. He should take the easy way out.

He couldn't wipe it away and it irritated him.

"One more thing, sir," Travis said. "There is a shipment due to arrive from Thailand. On the *Orient Venturer.* It will dock tomorrow afternoon unless we act."

Canfield sat back, gently drumming his fingers on the conference table. "I need some time to decide on matters. This meeting is adjourned," he said while nodding at Travis.

Everyone stood and filed out. Travis got as far as the door before closing it and turning back into the office.

"Sit down, Clive," Canfield said. "Glad you mentioned that incoming shipment. I think we need to do something about it fairly quickly."

"It came to me, sir, that because of what this man Cooper has been doing, the authorities may be renewing their interest in our business. Even if we got word to our man in the local customs-and-excise division he might not be able to prevent the ship being searched."

"Precisely, Clive. Of course, if they did make a search and there was nothing but the regular cargo on board…"

"No special cargo, no proof."

"Pity to have to lose that consignment. The Thai girls are high earners."

Travis shrugged. "There's a plentiful supply, sir."

"Exactly."

Travis crossed to a framed map on the wall. He tapped it with his finger.

"Pretty deep water where the ship is right now."

"Wouldn't be the first time a container got lost at sea," Canfield said.

"No time like the present, sir," Travis said reaching for the satellite phone on the table. He tapped in a number and waited until the call was answered.

Canfield took the phone, acknowledging the identification of the ship's captain.

"Canfield," he said. "Are you running to schedule? Good. I heard you've had troubled waters. All clear now? That's fine, Captain Muren. I hope the rest of your trip goes well. Goodbye." Replacing the phone Canfield returned to sit behind his own desk. "Problem solved, Clive."

AFTER TRAVIS HAD GONE Canfield smiled to himself.

Troubled waters.

Two simple words. In this case it was a prearranged signal that told whoever received it to dispose of any special cargo they were carrying. Venturer Exports had used the order a number of times when unexpected problems came up. There were no exceptions to the rule. If a threat appeared and there was time to implement the command it was issued quickly. The loss of cargo, financially, was to be avoided if possible, but if circumstances deemed so it was put into action without further thought.

There's a plentiful supply, sir.

Travis had put it plain and simple. In Canfield's business the supply of human fodder was limitless—and so, too, were the customers.

15

Ray Kepple shook his head in frustration, trying to work out where the contents of the bottle had gone. He brought it closer, staring at it with blurred eyes. He couldn't recall having downed the half bottle so quickly. Despite his condition he decided that he must have drunk the stuff. The problem was he could remember *why* he had been drinking.

The freight yard and the warehouse. Those bloody awful explosions after the man called Cooper had gone, leaving him tied to his office chair. The blasts, seeming to go on forever, had destroyed the fleet of trucks and reduced the warehouse to rubble. The force of the blast had demolished most of the control center and had blown Kepple's chair, with him tied to it, across the office. He had lain there, stunned, clothing and skin scorched, deafened by the blasts, barely able to move. Following the explosions and the rain of debris falling back to earth there was a lot of smoke. It drifted into his office and Kepple could smell the acrid tang. As his hearing returned he picked up the crackling of flames.

Cooper had done a real number on the yard.

Kepple was able to see why the man had been so effective in Holland, running rings around everyone. He wasn't held back by rules and regulations. He chose his targets, checked them out and went directly for them. Not like the cops and their pals on the task force. Cooper, whoever he was, got results.

When Paul Chambers turned up to inspect the damage he

had exploded with rage. His mood ranged from disbelief to incandescent fury. Ray Kepple was his main target. He blamed him for everything, including the weather. When Kepple pointed out that it had been Chambers's idea to keep the place low-key over the weekend the man almost lost it. He had to be careful because the police and fire crews were still around, poking and prying, asking questions. It had been a difficult time. Chambers had maintained that the explosions had been the work of a rival group who wanted to take over the business. The cops were skeptical, but when Canfield's lawyers arrived, backed up by orders from on high, the local authorities had to back off. Canfield, as usual, had used his influence to have the investigation stalled. It wouldn't last forever, but any delay would give Canfield and his backers time to negotiate themselves out from under. Even so it was a nervous time for Chambers and Kepple.

Later, when they were alone, Chambers had turned on Kepple again. He raged back and forth, venting his anger, and continued his verbal attack on Kepple until the man, driven to fighting back, told Chambers what he and Canfield could do with his job if they didn't like what had happened. He delivered Cooper's message with relish, enjoying the look on Chambers's face. Then he walked away from Chambers with a final wild threat that suggested if anyone did come asking questions he might reveal just what South East Containers had been doing because he wasn't carrying the can for it all.

Chambers had worked out his rage, eventually retreating to his car and driving off, leaving Kepple to survey the damage before using his cell phone to summon a taxi to take him home. His vehicle had been destroyed in the explosion and Kepple didn't think he had much chance of getting Chambers or Canfield to replace it.

He questioned the wisdom of the outburst as he rode home, but his resolve to not be made the scapegoat for Cooper's attack stayed strong. Later, alone in his house, drinking heavily, Kepple admitted to himself he had been careless. Chambers would do his best to shrug off responsibility, leaving Kepple high and dry. Hugo Canfield worried Kepple more than Chambers. He had only met the man once when Chambers had brought him to look over the site. That had been enough. The man frightened him. He didn't like Canfield but he respected the man's power and influence. Someone like Ray Kepple was unimportant to Canfield. Simply an employee paid to do a fairly menial task in Canfield's eyes. And someone who could be disposed of without much concern.

Kepple sat up. He was sure he had heard a noise outside the house. Moments later he sank back in the armchair, waving a dismissive hand. He had imagined the noise. If he hadn't it was most likely a stray cat or dog nosing around the trash can. He decided another glass of whiskey would send all the noises away. Before he had time to fill his glass he heard the noise again, and this time he didn't dismiss it. He placed the bottle and glass aside and hauled himself up out of the chair, swaying unsteadily.

"Bloody strays," he muttered, the words slurred. "I'll fix you bastards."

He stumbled toward the kitchen door, pushing it open and reaching for the light switch. As light flooded the kitchen Kepple realized two things.

The back door was open. And there was a dark-clad figure facing him.

Kepple's vision was a little blurred but he felt sure he knew the man. He tried to focus. When he managed to bring the figure into sharp relief he saw he had been right. He did know the man.

Canfield's minder. The one they called Sergeant Gantley. Ex-military copper. A big, powerful man. Broad across the shoulders and chest. Walked as though he was still on the drill field.

Gantley stood there and reminded Kepple of some immovable statue. He wore a black coat over a thick black sweater. And there were thin black leather gloves over his large fists.

"What are you doing here?" Kepple asked.

The question sounded superfluous. But Kepple didn't want to admit he knew what Gantley was there for.

Kepple turned, seeking refuge away from the man. His alcoholic stupor slowed him.

Gantley, moving swiftly for a man of his size, reached out and caught hold of Kepple by the collar of his shirt. He pulled the wriggling, sobbing man to him, and spun him around.

Kepple didn't even see the first blow coming. He just felt it as Gantley's massive fist smashed into his face. The powerful blow drove his head back, knocking his skull against the door frame. The black-leathered fist began to repeatedly pummel Kepple's face, crushing bone and tearing flesh. It didn't stop until Kepple, unconscious, hung from his hand.

Gantley let Kepple fall to the kitchen floor, turning him over onto his stomach with his foot. Then he bent over the inert form, took Kepple's head in his gloved hands and wrenched it savagely, hearing the neck snap.

When Gantley straightened up there was a contented smile on his face. It had been some time since he had killed a man with his bare hands. It was a satisfactory act for him. Any fool could kill with a gun or knife. He preferred this way. It still gave him a thrill.

Crossing the kitchen he rinsed the blood off his gloves under the faucet. Then he left the house by the kitchen door, closing it behind him. He returned to his car the same way he had approached the isolated house, crossing a field and walking through a small stand of trees. He climbed into the car and drove away from Kepple's house, using only his side lights, along the quiet lane, following it until he reached the main road. Forty minutes later he merged with the freeway traffic heading in the direction of London. When he reached the city he drove directly to his apartment block. Inside he changed his clothes, throwing what he had worn into his washing machine and switched it on. While the clothes were washed Gantley made himself a mug of tea, into which he poured a generous slug of whiskey. He watched a couple of hours of TV, then turned in for the night.

WHEN HE ENTERED Hugo Canfield's office the following day, around noon, at the Canary Wharf headquarters, Gantley saw that his employer had a visitor.

Canfield glanced across the office, over Paul Chambers's shoulder, meeting Gantley's gaze. Gantley merely nodded. It was all Canfield needed in the way of explanation.

"Sergeant Gantley," he said, "would you have the car ready for me in ten minutes? I want to go direct to the airfield. Make sure the plane is ready for takeoff."

"Of course, sir."

Gantley stepped out of the office and closed the door, leaving Canfield to deal with Chambers.

16

As soon as Gantley closed the door Hugo Canfield picked up his conversation.

"When I said back off, Paul, I didn't suggest taking everyone away and leaving the place wide open."

"It wasn't like that," Chambers protested. "We always scale things down at weekends. It would have looked odd if there had been extra activity. The site was well covered by the security system. How was I to know Kepple would let that bastard just waltz in and take a look around? I mean, we hadn't seen or heard from him since that last incident in Rotterdam. I figured he'd up and moved on."

"Too bloody right, Paul. He moved on here. You made a bad call, don't you think? Not the first you've made recently. Rotterdam. Bickell dead. The fucking farm. You handled it all carelessly. If Cooper had died the day he was supposed to we wouldn't be having our current crop of problems. Kepple was your responsibility. You hired the man. Not me."

"Now wait a damn minute. I hope you don't hold me responsible for everything that went wrong over there. The farm getting hit, van Ryden, DeChambre. Bloody hell, Hugo, I'll hold up my hands as far as Kepple is concerned but not for things that were nothing to do with me. I can't be expected to be in every place at the same time."

Chambers was almost shouting at the end of his protest,

then saw the hard expression on Canfield's face. He had gone a step too far.

Chambers became aware of the tense atmosphere in the room. He felt Canfield's animosity toward him and the first feelings of apprehension began to make themselves known. In the past he had always felt comfortable being around Canfield, despite the man's reputation. Canfield was all-powerful, almost arrogant in his dealings with others. That had never worried Paul Chambers. Since joining Venturer Exports his own standing had risen and he moved in wealthier circles, being introduced to a number of Canfield's associates. Now, doubt manifested itself and Chambers's nervousness showed as his hand trembled slightly, the contents in his glass shaking.

If Canfield noticed he said nothing as he crossed the room and refilled his own tumbler, savoring the aroma of the aged whiskey. In fact, he was enjoying the moment—letting Chambers sweat. The man deserved to be upset. His stupidity had cost the Organization dearly, and that was something Hugo Canfield could never forgive. It was bad enough they had lost cargo, money and facilities. With the multinational task force still hovering in the wings, just waiting to pounce, anything that drew their closer attention should have been avoided. Chambers had jeopardized Venturer Exports. He was going to have to pay for that.

"Hugo, let me put things right," Chambers said in an attempt to smooth things over. "I made mistakes. I've lost out, as well. South East Containers was my business, too. How do you think I feel about that? I'll make sure Kepple doesn't get away with what he's done."

His words had the sound of desperation. Chambers was floundering. He was aware he had committed a grave error and was eager to try and make reparation. He had no chance of doing that. In purely financial terms the cost of replacing the truck fleet was far beyond his means. Canfield could have made good the loss, but that was not the problem. It was less about the money, more about the damage to Canfield's reputation and his standing in the eyes of his influential friends. He would, of course, play down the events for his contacts. It would take some doing but Hugo Canfield was confident he could overcome the recent setbacks.

Chambers was another matter. His failure left Canfield only one course of action. Chambers could not be trusted any longer. The man had to be eliminated. Just as Kepple had been dealt with. More work for the dependable Sergeant Gantley. There, at least, was a man Canfield could depend on. There were never any doubts in Canfield's mind once he sent Gantley out. His decision made he moved on mentally, turning his attention back to Chambers in order to dismiss the man.

"I need to consider how to handle things, Paul. I need to get to Banecreif. I'll call you tomorrow. Go back to your apartment and stay put until you hear from me."

The dismissal was final. Chambers knew not to argue. He emptied his glass and stood. Canfield was already concentrating on another piece of business, as if Chambers had already left the room.

In the elevator on his way to the ground floor Paul Chambers went over the meeting. He was left with no doubt that any decision Canfield made would not be pleasant—for Chambers.

Outside the building Chambers saw Canfield's Bentley parked close by. The solid figure of Gantley was standing beside the car. Chambers had always found the ex-military cop slightly menacing.

When Gantley caught Chambers's eye he inclined his head, watching closely. There was a hint of a knowing smile on his lips.

Chambers walked to his own car, searching for his keys and actually fumbling them from his pocket. He pressed the button that unlocked the door and slid behind the wheel, jamming the key in and firing up the engine. Without looking back he knew that Gantley was still watching. Chambers pushed the stick into first, let out the clutch too quickly and stalled, the car jumping. Swearing Chambers restarted the car, managing to pull away on the second attempt. He didn't let out a breath until the office block had vanished from sight among the other tall Canary Wharf buildings.

He had a twenty-minute drive across the city to his apartment and Chambers felt every minute of the trip. The sheer volume of traffic forced him to drive slowly, stopping and starting every few yards. He hated driving in London. The place was becoming gridlocked. Worse every time he visited.

Still a distance from his destination Chambers's in-car phone rang. He pressed the hands-free button.

"Yes?"

"Paul, it's Greg."

"If it's more bad news I'm not really interested."

"I think you need to hear this, Paul. It's about Ray Kepple."

"Kepple? What's he fucking done now? Burned down the village pub?"

"He's dead, Paul. Someone broke into his place last night and beat him to death. Really did a job on him. He was barely recognizable. Face was caved in. He actually died from having his neck snapped."

Chambers was driving on autopilot, his gaze fixed on the car in front. He was recalling Canfield's cold attitude toward him during their office meeting. The indifference. The curt dismissal. And then the glimpse of Gantley outside the building. The quiet look that spoke volumes.

Gantley.

Hugo Canfield's minder.

Gantley looked after Canfield and also handed out punishment to anyone stepping out of line.

Canfield would have wanted the ultimate price for

Kepple's misconduct. Damn the man. He had allowed Chambers to ramble on about how he would discipline Kepple even while he had known Gantley had already done the job. And he hadn't even considered letting Chambers in on the matter.

"Paul, are you still there?"

The moment passed. Chambers took a breath.

"I heard, Greg. I don't suppose anyone saw or heard anything?"

"Nothing. Not surprising with Kepple living where he did. His closest neighbor was a quarter mile away."

"Local police handling it?"

"Yeah."

"Okay. We have to stay out of it. Let them screw around all they want."

Chambers severed the connection.

A cold sweat broke out on his forehead as he found himself reliving that moment when Gantley offered him that hint of a smile. He knew now exactly what it meant. Gantley had him on his list. Kepple's error had earned him a painful death. Now he was on the list. With everything falling down before his eyes Canfield was cleaning up loose ends. Making sure his surviving team was composed of strong people. He wanted the defaulters out of the picture. Weakness in one area could lead to weakness in others. Canfield would want to make sure there were no loose mouths left open.

The sound of someone hammering on a car horn startled Chambers. He snatched at the wheel and brought his car back into its own lane. He had let it wander. He hit the air-conditioning button, letting the cool air wash over his face. He realized his hands were shaking as they gripped the wheel.

Jesus, Paul, wake up. Clear your mind. Don't let the bastards do this to you, he told himself.

Chambers almost missed his apartment building. He had to

stamp on the brake, causing other drivers to swerve and give him the finger as he ignored them and swung into the parking lot.

He went into the apartment building and took an elevator up to his floor. As he walked along the thickly carpeted corridor, the cathedral silence of the place made him even more nervous. He had never noticed before how quiet the upper floor was. He looked back over his shoulder a couple of times, shaking his head when he realized what he had done.

Get a grip.

He slid the key into the lock and worked the handle. The door opened and he stepped inside. As the door swung shut behind him Chambers froze on the spot.

He was not alone.

He saw a tall figure, dressed in black pants and a leather jacket.

A lethal-looking auto pistol in his right hand was pointing at Chambers's heart.

"You were out, so I decided to stay around and wait," the man said. "I think you should sit down, Chambers. You don't look too well."

17

Paul Chambers decided his life was falling apart. The mistakes he had recently made, Canfield's loss of faith in him and the unspoken threat posed by Gantley—things could not get worse.

Then he realized he was wrong about that, too.

"I… How the hell did you get into my apartment?"

"You've got more important things to consider," the Executioner said.

Chambers paled at the implication behind Bolan's words. He looked around the room as if he had never been in it before, finally locating a chair. He sat down, rubbing a hand across his very dry mouth.

"What do you want? Haven't you already done enough?"

"You remember how this all started? You, me, in Rotterdam. The last thing you said to me was that I wouldn't get to see the sights. Wrong, Chambers. I've been seeing sights since then. None of them very pleasant. Innocent women and children caged up. Waiting to be sold like meat so you and your partners can turn a tidy profit. So scum like you can stay in an apartment like this. Must make you feel all warm inside."

"It's a business. We supply a hungry market, Cooper. And it's growing. What makes you think *you* can shut it all down?"

"You'll have to wait and see about that."

"So what do you want from me?" Chambers's growing fear spilled over, his voice rising to a high shrill sound. "Damn you, Cooper, your fucking hits against us have put me in the firing line. Canfield has more or less hinted I'm on my way out. He holds me responsible. Remember Kepple? Canfield had him killed. He sent his trained dog, Gantley, to beat Kepple to a pulp, then snap his neck. And it looks like I could be next. Gantley will be coming after me. Canfield is launching a tidy-up campaign. Cutting out what he thinks is dead wood…"

Bolan's face remained impassive. Whatever trouble Chambers had got himself into made little difference to the Executioner. His business pushed him outside the limits for redemption. There was no get-out clause for a man like Paul Chambers. By the very nature of his employment he was already in Bolan's sights.

"Look, I can give you information. But I want protection. I don't give a bloody damn what you think of me. I want to survive. We can trade," Chambers pleaded.

"Trade what?"

"Canfield is moving into something different. To add to his business dealings. A new venture."

"I don't expect it to be legal," Bolan said.

"Drugs. He's struck a deal with a Russian supplier. Opium from Afghanistan. Had a big consignment delivered a few days ago to his place up in Scotland."

"Where?"

"Canfield has an old house. Massive place. Pretty isolated. Up on the northeast coast. House is called Banecreif." Chambers rubbed his dry mouth. "I need a drink."

Bolan gestured in the direction of the bottles on a side table. Chambers picked up a whiskey and splashed it into a glass. He swallowed the contents in a single gulp and immediately poured a second.

"Well? Do we have a deal?"

"I'll let you know when we're in sight of Banecreif," Bolan said.

Chambers laughed and downed his second whiskey.

"You actually think I'm going to Scotland with you in tow? I might be desperate but I'm not suicidal."

"And do I look like I just came off the farm? Your choice, Chambers. You're my point man on this, or I walk out that door and you're on your own."

Chambers did some fast thinking. At least with Cooper at his side he might have a chance of staying alive. On his own, with Gantley hunting him, he had little chance. Paul Chambers had never considered himself a capable man in a fight. He always paid others to work violence for him and watch his back. Like it or not, the tall American holding the gun would seem the most likely man to prevent anything happening to him, and if Cooper managed to put Canfield down Chambers could take his chances. It wasn't foolproof but it was better than being on his own and waiting for Gantley to show, because sooner or later Canfield's trained dog would slip his leash and come looking.

"Okay, Cooper. I can't say it's what I'd choose if I had any other options. Only I don't. So we go together."

AN HOUR LATER Bolan accompanied Paul Chambers from his apartment. They picked up the rental car Bolan had left in the parking garage and drove across the city to London's Euston Station where they boarded the train that would take them to Scotland. The train would terminate in Glasgow and Bolan would pick up another that ran up country, his destination the far northeast of Scotland, taking him closer to Canfield's remote lair.

As they settled in the private compartment Bolan had requested when he had booked their passage, the Executioner was aware of his companion's nervous condition.

"Chambers, sit down and relax."

"Easy for you to say. Christ, I'm a walking dead man. That bastard wants me buried. If Gantley is looking for me the far north of Tibet won't be far enough away."

Bolan stowed his bag on the overhead luggage rack. He wasn't happy having to walk around with a cache of weapons but the situation called for extreme actions. Heading for Hugo Canfield's base he was not going in empty-handed.

"Right now we're ahead of the game. If we can stay that way there's a chance we might come through," he told Chambers.

"That's bloody pessimistic. 'Might come through?'"

"It's called being realistic. I don't guarantee anything, Chambers. Every situation like this comes with a fifty-fifty chance of survival. I accept that."

"Maybe you do. I figure those to be poor odds. Why the hell should I be in a mess like that?"

Bolan moved so fast Chambers had no chance to step aside. He felt a big hand close on his shirtfront. Bolan slammed him up against the compartment wall, the impact making Chambers gasp for breath. He found himself staring directly into chilled blue eyes.

"Quick to forget what you're involved in? Chambers, you trade in human lives. You buy and sell women and kids. Send them into virtual slavery. Into lives of sheer misery. The money in your wallet comes from the depravity some of those people have to endure. One of your own kind has turned on you and now you expect sympathy. Are you expecting me to forget what you do and hold your hand? Be thankful I don't pull out my gun and put a bullet through your head. Now sit down and shut up."

Bolan released his hold, allowing Chambers to shrink away from him. Chambers moved to one of the seats and pressed himself into the corner, staring out the window in cowed silence.

"THEY'RE ON A TRAIN for Glasgow," Canfield's man said from a pay phone at Euston Station. "I sent Breck and Munro after them. If they get the opportunity Cooper and Chambers won't even reach the Scottish border."

"If they do, at least we know they're coming," Gantley said. "Keep me informed, Harris."

Gantley put down the phone and turned to Canfield.

"Cooper's on his way. He's got Chambers with him, sir. They left London on a train for Glasgow. Breck and Munro are on board, as well. They might get the chance to intercept and deal with them."

"Hopefully we could be spared the need to expect them showing up here. If they *do* survive it still gives us time to arrange a welcome for them. Sergeant Gantley, don't bother to get any rooms ready. Cooper won't be staying long."

"Just a quick visit, then, sir?"

Canfield smiled.

"Very brief. Painful and brief. Especially for Chambers. Didn't take him long to change sides."

"I should have got to him sooner, sir. Before he could open his mouth to Cooper."

"One way or another Mr. Paul Chambers is going to find it's a very small world, Sergeant Gantley. One where he can't run away and hide."

"Yes, sir."

The ex-military cop finished pouring the whiskey. He sealed the bottle and placed it back on the wet bar. Without a word he placed the tumbler within Canfield's reach and left the room, closing the door quietly behind him.

Canfield picked up the tumbler, raised it to drink, then paused. His gaze turned hard, eyes gleaming as he struggled with the turmoil inside his head. Too much was happening that was causing him aggravation. When he'd retreated to Banecreif he expected a calm and restful time. Canfield hurled the thick tumbler into the wide stone fireplace. The glass shattered and the whiskey flared as the flames engulfed it.

"Damn you to bloody hell, Cooper," he said. "Damn you for making me feel like this in my own house."

On his feet he strode to the glass-fronted gun cabinet. He opened the doors and reached for a racked Franchi-SPAS shotgun. The weapon, customized for him in London, was finely balanced. The SPAS was a formidable tool in Canfield's expert hands. He liked hunting with the shotgun even though it was not primarily a sporting gun. When he turned it on either Cooper or Chambers there would be no hint of sport in his actions. This time around his targets would have a special significance.

He wanted the pair dead and buried and he cherished the hope that they actually got through to Banecreif. If his men on the train failed to stop them, Canfield could look forward to handling the matter himself.

Especially Cooper, the man responsible for so much death and destruction. He was the reason for the fragmenting of Hugo Canfield's organized and well-oiled machine. Because of Cooper, Canfield had lost merchandise, money and people. His reputation had been tarnished and so had his credibility. If the news spread to his potential new partners it might sour their decision to do business with him. Canfield understood how they might view the attacks on Venturer Exports. The drug business thrived on being able to move its products around with comparative ease, taking any small losses without suffering too badly. The fact Canfield was under the eye of a multination task force looking into his trafficking might not bother them. The blatant strikes against him by Cooper, who ignored the restraints placed on a lawful investigation, might easily do more to scare them off.

The problem was Canfield's and Canfield's alone. He needed to clean up his own mess. Prove to his future partners that Hugo Canfield was capable of maintaining order. Only he could solve it, and solving it meant getting rid of Cooper. The man's sheer audacity was bringing him here to Banecreif. Canfield saw that as Cooper's mistake. If he did survive the rail trip he would be on Canfield's home ground. Here he was the master. His knowledge of Banecreif and the surrounding terrain was indisputable. That gave Canfield the advantage. He would use it to the limit.

And this time Cooper would not walk away so easily.

In fact, he wouldn't walk away at all.

18

Breck waited for his partner to join him in the buffet car. He handed Munro the cup of coffee he'd ordered. Munro ignored his partner while he blew air across the steaming surface of the drink. It was one of his partner's habits that annoyed Breck. He held back from saying anything because it would only encourage Munro to continue doing it.

"Aren't you going to ask me if I found 'em?" Munro asked abruptly. There was a thin smile on his lips. "Pay attention, son, or life is goin' to pass you by."

They had each taken one end of the train, working their way back to the central point, that being the buffet car. Breck had seen no sign of Cooper or Chambers. The smug expression on Munro's lean face suggested he had been successful.

"Have you found them?"

Munro took a mouthful of coffee, nodding. He led Breck away from the counter to avoid being overheard. "Third carriage along. Compartment 12B. Easy as that."

Breck glanced out the window behind him. "Be dark in a couple of hours. Reckon we should wait until then?"

"About right. What do you think? Take 'em down and dump 'em off the train while it's still dark?"

"Makes sense to me."

"That Yank will be armed," Munro said. "And he's not slow to use his gun from what I heard."

"So we'll be careful. Here, you're not going soft on me, are you?"

"Like I would. Anyhow, what sort of a question is that to ask?"

"Since you started going around with that skirt from the club I reckon you have."

Munro wagged a finger at his partner, grinning widely. "Jealous. You are bleedin' jealous, Marty Breck." He swallowed more coffee. "She never did fancy you. Thought you were too rough for her. She prefers the sensitive type like me."

"Says who?"

"Who is she with, partner? Need I say more?"

Breck shrugged as he reached into his jacket and took out his cell phone. "Better let Gantley know we spotted them."

He spoke quietly when his call was answered, finally completing his conversation. He shut the cell and put it away. "Same as before. If the chance comes up we do it. If not we stay on their tail until they reach Banecreif."

"Never been to Scotland," Munro said.

"Sheltered life, son. You need to get out of the smoke more often."

"Right now I fancy a meal. There's a proper restaurant car back that way. Help pass the time."

"Very smart, Sherlock. And what if Cooper and Chambers decide to do the same? Chambers knows us."

Munro accepted the fact grudgingly. "Well, they do sandwiches here. What do you fancy? Chicken? Chicken with salad. Or they do a nice chicken with chicken."

"Just get something, huh?" Breck glanced at his watch. It was going to be a long wait.

NEITHER COOPER NOR Chambers left their compartment. Food had been ordered and was delivered to the door. On watch farther down the car Breck saw an opportunity to get them inside the compartment. Give Cooper and Chambers ample time to eat their meal before they moved. He returned to the buffet car and an increasingly fidgety Munro.

"It's getting dark, Marty," he said. "Time to move?"

"We give 'em a couple more hours. I just saw food being delivered. Let them eat, then we go. Wait until things quiet down."

"That's generous of you."

"No. It gets us a way into that compartment. Knock on the door and say we've come to collect the tray. They open up and we go in hard and fast."

Munro peeled open his sandwich and studied the contents. "Does that look like chicken to you?"

"A couple of hours. We take turns to watch the compartment in case the waiter turns up first. Now eat your bloody sandwich."

IT WAS DARK BEYOND the train windows. No one had gone near the compartment. Breck joined his partner and they made their way along the corridor to 12B. From inside their jackets they pulled out the suppressed 9 mm Glock pistols they carried in shoulder rigs.

"Nice sharp knock," Breck said.

Munro nodded, rapping on the door.

"Restaurant service, sir," Breck said. "Come to collect your tray."

The door clicked after a few seconds. It opened. Paul Chambers stood there. As he recognized the two men he put out a hand as if to ward off any threat.

"No way," he shouted.

"Hey, Paul," Munro said and stepped inside the compartment, his Glock already rising.

Breck tried to warn his reckless partner but he was too late. Sudden movement from just behind the door caught Munro off guard. The dark outline of a fast-moving figure loomed over him. An arm swept down. Munro gave a strangled cry as the solid metal of a pistol smashed across the back of his skull with tremendous force. He stumbled across the compartment, out of control, slamming into the far wall.

Already committed Breck followed his partner over the threshold, aware of the threat behind the door. He moved fast, starting to crouch, angling his Glock to punch a round through the panel. His intention might have been sound, but the execution was not fast enough. The door was driven at him, catching his shoulder, driving him off balance. He hit the compartment floor, the Glock firing as his finger jerked the trigger. Breck rolled, desperation leading his frantic moves. He heard the compartment door slam shut, caught a blurred glimpse of an armed figure. He dragged the seemingly reluctant Glock around to take a shot. He never made it. The muzzle of the other man's pistol winked brightly—once, then again. Breck felt the impact of the pair of slugs as they cored into his chest. The force at close range slammed him to the floor, his arms spread wide as he sucked in air, struggling against the lethargy that was drawing him into a silent and shadowed place.

BOLAN STEPPED BACK, still gripping the Beretta 93-R Len Watts had supplied. It was as if a blanket of silence had cocooned the compartment and it stayed that way until he let out the breath he'd been holding.

Reality rushed back. He could feel the rhythmic cadence of the speeding train. The occasional creak of metal from the gentle sway of the car. Bolan backed across the compartment, moving the Beretta to cover everyone.

That was when he saw Chambers. The man was crumpled in a corner of the compartment, limbs twisted awkwardly. The loose bullet from Breck's pistol had blown in through his left eye and angled up to erupt from the top of his skull.

19

The Executioner collected the Glocks the intruders had carried and dropped them in his bag, along with the spare magazines they had. He knew from past experience that adding to his arsenal was recommended.

His only choice was to leave the train at the earliest opportunity and make alternative travel plans. It wouldn't be the first time he had been forced to rethink a mission. Flexibility in these situations was often necessary. Bolan had made such moves on many occasions before.

He secured his bag by its long strap, swinging it across his back. The Beretta was back in its holster beneath his zipped leather jacket. He opened the compartment door and checked that the corridor was clear. He made his way along until he reached the end. At the junction where the car joined the next one there was an exit door set in the side. Bolan waited until he felt the train start to reduce speed. It was making the pull up one of the long gradients as it coasted through the Scottish lowlands. Working the door release Bolan eased it open until the gap was wide enough for him to push through. He used the grab rail set in the car side, searching for the foot step, and swung clear of the door, slamming it shut once he was secure.

The chill draft caused by the train's motion buffeted him and pulled at his clothing. Bolan hung on to the grab rail, thinking how well it had been named. He peered around. There was enough illumination coming from the train's windows and from the pale moon to show him the terrain. From the tracks the ground fell away in a long grassy slope. Some way ahead he could see clusters of lights, indicating some habitation. A town. That meant people and maybe the chance to gain some kind of transportation.

The sudden shriek of the train's whistle sounded. Following that, the train's speed reduced more. Bolan checked out the slope some feet below his level. It still seemed to be moving by at a good speed but he figured it wasn't going to get better. He was about to take a calculated risk. One that might leave him injured. If he decided to stay on the train he could find himself in the hands of the authorities and, if Canfield learned about it, the man's influence would be asserted. His contacts would home in on Bolan and freedom might become a thing of the past.

As the train reached midpoint along the gradient its speed dropped down another notch. Bolan swung around so he faced the direction the train was moving. He waited for the clearest patch of slope and went for it. He pushed out from the step, relaxing his body and hit the soft surface of the slope with enough momentum to hurl him forward. His feet made contact. He let himself go, loose limbed, skidding across the grassy slope. He slammed facedown, his arms crossed to protect it.

The hard shock stunned him and he was barely aware of being flung downslope. The hard contents of the bag dug into his chest and ribs as he bounced and slithered across the face of the slope.

His wild ride came to a dead stop as Bolan slammed into a thick tangle of thorny bushes. He didn't attempt to move until his senses settled. The first thing he did was check his arms and legs. Then he sat up and dropped the bag. Bolan stood slowly, turning to check out the train. He could still see the faint glow of lights as it continued up the gradient.

The sooner he started to move, the better. Walking would help keep his battered body from stiffening up. He checked out his surroundings. The lights he had seen from the train were slightly west of his position, a couple of miles away. Bolan spotted moving lights below him—vehicles on a road a quarter of a mile distant. Bolan brushed himself off, slung the bag over his shoulder and headed in the direction of the road.

IT WAS CLOSE TO MIDNIGHT when Bolan closed the door of the room he had taken at the roadside lodge. The lodge was the U.K. equivalent of a motel, there to provide accommodation for long-distance travelers. The young man on duty at the desk had processed Bolan's request for a room with barely any interest. He was eager to get back to his viewing the international soccer match on the television set in his cubbyhole behind the desk.

"You have a car?" the young man asked in a Scottish dialect strong enough to almost baffle Bolan.

"No. Local sales man dropped me off. He'll pick me up in the morning. We had a long day."

"So haven't we all." Bolan's key card was slid across the desk. "Straight along the corridor. Room fourteen. You take your breakfast at the diner across the way. It's in the price."

Bolan nodded, but the man had already turned back to his TV, absorbed in the droning reflections from the commentator and his group of former players as they analyzed the match.

The room was comfortable and functional, equipped with a TV and a kettle for making hot drinks from the supply on a sectioned plastic tray. Bolan flipped the switch. As the water boiled he crossed to the room and closed the curtains. He checked the bathroom. The shower beckoned. Bolan made himself a mug of instant coffee, sitting on the edge of the bed as he drank it. He stripped off his clothes and padded into the bathroom. He caught his reflection in the mirror over the sink. His torso was crisscrossed with bruises and the still-healing bullet tear. He had half expected it to start bleeding again. He counted himself lucky that his leap from the train had let him off so lightly. Bolan turned on the shower and stood under the hot water. He soaped himself, then leaned against the tiled wall and let the water ease away some of the aches and pains.

His strike against Canfield's home base would still go ahead. It would take him longer to reach the place, but that might work in his favor. Anticipation of the coming attack would play against Canfield. He might lose some of his confidence. Start to doubt his own safety as he debated where and when Bolan would show. It was a strategy that could give the Executioner an edge. Anything that took the edge off Canfield's force was welcome. Bolan had no idea of the strength of Canfield's security. He was going in blind. It didn't worry him too much. It wouldn't be the first time he had gone up against an unknown force. He had the advantage of time on his side.

Out of the shower Bolan dried himself and wrapped a towel around his waist. He prepared another coffee, stretched out on the bed and checked his phone. He saw the power was in need of charging, so he took the unit from his bag and clicked in place the converter that would allow him to use the U.K. socket. He connected to the cell phone, saw the power indicator rise and hit the speed dial that would link him to Hal Brognola.

"Striker, where are you?"

"A long way from home," Bolan said.

"How close are you to wrapping this up?"

"Close enough. You got anything for me?"

Brognola held back for a moment.

"Good news and bad news," he said. "On the bad side there's no way of making it any easier to say."

"Just say it, Hal."

"A ship on its way to the U.K., the *Orient Venturer,* dumped one of its containers over the side. They didn't know they'd been spotted by a trawler out of a British port. The trawler hove to where the container had been dropped and marked it with a buoy. A British Navy vessel was called and it sent down diving teams to locate the container. When they raised it and got it open they found twenty-five bodies inside. Young women and kids. Later identified as Thai. The call went out and the authorities were waiting when the container ship docked. Captain and crew were arrested. No one will talk but we lucked out when the Bear did some hard probing into the container ship's background. This is the good news. Aaron found one hell of a maze as far as ownership was concerned. Blind alleys and phony registration. But bless that man, he finally pinned it down. Bottom line is that the *Orient Venturer* belongs to Hugo Canfield's organization. He can deny it until hell freezes over but he's the man."

Brognola sensed Bolan's feelings through the protracted silence that followed his revelation. He let Bolan have his moment, knowing how the man would be hurting. If emotion was ever allowed to break Bolan's stoic image, it could be guaranteed when he was faced with more innocent suffering. The facts about the women and children would hurt Bolan more than a 9 mm bullet.

"Hal, how far has this information gone?"

"I haven't spoken to anyone."

"Leave it that way. We started this mission one-to-one. I'll finish it that way."

"No problem. A little more feedback. Aaron's digging into the data he downloaded from van Ryden's computer has paid off, too. Names on Canfield's payroll. High rollers in government positions. Customs. Police. Canfield has connections. Those names covered individuals in Europe, the U.K. *and* the U.S. Looks like van Ryden was hedging his bets by keeping lists. Covering his ass in case he needed protection himself. That's a lawyer for you. The task force will be drooling for weeks when they get their hands on that intel."

"Tell Aaron nice work."

"I'll hold back on this until I hear from you," Brognola said. "I guess Canfield is in for a surprise when you show up."

"That's the idea, Hal."

20

Banecreif was more than five hundred years old—a sprawling stone mansion with extensive grounds. Isolated—the closest village was over ten miles away—it stood on the coast, the east side of the massive building overlooking the cold gray waters of the North Sea. From the base of the east wall a sheer rock cliff dropped eighty feet to the inhospitable waters.

Since he'd purchased the house Hugo Canfield had invested a great deal of money in the place. He added modern refinements. A powerful generator supplied electricity to light the house and provide heated water for the bathrooms he had built. The kitchen was equipped with professional stoves and freezers. There was no permanent staff. When Canfield was away a local couple kept the house running. If he was expecting business guests he flew in catering staff.

With the current situation Canfield had Sergeant Gantley, plus a five-man security team at the house. His personal helicopter had brought them to Banecreif from the closest airfield. It was standing on the concrete landing pad next to the house.

Sergeant Gantley looked after security and supervised the kitchen. One of the ground-level rooms served as a small but efficient control center. From there it was possible to view the incoming images from a number of security cameras that had been installed around the property. Total security systems had yet to be completed, with motion sensors and infrared detection still to be added. Fortunately the house was far enough off the beaten track not to attract many visitors. Canfield maintained a low profile when he was at the house and his roving patrols were enough to keep any unwitting trespassers away.

Hugo Canfield always felt secure at Banecreif. The peace and quiet allowed him time to think out his problems and plan future enterprises. He had installed expensive communications systems—satellite phone lines, high-speed Internet. Distance was no problem. He could speak to anyone he wanted, anywhere across the globe.

He was on the phone to his Russian contact in Leningrad. Pavel Molenski was head of the drug syndicate Canfield was hoping to do business with.

The conversation was not going well.

"Hugo, I hope you are keeping well? I have heard life is a little difficult at the moment."

"A few local problems, Pavel. Nothing to worry about."

"But that *is* the problem, Hugo. Friends are concerned. Questions have been asked. About your suitability to join us. And as much as I admire your past record, these recent setbacks are starting to give me reason to doubt."

"No need, Pavel. As I said this is a local disturbance. One that I will settle very soon."

"First your setup in Holland. Now your U.K. base. My sources tell me that your organization has been severely hit."

"Nothing that cannot be brought back on-line. Trust me, Pavel, I won't allow this interference to put our deal at risk."

Pavel's strong Russian accent came through clearly. "It has been decided, Hugo, to give you exactly one more week. If nothing has changed by then, if you have not completely cleared up this mess, we will be expecting the return of our merchandise and all future deals will be off."

"Don't do this to me, Pavel. Not now. I've made commitments to my contacts here. I can't renege on my promises."

"Understand me, Hugo. You made a commitment to *us*. We

supplied the merchandise. It seems clear that you will not be able to go through with your end of the deal. We have to protect our interests. If you are compromised we could be drawn into the area of suspicion. One week, Hugo, then we collect our goods. And we can do it peacefully, or with extreme force. Please do not make it that we need to use force. That would be extremely foolish on your part."

The phone went dead. Canfield listened to the buzz of the line. He experienced a growing anger as he recalled the Russian's words. The implicit threat.

"The hell with you, Pavel."

He slammed the phone down and strode across the room, standing in front of the blazing fire in the ornate stone hearth. Canfield stared into flames, his thoughts working overtime. First Cooper. Now the fucking Russians. Whining because they were scared their consignment of drugs, stored in the temperature-controlled cellars beneath Banecreif, was going to be lost. Crying like babies who wanted their toys back. They were pathetic. They were greedy. Wanting everything instantly. Suddenly they were acting as if they were the top dogs. Pushing into every corner of his business. Uneducated, nonthinking thugs. Maybe he had been wrong to negotiate the deal. It was a mistake on his part. They were going to have to wait until he had the Cooper affair handled. Then *he* would show them how negotiate.

He heard a clock chiming at the far end of the large room that served as his office. Canfield turned and crossed to the oak desk and sat down in the huge leather chair. He reached for the internal phone and called for Sergeant Gantley to join him.

The ex-Army cop was there in minutes. He was an imposing figure in his dark military-style fatigues. He carried a SIG-Sauer P-226 in a high-ride holster on his right hip. The pistol, with its stainless-steel parts and wood grips, was Gantley's personal weapon.

"Any sign of Cooper?" Canfield asked.

Gantley shook his head. He had his security detail on roving patrols in and around the massive old house. "Nothing from Breck or Munro, either, sir. I'm trying to get in touch with Harris," Gantley said. "Maybe he can give me an update."

"I've just been speaking to Pavel," Canfield said. "He had the nerve to actually threaten me. This Cooper mess has those Russians wetting their pants. He's ready to go back on the deal. Told me we have a week to sort this out, or they'll demand the drugs back."

"Russians? They couldn't even keep their own country together, sir. Now they all think they're Al Capone. Never met one I couldn't drink under the table, sir."

"Just thought I'd let you know, Sergeant Gantley. First things first. We deal with Cooper, then sort out these bloody Russkies."

"Yes, sir."

GANTLEY MADE THE ROUNDS, checking his team. They were well armed. Two outside. Two more on the roof and one manning the security room, watching the camera monitor screens. Each man was carrying a holstered Beretta 92-F and an HK MP-5A4. The long-established submachine gun still performed well and Gantley trusted the weapon. The MP-5s were loaded with 30-round twin magazines for extended firepower.

He climbed to the roof, walking the stone-flagged flat area bounded by a three-foot-high buttressed wall. From there he was able to look out across the surrounding terrain.

He saw undulating grassland and timber and the thin gray snake of the narrow approach road. Moving around to the east side he stared out across the water. Mist hung over the jagged coastline extending away from Banecreif. Strong currents sent icy waves crashing against the base of the rocky cliff, the spray leaping high up the dark, weathered rock. Gantley felt the touch of rain and saw gray cloud sweeping in off the sea. He made contact with the roof sentries. The men wore thick parkas over their clothing against the chill. It started to rain heavily.

"Anything?" Gantley asked.

"Nothing, sir. If he's coming he's taking his time."

"That could be deliberate," Gantley said. "Trying to make us sweat."

The sentry smiled. "Hardly likely in this bloody weather."

"Well, don't slack off just because he hasn't shown yet. From what I've learned Cooper is no quitter. He'll show."

Gantley started back down into the house. His cell phone rang and he answered.

"It's Harris. You need to hear this. Took me some time. There's been a shut down on information coming from the cops. My contact in the information office finally came through. When the train arrived in Glasgow Breck and Chambers had already been found dead in the compartment Cooper booked. They had both been shot. Munro was found alive but with the back of his skull caved in."

"Cooper?"

"No sign of a fourth man. He could have jumped the train anywhere after it crossed the border. He could be long gone."

"No, Harris, he's not gone. The man is on his way here." Gantley checked his watch. An hour after midday. "He's had plenty of time to make new travel arrangements. Keep me informed of any developments."

Gantley ended the call and put his phone away. He crossed to stand at the wall again, scanning the surrounding countryside, nodding to himself.

"Come ahead, Mr. Cooper. I'm ready and waiting for you."

21

Using the available guest computer Bolan had checked out Banecreif on Google's map site. It was a long drive down a rugged road that would take him to the easterly edge of the Scottish highlands. The road ran along the coast, the North Sea bordering the route. Remote. Isolated, with only a few scattered villages along the way. It would take Bolan the best part of a day to reach his destination. He didn't mind that because the delay in his travel would leave Canfield wondering when his unwelcome guest might turn up.

Checking out of the lodge Bolan asked the young woman behind the desk, the day-shift receptionist, to call him a taxi, explaining that his pickup had been postponed and he needed to locate a car rental agency. The closest agency was in the next town, a forty-minute ride away. The taxi turned up in short time and Bolan settled in the backseat. The journey took just over thirty minutes after Bolan promised the driver a bonus if he could get him to his destination quickly.

At the rental agency Bolan made the necessary negotiations and hired a late-model Volkswagen Toureg SE. The big 4x4 had auto transmission and even a touch-screen DVD navigation system. Its powerful engine would provide Bolan with the kind of horsepower needed to cover the long distance to the Scottish Highlands.

Leaving the rental agency Bolan spotted a convenience store and pulled in. He stocked up on a few sandwiches and bottles of water. Behind the wheel he tapped in the coordinates for his route and watched as the sharp image came on the screen. Pushing the stick into first Bolan settled into the comfortable leather seat and moved off.

LATE AFTERNOON, hours into his drive, Bolan was away from the sprawling bustle of Glasgow and heading north, toward Inverness and the eastern side of the country where he would eventually link up to the coast road that would lead him to Banecreif. He saw that he was heading into rough weather as dark clouds rolled in from the east, gathering into a storm bank the farther he drove up-country. The road ahead stretched across low hills with little habitation save for a few farms scattered across the landscape. His original estimate was that he had roughly two hundred and seventy miles to cover—around six hours' driving. With the weather backing up, threatening rain, Bolan added to that time. However it worked out, it was going to be late by the time he reached his objective.

The realization did little to unnerve Bolan. A strike in the wee hours might work in his favor. It was the time when the most alert opponent lost a degree of his deductive powers. When the body naturally reached that twilight condition, slowing down. Leaving perceptions at a low ebb. Something to be taken advantage of.

When Bolan spotted a truck stop he pulled in. The small restaurant and store was hosting only a couple of drivers from the long-haul trucks parked outside. Bolan picked up a thermos flask from the store section, went to the restaurant counter and ordered a black coffee. At his request the red-haired woman serving filled his flask with more coffee. Bolan allowed himself a leisurely break, downing a second mug of coffee before settling his bill and leaving. He took a few minutes to walk around the parking area before he returned to the 4x4.

As he settled himself behind the wheel, securing his seat belt, the first fat drops of rain hit the windshield. By the time he had driven out of the parking lot and turned back onto the road the rain had increased to a hard downpour. Bolan flicked on the wipers, the built-in sensor determining how fast they needed to operate in order to clear the glass screen. It became gloomy enough that Bolan needed the headlights, as well. He set his speed and activated the cruise control, letting the vehicle take the strain.

Bolan drove through Inverness into a rain-filled night, the road swinging toward the coast. Beyond the town the strip of road ahead was dark and empty, leaving Bolan the opportunity to consider what lay ahead for him at Banecreif.

He had his mission to complete.

Retribution to deliver to Hugo Canfield.

THE UNBROKEN STORM followed Bolan all the way to his turnoff. He lost time negotiating the empty, winding main highway, only the powerful headlights of his vehicle breaking the darkness surrounding him. The navigation system performed its task well, and Bolan easily found the narrow, single-lane road that led to Banecreif. According to the screen readout the road ran for two miles, dead-ending at Canfield's property. He cut the lights as he rolled the Toureg onto this feeder road, taking the first chance he got to turn the vehicle around and reverse into the cover of the trees and bushes edging the road. Bolan killed the engine. The drum of falling rain on the roof matched the distant crash of waves hitting the rocky shore close by.

He pulled his blacksuit and boots from his bag and changed. His shoulder rig held the Beretta 93-R. Len Watts had also provided an Uzi, still one of Bolan's favorite weapons. He slid a sheathed knife onto his belt. Snapping on a combat rig Bolan made sure the pouches held plastic ties and extra magazines for the Beretta and the Uzi. It was basic equipment, but enough for what he intended. He pulled on a black baseball cap to complete his transformation, slipped out of the vehicle and locked it, dropping the key into one of the blacksuit's zippered side pockets.

Using the faint moonlight Bolan headed in toward the dark bulk of Banecreif. Even at the distance he was from the house Bolan could see how it dominated the headland where it stood. Cold and brooding.

HUGO CANFIELD FOUND IT hard to sleep.

The early hours were the worst. Night was still hanging on, reluctant to relinquish its hold to the coming dawn. Canfield hated waking because he could never get back to sleep. This time was even worse. He couldn't get Cooper out of his mind. The man stalked through his thoughts. A spectral figure bringing death and destruction with every step. He had certainly done that to Canfield's operation.

It angered and interested him at the same time. The anger was easily explained. His interest in Cooper another matter. The man intrigued him. Canfield wished he could learn more about him. No getting away from the fact that Cooper was a hell of an opponent. He came through every confrontation ready for the next. Gained his information and acted on it. He had a relentless drive to him that pushed him ever forward, his mind like a guided missile, directing him to the next target. In a perverse way Canfield likened himself to Cooper. In their respective businesses they knew what they wanted and simply went for it, casting aside doubt and uncertainty.

If Cooper had allied himself with Hugo Canfield they would have made a formidable team. They would have been unstoppable.

Canfield pushed that out of his mind as quickly as it presented itself. Cooper was on the side of the good and righteous. No doubt about that.

The mix of conflicting thoughts denied Canfield any

further rest. He left his bed, showered, shaved and got dressed. He made his way downstairs to the kitchen, craving coffee. He found Gantley already there. A mug of steaming black coffee was pushed across the work surface. Canfield took it.

"How did you know?" Canfield asked.

"It's what you pay me for, sir. And I heard you in the shower when I passed your room ten minutes ago."

"So, is everything secure?"

"As we can ever make it, sir," Gantley said.

"Can we stop him? Given his recent record."

"A bloody good try is what we can offer."

"Not the best summation, Sergeant Gantley, but an honest one."

BOLAN WALKED STEADILY, head down against the rain driving in from the seaward side of the track. The unpaved surface of the road had already become a soft morass of dark mud. He had only walked for a few hundred yards before the chill began to penetrate the blacksuit. There was nothing he could do to change that. Bolan kept moving, his mind focused on his objective.

He was there to make sure Hugo Canfield was taken down. That his organization was neutered. Venturer Exports would be reduced to ashes and scattered beyond repair.

That was going to require Bolan going on the hunt.

He had no qualms about that. All he had to do was recall the deaths of two task-force agents and the twenty-five Thai women and children dropped overboard from Canfield's ship while locked inside a steel container.

Bolan wouldn't derive satisfaction from whatever happened at Banecreif, but he would achieve some kind of closure for the dead.

And that would have to do.

22

Faint dawn light was edging away the night. The rain persisted, laying a misty curtain across the landscape. Bolan didn't mind that. It would offer some additional distraction for his approach. With Banecreif looming in front of him Bolan took to the ground, working his way through the wet grass, using every patch of shadow he could find until he was close enough to pick out the sentries.

Bolan studied the sentry as he slogged his way through the heavy waterlogged grass. Even though he was clad in a waterproof coat the man was probably chilled to the bone and hoping to be relieved. Bolan figured this would be the best time to take the man. He had probably been on duty for a long few hours. He would be tired and ready to get under cover.

The man moved by him. Bolan was no more than twenty feet away and was able to see the MP-5 the guard was carrying over one shoulder, his hands shoved deep into the pockets of his jacket.

The sentry paced on, pausing at the perimeter of his patch to look around, before slowly, reluctantly, turning and retracing his steps. By this time Bolan had moved in closer, so that when the sentry drew level with him, Bolan was almost under his feet. As the man reached the ideal position Bolan swept his legs from under him, dropping him flat on his back. Unprepared the guard hit the ground with a hard thump, gasping as the air was forced from his lungs. Before he could recover

Bolan slammed a bunched fist against his jaw. The sentry grunted and lay still, momentarily stunned. It was enough time for Bolan to strip away his MP-5 and handgun, turn the man facedown and use a couple of plastic ties to secure wrists and ankles. He rolled the man back over and as the sentry shook away the dizziness Bolan slid the fighting knife from its sheath and pressed it against the man's exposed throat, applying just enough pressure so that the fine sheer edge cut into flesh, drawing a little blood and creating a prickly stinging sensation.

"Listen good," Bolan said. "You have an easy choice. Give me the answers I want, or I lean on this knife a little harder and open your throat all the way."

The sentry stared up at Bolan, only just able to see his face in the dawn light. But there was enough to recognize the hard, icy gleam in the eyes staring back at him.

"I say anything Gantley will—"

"Gantley isn't the one you need to worry about, friend. It's me you're going to have to deal with. Right now I'm the most important man in the world."

Bolan emphasized his words by drawing the blade a little deeper across the sentry's throat, causing a warm trickle of blood to slide across taut flesh.

"Jesus…"

"I'd suggest it's a little late to start getting religion. Are you ready to answer my question?"

The sentry stopped trying to free his bounds wrists and nodded. "What?" he asked.

"How many more of you are there? And don't make up numbers. I'm going to leave you here. Mess with me and I'll come back and show you just how persuasive my friend here can be."

"Okay, okay. One more on the ground like me. Two on the roof. One inside manning the security cameras. And Gantley."

Bolan took hold of the sentry's collar and dragged him through the grass until he reached the trees. He used the knife to cut a wide strip from the man's waterproof coat and gagged him, propping him against the trunk of a tree. He searched the sentry's coat and found a spare magazine for the MP-5. Returning to the spot where he had taken the man down Bolan picked up the MP-5. He swung the Uzi across his back, moving forward, his eyes searching for the second sentry.

It was the sentry who found Bolan. As the Executioner circled a heavy stand of tangled undergrowth the sentry appeared off to his right, picking up speed as he fixed Bolan's position. The guard called out, raising his MP-5 and let go with a loose burst that chopped at the undergrowth, showering Bolan with debris.

Bolan dropped and rolled, propping himself on his elbows and returned fire. The sentry jerked aside, cursing wildly, and then hauled himself to a stop. His weapon tracked back in Bolan's direction but he was a couple of seconds too late. Bolan's second burst caught the man chest-high, a follow-up adding to the devastation as the 9 mm slugs cleaved into his body, tearing into his lungs and heart. The man uttered a high squeal, falling back and slamming to the ground.

Bolan scrambled to his feet and dug in his heels, angling across the open ground for the cover of the house. In his mind he was calculating how soon the sentries on the roof might respond.

The chatter of concentrated automatic fire answered his question as a pair of MP-5's opened up. Bolan heard the sodden thumps as 9 mm slugs tore at the rain-soaked ground around him. He ducked and weaved, presenting a constantly shifting target, feeling the impact as slugs struck closer than he wanted. The shooters were having to lean over the parapet as Bolan got closer to the house, the angle they were having to deal with making accurate fire difficult.

Bolan reached the rough stone wall, slamming against the unyielding surface and pausing for a moment. Shadows at the base of the wall helped to conceal him but he was aware that some of the 9 mm projectiles were also getting closer to the angle where the ground met the wall. By the law of averages he was soon going to feel one of those slugs. He glanced left and right. He saw a low-sited window a few yards away. He needed access to the house and a window was as good a way of entering as a door. He edged along the wall, taking himself away from the bursts of fire, albeit briefly.

The window was large, the sill no more than a couple of feet from ground level—an old, wooden sash-style window. Bolan pulled away from the window, raised the MP-5 and triggered the remaining magazine capacity at it. The burst of sustained fire shattered the glass from the frame and shredded the wood. Throwing his arms up to cover his face Bolan took a run at the empty gap and launched himself through the window, taking the remaining glass and wood with him. He landed on his feet, glass showering around him.

The first thing he did was eject the empty magazine and snap in his remaining full one. A glance around the room showed it in shadow, devoid of furniture. The door was on the far side. Bolan crossed to it, easing the handle and edging the door open to show the empty passage beyond.

23

The moment the sound of gunfire reached the security room, the guard in charge, Lou Trencher, snapped out of his half-sleep state and hit the exterior lights. Instantly the monitor screens were illuminated by the powerful lamps mounted around the outside of the house.

Damn, I should have had them on already, he thought.

Trencher knew he was in trouble. Once Gantley found out he had been slacking at his post it wouldn't matter if an intruder was out there. The former military cop would kill Trencher himself. Sergeant Gantley had a fetish about running the security team like a small army. And he had no patience with anyone who slipped below his standards.

The first thing Trencher saw was a body stretched out on the ground. He focused in with the camera controls, bringing the motionless form into sharp relief. He couldn't identify the man because he was lying facedown, but he did see the blood oozing from the ragged bullet wounds, being sluiced away by the rain still sweeping in across the grounds.

Trencher keyed the Send button on his internal handset.

"Intruder alert. West wall."

Trencher heard the rattle of more automatic fire. It was coming from somewhere overhead. The roof guards. They must have spotted the man. What was his name—Cooper.

Close by Trencher heard more gunfire. Then the shattering of glass. He realized it was coming from the room just along the passage from his security cubbyhole.

Is Cooper breaking in? he wondered.

Aware he had some making up to do Trencher snatched up his own MP-5, swinging around and stepping out into the passage. He flattened against the opposite wall.

He heard the rattle of the handle, saw the door pulled open. The room inside was dark. Trencher could hear the sound of rain splashing in through the shattered window.

Where was Cooper? *Why didn't the bastard show himself?*

He eased away from the wall, his finger curling against the submachine gun's trigger.

In the distance he heard someone shout his name. He recognized the harsh bark.

Sergeant Gantley.

The angry call drew Trencher to an involuntary halt, head turning in the direction of the sound.

What did the man want now?

Fuck you, Trencher thought, I got more important things to do.

He swung back toward the point of his interest. The empty doorway.

Only it wasn't empty any longer.

A black-clad figure stood there, the muzzle of his own weapon already tracking Trencher.

Oh, shit, Trencher thought.

Second time he had screwed up tonight.

Bolan hit the armed man with a solid burst from his MP-5. The blistering stream of 9 mm bullets cut into and through the guard's midtorso, kicking him back across the passage until the stone wall brought him to an abrupt stop. Trencher's finger squeezed back against the MP-5's trigger and a burst hit the ceiling overhead, flattening and spinning across the passage. Trencher slid to his knees, dropping his weapon and clutching at his wounds. The last thing he saw was the dark-clad figure turning and heading along the passage.

The Executioner had seen the flight of stone steps that led from the ground floor. The steps were set against the wall, steep, and disappeared into apparent darkness. As he sprinted up he felt the flow of chilled air that met him. The stairs curved slightly to the left and as Bolan followed the turn the cold air increased. His initial guess had been correct—the steps led to the roof. Above him now he made out the shape of a heavy wooden door, partly ajar. The last few stone risers were wet from rain that had blown in through the gap.

He drew himself tight against the cold wall, using his foot to edge the door wide, giving it a final hard shove. The door swung wide, banging against something solid.

Bolan went through fast, dropping to a crouch and veering to the left, his MP-5 tracking ahead, searching for targets.

He had two armed men on the roof. Aware of his presence. Now that the high-mounted lights had been activated there was a degree of illumination spilling across the rain-swept flat area.

That light would expose the two guards *and* Bolan.

A hunched shape cut through Bolan's field of vision, firing as he moved. Bolan heard the hard snap of the slugs as they struck the stone behind him so he changed direction, following the man and also searching for guard number two.

More automatic fire. Bolan felt hot stone chips bite his left cheek. He swung around in response, seeing the still-moving shape. He pushed the MP-5's muzzle around and kept the guard in his sights for a couple of seconds. His finger eased back on the trigger, sending a burst at the man. The guard stumbled, a muffled curse on his lips. He still managed to fire back, his slugs clanging against a metal ventilation duct only a few feet away from Bolan. Bolan dropped, rolled, then dragged himself away from his position, working his way into a stand of heating and ventilation ducts, letting the complex shadows conceal his black shape. It wasn't going to hide him for long, but he needed a moment to check out the relative placing of his opponents.

He was a second away from raising his head when the faintest crunch of a boot against the stone roof slabs reached his ears.

The sound came from too close to his right.

The second guard. Moving in for the kill.

Bolan rolled over on his back, sensing the dark bulk rearing above him. In the fragment of light that fell across the section Bolan saw the rain-slick face, arms extending the man's MP-5, the shiny surface of the waterproof jacket. The light gave his eyes a cold, metallic gleam.

His MP-5 had moved with Bolan, an extension of his body, and he triggered the weapon the instant he locked on to the guard. Bolan kept his finger on the trigger, expending the remaining half of the magazine, pumping the 9 mms into the man's torso. The close range pushed the slugs through, blowing out the spine in a bloody spatter of flesh and splintered bone. The guard gave a strangled groan as he toppled away from Bolan and crashed down hard on the stone roof slabs.

Bolan threw the empty MP-5 aside and pulled the Uzi into position as he turned back to face the remaining guard. He worked his way out from the stand of pipes as the man, ducking and weaving as he sought a clear shot, was silhouetted against the bright glare from one of the spotlights.

The guard realized his error and turned to step out from the light.

Bolan's reflex action triggered the Uzi. He used a tried-and-tested figure eight, stitching the guard from chest to crotch, the man jerking from the impact of the 9 mm burn. He bounced against the stone slabs, his MP-5 slipping from his grasp. A second burst from the Uzi took a section of his skull off, ending the fight.

A moment of calm descended as Bolan eased to his feet, though his left shoulder ached from slamming against something when he had dropped to the roof and he had a faint ringing in his ears from the harsh chatter of automatic fire.

He turned his face to the falling rain, letting the cold water refresh his senses.

He didn't hear the soft footfall behind him. Only sensed that he wasn't alone a split second before something struck him across the back of his skull and he dropped to his knees, the shadows turning even blacker.

24

Bolan felt fingers working his combat rig loose, dragging it off his body, then freeing the holstered Beretta. He struggled against the dark mist fogging his senses, aware that the knife was being stripped from its sheath. The Uzi had gone from his grasp as he had been driven to his knees. He struggled upright, swaying as he gained his feet, turning about at the harsh voice ringing out.

"All right, son, so you're the tough man? Christ, you don't look so hard to me."

The man facing Bolan was his height, broader across the shoulders and chest. His hair was cropped close to his skull, glistening with rain. He wore dark military fatigues, heavy boots on his feet. Bolan saw him unclip the holstered pistol on his hip and place it on one of the exhaust ducts. Then he was flexing massive fists, covered by thin black leather gloves, as he faced Bolan.

This *had* to be Sergeant Gantley. Canfield's minder.

"Fuckin' Yanks. Too much money and fancy ordnance. All that bullshit about being the best."

Bolan didn't reply. He was using every second to recharge his reserves because he was going to need them. It was why Gantley had deprived him of his weapons. The man was ready to use his hands.

They squared off in the predawn paleness. Rain still sweeping in across the slabbed roof of Banecreif.

"Come on, then, Cooper," Gantley taunted. "What is it you arseholes say—give me your best shot."

Even in the low light Bolan could see the perverse smile edging Gantley's thick lips. He realized that the man was anticipating the upcoming conflict and expecting to enjoy it.

Gantley moved forward, impatient because Bolan was refusing to move. In his eyes that would only confirm what he felt about Americans.

All show and no go.

Bolan let him close in, saving his strength for what was to come. Gantley had left him no choice. He was going to have to fight, or allow Gantley to beat him to death.

The Brit swung a powerful fist. His left. A clumsy feint. Bolan eased away from it, his eye on Gantley's right, which was looping around in a blur. He ducked under the powerful swing and leaned in to deliver two hard punches to Gantley's ribs. Bolan concentrated his power into the blows and though Gantley's muscular torso absorbed much of the impact there was enough to make him grunt and step back. Bolan caught the lips peeling back from Gantley's teeth in an angry snarl.

He can be hurt, Bolan thought, and he doesn't like it.

The next attack came swiftly. Despite his bulk Gantley could move fast, his upper body weaving. His long arms enabled him to swing early, still just beyond Bolan's stretch. He didn't feint this time, simply lashed out with both fists. His left caught Bolan across the side of his face, knocking the big American off balance. The blow was hard, not crippling, but left Bolan smarting, blood running down his cheek from a fresh gash.

Bolan pulled away, saw the thin smirk on Gantley's rain-slick face as he retreated. Then he brought himself to a stop, catching Gantley off-kilter for a second. It was enough time for Bolan to slam his fist full into Gantley's mouth. The blow split Gantley's lips, blood blossoming as flesh was hammered back against his teeth. Bolan held his attack, throwing hard punches to Gantley's mouth and cheeks, rocking the man's head from side to side. Gantley took steps back, seemingly confused by the sudden and unrelenting attack. Bolan changed tack without warning, using his booted foot to deliver hard sidekicks to Gantley's left knee. The blows hurt Gantley. His leg was weakening, his reflex blows uncoordinated, missing more than connecting. He could not contain his anger. Gantley was not used to being hurt, even opposed, and he had to gather himself with a great effort, sucking in his rage and concentrating his efforts.

One of his large fists caught Bolan's left wrist, yanking his arm to pull Bolan in close. He batted aside Bolan's free arm, then swung him aside with the ease of a child casting off an unwanted toy. Bolan was thrown across the roof, losing his grip on the wet stone. He went to his knees, throwing his hands out to prevent contact with the solid slabs. He knew immediately that he had to get back on his feet. Gantley would be moving in. Before Bolan could stand upright Gantley's thick arms encircled his neck, closing tight like the coils of a snake as he hauled Bolan to his knees. Bolan could hear him snorting through his bloody mouth as he bore down.

Bolan sucked in a breath before Gantley's stranglehold cut off his air. Knowing his time would be short Bolan reached up and back, getting a grip on Gantley's fatigue jacket. He hauled hard, letting his body drop from the waist. The leverage worked and Gantley was dragged up and over Bolan's head, in a perfect shoulder roll. As he thudded to the stone slabs his grip on Bolan's neck slackened and Bolan rolled free, turning his body and slamming his right boot full into Gantley's face. Gantley's nose simply collapsed under the kick. Blood erupted from the crushed organ.

Rolling again to gain distance Bolan staggered to his feet. He saw Gantley doing the same, and not wanting to give the man any leeway he launched a full roundhouse kick that hammered into Gantley's chest, driving him backward. Continuing his forward run Bolan had almost reached Gantley

when the Brit hooked his own right leg around and kicked
Bolan's legs from under him.

The drop to the slabs left Bolan struggling for air. He saw
Gantley rise over him, fists opening and closing in unison.
Bolan drew his legs under himself and pushed upright. He
swung at Gantley, drawing blood from the man's left cheek.
Bolan didn't see Gantley's left sweep up out of nowhere. It
struck him across the side of his face with a meaty thump.
Bolan recoiled from the blow, tasting blood in his mouth. He
backpedaled and slammed against the buttressed stone wall
edging the roof, gasping from the impact.

The man was not going to give him time to recover. Even
as the thought crossed his mind Bolan sensed movement, saw
the shadow that fell across the stone slabs at his feet. He
heard the grunt of exertion as Gantley launched another fist.
Bolan yanked his head to one side, the solid knuckles raking
the curve of his jaw. Although the full force of the blow was
reduced, there was enough energy to spin Bolan off balance.
Bolan heard the scuff of Gantley's boots as the man moved
to keep up with him. He threw up his left arm and took a solid
blow just below his shoulder, then hauled himself around and
countered with his right fist, slamming it hard into Gantley's
ribs. The blow drew a grunt from the man and he retreated
briefly, giving Bolan time to slam a booted foot against the
Brit's knee again.

Gantley pulled back, struggling to maintain his balance and
Bolan thrust himself forward, driving his shoulder into the
man's broad chest, then launching a forearm smash that
impacted against Gantley's cheek. The sheer force of the blow
fractured the cheekbone. Bolan delivered a second punch, increasing the damage. Flesh tore and a shard of splintered
cheekbone showed white before blood discolored it.

The pain he must have felt only increased Gantley's fury.
He caught hold of Bolan's blacksuit with both hands and

hurled him across the stone flags. Losing his balance Bolan
had seconds to throw out his arms to break his fall as he went
down for the second time. He landed hard, bouncing and
tumbling across the weathered slabs, scraping his face against
the rough surface. He felt the wash of warm blood streaking
across his cheek and mouth. The low stone wall edging the
roof brought him to a bone-jarring stop.

Bolan could hear the heavy crash of the surging tide
slamming against the rocks at the base of the east wall behind
and below. Twisting his head he saw Gantley advancing.
Blood streamed down his face and spattered the front of his
fatigues. Gantley still looked every inch the hard man he was.
His solid bulk did nothing to hinder his movements and he
lunged forward without warning, slamming into Bolan as he
pushed to his feet, aware of the low wall at his back. He was
too late to move aside and Gantley crushed him against the
stonework, massive hands clamping around Bolan's throat.
Bolan felt his spine driven against the lip of the wall. He
braced his booted feet and pushed back against Gantley's
sheer bulk. The man was snorting with the effort he was
putting into his attack. Hot breath fanned Bolan's face. He felt
Gantley's thick fingers squeezing down on his neck, starting
to deny him air.

Bolan sensed déjà vu. Gantley's arms were around his
neck again. If he was unable to draw in oxygen his responses
would begin to falter. He spun through his options, realizing
they were few. Gantley had him pinned against the wall so
there was no retreat that way. The man's brute strength, spread
against Bolan, held him near motionless. Only Bolan's arms
were free. He spread them for a moment, closing his hands
into fists, then struck out at Gantley's face—first against the
already damaged cheek, then to the other side of the Brit's
face. Every ounce of Bolan's not inconsiderable strength went
into the blows, delivered without mercy. He maintained the

two-sided attack, slamming his knuckled fists against Gantley's face, seeing it turn even more bloody and raw.

Gantley increased his grip on Bolan's throat and it became a simple contest between the two—who would quit first. Bolan centered his whole being on his unrestrained physical assault on his opponent, his fists aching from the contact with Gantley's head. And it was Gantley who jerked back, gasping from the relentless blows slamming into his battered flesh. As his grip on Bolan's throat slackened Bolan planted his left hand on Gantley's chest and accelerated his withdrawal, pulling back his right arm to aim a telling blow that landed square against Gantley's already smashed nose. Blood erupted in bright streams.

Howling with pain Gantley stumbled back, raising his hands to his ruined face and Bolan went directly for his unprotected stomach and ribs, pounding in blow after blow that brought the former military cop to a stop. Gantley let out a shuddering moan, starting to fold. Bolan dropped his hands on Gantley's shoulders, pushing down as he swept his right knee up to smash into Gantley's face. The blow straightened Gantley, his face a caved-in bloody mask. He didn't even see as Bolan stepped in close, turning, then hauling Gantley over his shoulder in a body throw that launched the Brit off his feet. There was a surreal moment when Gantley seemed to hang in the empty air, then a long scream as he vanished over the buttressed wall, out into empty space before the long drop to the granite rocks at the base of the house.

Gantley's scream faded as he fell, ceasing the instant he struck the rocks.

25

The Executioner retrieved his Beretta after he finally located it, then crawled on hands and knees back to the base of the wall where he leaned against the stone, head hanging, dripping blood. Waves of nausea engulfed him. The only way he might have described his condition was as one big bruise. He was aching from head to foot. Bloody and sick. Even his hands hurt. His knuckles were raw and bleeding. He raised his aching head back against the cold, rough stone of the wall, wishing the rain would wash away his pain. He knew he had to move soon. To go find Hugo Canfield and complete his mission.

In the end he didn't need to do even that.

Something told him Canfield would find him, and Bolan was too exhausted to climb to his feet there and then.

From where he sat he could see the door that led back down into the house. A square of light against the graying dawn. He fixed his gaze on the doorway and waited. Something stirred in him, warning that Canfield was going to come to him. Bolan's battered right hand grasped the Beretta, drawing it close to his side where it was hidden by his thigh. He moved the selector lever to tri-bursts.

He waited.

The minutes crawled. When he breathed Bolan felt a stab of pain across his ribs down his right side. He laid his left hand across his body, pressed over the ache. He hoped they were simply bruised and not cracked.

He saw the shadow first, moving against the stone wall just inside the open stairwell. Bolan fixed on it, watched it pause, then rise higher. He could see the head and shoulders. The extended outline of a weapon. The form grew larger. It was the bulk of a tall man carrying an easily recognizable SPAS combat shotgun.

The man chose his weapons well, Bolan thought.

His grip on the Beretta tightened.

Hugo Canfield stepped through the open door, moving quickly to one side to avoid being framed. His searching eyes picked up on Bolan's motionless form, the shotgun coming around to center on the Executioner.

"Tell me you're still alive, Cooper. I want you alive, you interfering son of a bitch, so I can blow you to hell and back."

Bolan didn't respond. He needed Canfield to walk closer so he had a clear shot.

"Just move. Enough so I know you can see who it is putting you down. Damn you, Cooper, fucking move. You hear me? Thought you'd won? I'll get through this. Rebuild. Come through even stronger. Do you bloody well hear me..?"

Bolan heard him.

He showed he had heard by bringing up the concealed Beretta.

He saw the shock on Canfield's face in the instant before he fired.

He placed a triple burst that cored between Canfield's eyes and into his brain. He followed with two more, dropping the man where he stood, his finger frozen on the trigger of the shotgun. Canfield sprawled on the rain-soaked roof of Banecreif, his shattered skull leaking blood and brains across the slabs.

"You talk too much," Bolan said.

He let his gun hand drop to his side. Despite the wet and the cold he was too tired to move for the moment, so he stayed where he was as dawn crept over the horizon.

HAL BROGNOLA ANSWERED his phone and for a moment failed to recognize who was on the other end. It was only when he picked up the word *Banecreif* that he realized it was Bolan.

"Hey, Striker, you sound a little rough."

"It's been one of those days."

"You get your result?"

"The organization is minus its head boy. Banecreif might be open for a new tenant. After some redecoration."

"Do I pass our findings along to the task force now? They are going to think Christmas has come early. I've already had reports of Canfield's associates starting to jump ship and getting lawyered up."

"The whole package. Have a word with Aaron. He should have completed his excavations into the databases we downloaded. I figure the task force will be knocking on quite a few doors in the next week or so."

"Hey, thanks for your input, pal. We can start to pick up the pieces and step in. No doubt there's going to be some raised voices heard but with Canfield out of the frame and most of his major setups out of action…well, I guess you see the situation should work in our favor once we start producing the downloaded data."

"Before I moved out I found the drug stash Canfield had on-site."

"His new venture?"

"Yeah. Hell of a size, too. I didn't like to leave all that white powder lying around in the basement. Anyone could have wandered in and found it."

"I understand."

"Happens that Canfield kept a fuel backup in one of the outhouses with Banecreif being off the track. Diesel and gasoline. I jury-rigged supply hoses to feed in through the extraction vents to the basement. Those storage tanks held quite a few gallons. Made one hell of a blaze."

"Are you clear, Striker?"

"Way down the road. Couple of police cruisers went by a while back, but I'm observing the speed limit and out of uniform."

Brognola sighed.

"Thank God for that. Hey, you sound bushed. You need any help?"

"The final quarter got a little rough. I held my own but took some whacks."

"You fit to drive?"

"Slowly."

"Keep your cell handy. I'll see what I can fix through the U.K. task force. Make a rendezvous for you. Hell, they owe you that much. No, dammit, we *all* owe you."

"Keep an open file on this dirty business, Hal, because it isn't finished yet. If no one else does I'll be coming back to it. Sooner or later I'll be coming back. And that's a promise."

D0769947

When Your Child
Wanders
from God

When Your Child Wanders from God

Peter Lord

SPIRE

Published by Fleming H. Revell
a division of Baker Book House Company
P.O. Box 6287, Grand Rapids, MI 49516-6287

Spire edition published 1998

Third printing, June 1999

Previously published by Chosen Books under the title *Keeping the Doors Open*

Printed in the United States of America

ISBN 0-8007-8656-4

Unless otherwise indicated, Scripture quotations are from the NEW AMERICAN STANDARD BIBLE®. Copyright © The Lockman Foundation 1960, 1962, 1963, 1968, 1971, 1972, 1973, 1975, 1977. Used by permission.

Scripture quotations marked KJV are from the King James Version of the Bible.

For current information about all releases from Baker Book House, visit our web site:

http://www.bakerbooks.com

To our children

John, Richard and Debbie, Susan and Eli,
Jimmy and Melinda, Ruth and Keith

for their love and patience
beyond the call of duty

Many thanks to
Christine W. Greenwald
for her editorial expertise
and finishing touches
on this manuscript

Contents

Introduction

Some time ago our son Richard, a husband, father of five boys and pastor, said to me, "Rearing children is not a science, it's an art. In a science, you do the same things over and over again and come up with the same results. But in art each piece is an original."

Richard is right: Each child *is* an original, a unique individual, unlike any person in the whole world. And in the spiritual realm, children who come to God grow in the Christian faith at their own paces, in God's time. Yet how difficult it is for us as Christian parents when our children struggle with temptations and rebellions, when they reject God. We worry and wonder: Will they ever come back?

It is then we must, as the great missionary and devotional writer Oswald Chambers put it in his classic book, *My Utmost for His Highest*, "Let God be as original with other people as He is with you." If we have the promise of God for our children, we can know with certainty that He will fulfill it in His own time, in His own way.

In Section 1 of this book I discuss the process by which parents and their children can move from fear and rebellion to faith and redemption, from sorrow to joy. In Section 2 I share principles my wife, Johnnie, and I have learned as we have tried to follow God's patterns for parenting, allowing the Holy Spirit to work in each of our children in His own original way, using us as He wills in the process.

This book is a testimony to the grace of God. We have made our share of mistakes in rearing our children, but God is good, and is dealing with each of them as only the Father of all fathers, the inventor of fatherhood, knows best to do.

My prayer for this book is:

Dear God our Father, God of mercy,

Create in the hearts of all the readers of this book revelation about Your grace, mercy and power: Your grace that forgives and offers second, third and many more opportunities; Your mercy that triumphs over judgment; and Your power to turn any life and situation around. We thank You for Your ability to do exceedingly abundantly above all that we can ask or even think.

Praise Your holy name! Amen.

Peter Lord
Titusville, Florida
Fall 1991

When Your Child
Wanders
from God

Section 1

The Process

1

Building Blocks:
The Basis for This Book

At five o'clock one spring morning in 1972 the telephone rang in our Titusville, Florida, home, waking my wife, Johnnie, and me from a sound sleep.

"We have your son here," said a deep voice on the other end of the line. Identifying himself as the desk sergeant at the Orlando jail about forty miles away, he explained that our twenty-year-old son, Richard, had been arrested and charged with possession of narcotics.

I do not need to tell you that this is a most unpleasant way to awaken early in the morning. Neither do I need to explain why I have no trouble remembering how it felt to see my firstborn behind bars later that day. The scene is indelibly fixed in my mind some twenty years after it happened.

There was Richard in dirty dungarees and T-shirt, barefoot, with his long, uncombed hair falling over his shoulders. He was subdued and quiet. I do not know what he expected us to do, but we had told him over and over that if his drug use led him to jail we would not bail him out.

Difficult as it was, and despite the sadness and hurt we felt as we stood in the jail corridor talking with him, we stuck by our word. When we headed for home we left, instead of bail money, strong assurances of our love and our willingness to help him when he was ready to change.

Underneath all of the other emotions we experienced as we drove home that day was a quiet confidence that God was in control. We were learning that the most important tools for relating to our Lord Jesus—tools we had each learned through our own personal crises of faith, tools we will discuss later in this chapter—applied also to this crucial arena of training our children to be responsible and (we prayed) God-fearing Christian adults.

But, like millions of Christian parents before us, we faced a grim reality: Despite our prayers and concerted efforts to raise our children according to our under-standing of biblical principles, our eldest son was not behaving in either a responsible or a Christlike manner. He had, at least for a time, left God. And, as you will discover in the pages of this book, over the years we have experienced varying degrees of anxiety and crisis over our four other children as well.

But praise God! This book is about His graciousness, both in teaching and molding our children, and in teaching and molding Johnnie and me through our parenting ups and downs. I have made many mistakes in rearing our children, and in being a husband (which is a vital part of rearing children). Yet our Father and Lord has helped us and is restoring the years the locusts have eaten (see Joel 2:25). He has done exceedingly above all I asked for or imagined!

What to Look For

Most likely you have purchased this book because you, too, are a parent in crisis—a parent who is watching, brokenhearted, frustrated and maybe very angry, as your child or children seemingly turn their backs on the values you have tried to instill in them. They, too, have left God. It is my desire that you will find in this book two kinds of help.

First, I hope you will find workable encouragement for your present crisis. Second, I hope you will find guidelines for preventing or at least alleviating some future crises by improving your parenting know-how and sensitivity. Parenting is one of the few professions in life for which most of us have little or no training. We're bound to make mistakes, but each lesson we learn makes us better equipped to handle the next challenge.

There are also two traps any writer on this subject must take care to avoid, and each reader must be on the alert for them, as well.

The first trap is this: looking for a "sure-fire" formula for rearing children.

In my own experience in rearing both our natural children and the spiritual children over whom the Father has given me watchcare duties, I have found that child-rearing at its best is not done by factory and formula; it is done by research and development. Let me explain.

Most modern factories use the assembly line method. If the workers perform the same functions in the same way under the same conditions they will end up with the same products. So the Pontiac 6000s that roll off the line might vary in color and a few accessories, but they are basically alike.

Using a formula is appealing. It looks easy and foolproof. In fact, many books, seminars and sermons on child-rearing offer formulas: "Fifteen Steps to Rearing Successful (or Godly or Christian) Children."

These formulas usually come from two basic types of people. The worse of the two is the writer or speaker who has never reared a child successfully but has devised a theory by threading together various Bible verses.

Why is this so bad? Because by using half a verse here and a third of a verse there he or she can prove almost anything from Scripture. And most of what he or she "proves" is not consistent with God's Word. The Scriptures offer plain and simple truths, guidelines and principles. They do not need elaborate interpretation. They were written for the common man and woman, and can be understood easily and simply.

The other formula-oriented person is the one whose children turned out to be godly. These sincere and earnest Christians sought God's wisdom on their knees in rearing their children for His honor and glory. Their mistake is in believing that what worked for them will work for everyone else.

And why doesn't it? Because the formula assumes that all children are the same at the beginning. If parents begin with the same "raw materials" each time and apply certain "tried and true" methods, they will end up with the same results.

But no child is the same. One of the most amazing things about children is how they can come from the same parents and be so completely different in almost every way! They are living beings, life forms. Written into each one at the moment of conception are inherent qualities that, through their parents' cooperation with God or lack of it, can be developed or squashed.

When you build something you have the privilege of designing what you want and then producing it. When you grow a life form, the predetermined design is already there and you can only cooperate with it. Each child is a completely individual package of potential. Each will end up not as a clone, but as a special expression of God's creative power.

This is where research and development comes in. You see, in industry the research and development department is where prototypes are created. Each project is new, different. Special attention is given to every detail because the end result will be like no other.

Thus, as parents prepare to raise each child they must approach each one as a separate project—as an exercise in research and development, in growing and shaping, not building. To do this they need the Holy Spirit's help to find out how best to cooperate with the life of each child in maximizing the unique combination of qualities God has given him or her.

So while I won't be sharing a formula for successful child-rearing I will be sharing the principles that Johnnie and I have learned from our Lord and Father as we have muddled our way into and through a variety of child-rearing crises, both small and large. But principles have a thousand applications—applications that will differ in every circumstance and must be interpreted to us individually by the Holy Spirit.

So leave behind the first trap of looking for a formula. Instead seek the hope and encouragement that God in His grace and mercy will draw both you and your children closer to Himself.

The second trap is this: falling into guilt trips.

The last thing I want to do is act as the devil's travel agent and send parents with erring children on another guilt trip. Many books, articles, sermons and conferences on parenting convinced me more of my failures than of the power of God to take my attempts at parenting and use them to teach our whole family more about Him.

Remember, we have all made mistakes. But if we have repented and asked God to forgive us and help us to listen for His guidance as we parent, we need feel no more guilt. If we do, we can know it is motivated by the devil, who delights in halting our forward progress by accusing us continually of past failures.

The devil even uses Scripture to make parents feel guilty. Think of that verse so often quoted by writers and teachers: "Train up a child in the way he should go, even when he is old he will not depart from it" (Proverbs 22:6). How easily the devil can twist this wonderful text to accuse and wound already hurting mothers and fathers!

"If you had done right your children would have turned out right," Satan whispers. "You failed, and that is why they have gone astray."

There is enough logic in Satan's accusation to drive even fairly strong Christians to heavy guilt. But a fundamental mistake so many of us make as parents is to believe the enormous lie implicit in Satan's twisted logic.

What lie? you ask. Just this: Children become godly because their parents do the "correct" things in raising them.

This is simply not true. *Only God can make anyone godly*, and we will explore that concept further in the following chapters. But to believe that our parental actions can produce godly children reduces genuine Christianity to a formula, and God will not be reduced to a formula. He is sovereign, bigger and stronger and wiser than we can ever imagine, and to think that the building of godly children rests on our puny efforts alone is ridiculous.

Building Blocks

When Your Child Wanders from God is founded on two vital premises, or building blocks. Unless we understand and incorporate them into our lives, the rest of the book will be meaningless. Please read the remainder of this chapter carefully and prayerfully, asking God to help you make these building blocks the foundation for your whole life with Him, including your vitally important mission as a Christian parent.

Building Block 1: *Christian parents need to relate intimately to God the Father, Son and Holy Spirit—to come to know Him—through study of and meditation on Scripture and two-way communication.*

How basic, you say! Yes, it is, but far too many Christian parents rely on a Sunday morning spoon-feeding session and nightly table grace to nurture the relationship begun with God when they accepted Jesus as Savior. Then they flail and flounder through parenting situations wondering why God doesn't give them the wisdom and assistance they need.

But the emphasis in Scripture is on knowing God. The word *know* in the Bible is used to mean much more than does our common usage, which implies "to know about." *To know* in the Bible indicates an intimate personal experience; in fact, it is the word used throughout the Scripture to describe sexual intercourse. To achieve intimacy with God, a personal and deep relationship with Him, is by far the highest pursuit in life.

The apostle Paul, from his jail cell in Rome, wrote to the Philippian church that all the things he had done and experienced were dung—manure!—compared to the value of *knowing* Christ Jesus as his Lord. And this was the man who started at least thirteen churches and was the primary apostle and witness for Jesus Christ in his day.

How Can We Know God?

We get to know God the same as we get to know most people: in private. By being alone together people are freer to share at the deepest levels and thus to know each other's hearts.

The best and easiest way I have found to know God is to establish a regular quiet time and place, away from the distractions of life, where I can give full attention to my heavenly Father and the Lord Jesus Christ. It is possible, of course, to hear God speak anytime and anywhere He wishes and chooses to speak. But by learning to hear Him speak in private we will more easily recognize His voice at other times, including those of chaos and stress.

Besides, one of the greatest honors we can give to anyone is our time and undivided attention. I've learned that when I make and keep appointments with God He is pleased to meet with me.

Sitting at Jesus' feet and listening to His Word is the one essential no Christian—and no Christian parent—can disregard. Let me say it again—this is one of two building blocks on which this whole book rests.

Jesus emphasized the importance of this building block in this story:

> Now as they were traveling along, He entered a certain village; and a woman named Martha welcomed Him into her home. And she had a sister called Mary, who moreover was listening to the Lord's word, seated at His feet. But Martha was distracted with all her preparations; and she came up to Him, and said, "Lord, do You not care that my sister has left me to do all the serving alone? Then tell her to help me." But the Lord answered and said to her, "Martha, Martha, you are worried and bothered about so many things; but only a few things are necessary, really only one, for Mary has chosen the good part, which shall not be taken away from her."
>
> Luke 10:38–42

In their very helpful book *Discover Your God-Given Gifts* (based on Romans 12:6–8), authors Don and Katie Fortune point out that this passage shows Martha exercising her inborn gift of serving, and that Jesus no doubt complimented her on many occasions for the fine hospitality and quiet refuge she offered Him. But in this instance He wants her—and us—to see that our *service* to God is empty unless we truly *know* Him.

My quiet time has proven to be the best, most enjoyable and most profitable time of my life. Here I have found faith, encouragement, motivation and instruction for my whole life—including my tasks as a Christian parent. I compare my quiet time with my most intimate moments with my wife. Why? Because these are the closest times I have with the persons I love the most.

Developing a Profitable Quiet Time

There are many ways to spend quality time alone with God, and eventually most people develop their own styles, times and places. Having regular quiet times and keeping them private are important aspects, but they may vary occasionally as the circumstances of your life change. Don't "get the guilts" about this. Simply do your best to reestablish regularity and privacy again as soon as possible.

Many people include thanksgiving, praise and worship in their quiet times. Some use this time to read Christian literature. Whatever else you choose to include, two components are crucial: meditation on Scripture and prayer.

Meditating on Scripture.   First of all, recognize that the Author of all Scripture, the Holy Spirit, lives in you. He knows His own Word, and He knows you and your situation. So go to your private place with a Bible, a pen and a notebook to record your impressions and your prayers. Pick a Bible book and plan to work through it. I suggest starting in the New Testament, preferably with one of the Gospels.

Then meditate on the Scripture you've chosen by reading slowly, always listening for the voice of the Author, who came to guide us into all truth. It is not the amount of Scripture we read that is beneficial, but the amount of truth that winds up in our hearts. A person can own a grocery store, work in it several times a day and still starve to death. Only by consuming food does he gain the nourishment he needs. The same is true in our spiritual lives.

How does Scripture meditation differ from Bible study? A person studies with his or her left brain, and meditates with his or her right brain. It works like this.

The left brain stores all the information that comes into each of our lives. With this information we reason, figure and conclude. But we can reason only on the basis of the facts stored in this "computer." If we have only partial facts or incorrect information our conclusions are confined by those limits.

The right brain, on the other hand, has fascinating capacities like imagination—the ability to see what is not present in time or space. It receives new information and can pick up messages from the spirit worlds, both God's and the devil's.

Thus, when we study the Bible we use our accumulated information (true or false) to form conclusions. Remember, we act according to what we believe to be true whether it is true or not. That is why some Christians who lived during the Civil War were able to claim that God condoned human slavery. Their study of the Bible and the information they had accumulated from the outside world through the left brain combined to present what they thought was a correct conclusion.

To meditate on the Bible we open our minds to the Holy Spirit. We allow Him to call up information from the left side of our brains and to communicate through the right side as well. He may bring to mind a certain fact or point out false information and then renew our minds with right and true information. He may inspire our imaginations to picture different Bible characters in recorded incidents, and help us apply that understanding to our own situations. And He may give us His intuition to discern the correctness of motives and actions, our own and those of the people around us.

Meditation is a wonderful way to read the Scriptures, to let the Author, who knows you and knows His own Word, put together just the nourishment you need. I wish someone had taught me how to meditate early in my Christian life. Sitting at Jesus' feet, listening to His Word and writing down my impressions has been immensely helpful and practical as I have worked through difficult child-rearing problems.

Profiting by Prayer. The second crucial component of the quiet time is prayer. That's how most Christians through the ages have fellowshiped with God; the majority of them never had Bibles, or access to Bibles, and couldn't have read them anyway. Yet they were able to know, learn to trust and maintain fellowship with God through prayer.

How did they do it? After all, many new Christians start out enthusiastically in prayer, only to stop praying, eventually, in any meaningful way. That's perfectly natural because few of us practice prayer as a means of fellowship with God. Instead it is simply a one-way conversation, often filled with "gimmes." Understandably, most intelligent people become bored.

But when prayer is a conversation between you and the God who loves you it is wonderful experience.

How good God is to allow the Holy Spirit to live in us and guide us in our praying, since so often we do not know how to pray (Romans 8:26–27)! As we fellowship with Him during our quiet times we are free to ask Him anything on our hearts, and He is free to speak to us about the burdens He knows we carry.

One day as I was asking God how to pray for one of our daughters, He said, *Ask Me to protect her.* That is exactly what I did. Imagine how I felt when I heard, later that afternoon, that she had been in an accident. Her car was fully demolished, but she came out of the smashup completely whole!

Prayer time should be conversation time, when I can pray or act with God's wisdom and power. I have found that when I do as He says, it frees Him to do as He wills and wants to do.

Meditation on Scripture, which trains us to hear His voice, is critical to this kind of praying. Without the ability to hear His voice, we will pray only from our own points of view.

Building Block 2: *Christian parents need to cooperate with God by carrying out whatever actions He impresses on us as we relate to Him.*

This entire book is built around the absolute necessity for hearing the God who guides us into all truth and gives all wisdom and support with supernatural power. We need to spend time with the One who cares for us and our children more than we can ever imagine, who knows our heartaches and our children's problems, and who can offer real and permanent answers.

William Hay M. H. Aitken wrote,

> Whatever happens let us not be too busy to sit at Jesus' feet. We shall not . . . lose time by enjoying this; . . . we shall redeem the time . . . and we shall gain in blessedness and enjoyment of our work, and gain in the quality of our work; and, above all, we shall gain in that we shall give Him pleasure where otherwise we might only grieve Him. And this is indeed the crown of all our endeavors. *He who pleases Him does not live in vain*

God has often impressed upon me, as I have shared my concerns about my children with Him, that I was to pray a certain way, make a telephone call, write a letter or arrange for some one-on-one time with one of my children. When I obey those impressions and act on the directions He offers, another piece of the puzzle or problem concerning that child falls into place, whether I know it at the time or not. But if I fail to obey that impression, I hinder His Spirit from continuing to work in my child's life.

What a blessing to be able to take each of our children's problems or needs, each distressing incident or behavior, each call for concern, into our quiet times with the Lord! As we meditate on Scripture and talk with Him, He gives us wisdom, unconditional love for our children, creativity and ideas for handling each situation.

Now obviously this building block stands in direct opposition to the way so many of us deal with our children: flying blind as we *react*—both emotionally and physically—to our children's attitudes and behavior. How often, instead of taking a concern to my quiet time and waiting for my Father's directions, I have answered with anger or harshness or lack of compassion, and made a parent-child situation much worse!

Remember: Cooperation with God takes practice. It becomes part of the spiritual nature only after we learn to know His voice and relate to Him intimately. But the rewards are worth the effort, for we will begin to see Him work. And as we "cast our cares on Him," allowing *Him* to be responsible for developing godliness in our children, the burdens of parenting will become lighter and the road ahead brighter.

In the next chapter, by sharing some of the events that led Richard, Johnnie and me to that sad encounter in the Orlando jail, we will deal more specifically with the way to hear God's word for a particular problem with a particular child.

2

The Word of Faith

Principle: Faith stands on who God is and what He says. Before you can believe a promise for your child you must get a promise from God. Faith comes by hearing a word from God.

Scripture: Isaiah 55:8-11; Romans 10:17

That Saturday morning in the spring of 1971 started as so many others had, with our family at different stages of wakefulness. Saturday at the Lord house was a day for sleeping in, family togetherness and catching up on household jobs.

Susan, our eighteen-year-old daughter, was eating breakfast. My wife, Johnnie, and Ruth Ann, our ten-year-old, were getting dressed. Richard, nineteen, and one-year-old John, our baby, were still in bed. (Jimmy had not yet joined our family.)

As I prepared to do some chores, a knock sounded at the door. I answered and found Bill, our church's minister of youth and music, standing there.

"I need to talk to you and Johnnie," he said quietly.

I called Johnnie, and we invited Bill into the living room and sat down, a bit puzzled by his serious expression.

"Has Richard talked to you?" Bill asked.

"No," we replied. "What about?"

Instead of answering, Bill asked, "Is Richard around? I'd really like him to be here while we talk."

It took a few minutes to get Richard out of bed, but finally all four of us were seated in the living room together.

Then Bill said, "I gave Richard a week to tell you something, and told him if he had not done so by today I would come and speak to you."

Bill was about to drop a bomb on us, a bomb that would begin a new phase in our parenting experience and change our lives forever, especially our relationships with God and each member of our family.

He said simply, "Richard is on drugs."

Richard, our eldest child, had been elected the most popular boy in the graduating class his senior year in high school. He had always been a nice, easygoing fellow. We were sorry he had dropped out from his freshman year in junior college, but he seemed happy working at a local men's clothing store.

But Richard on drugs? *Our* Richard on drugs? This was a time when drugs were still just coming onto the American scene. Our shock was heightened by the terrible stories we had heard about drug users—the life-threatening risks and the sullen attitude of rebellion. And I was a pastor, a leader in the church and community. What would our congregation say? Would the members still want me as pastor if I was a failure as a parent? Worst of all, had I failed Richard?

All of these questions raced through my mind in a matter of seconds before Johnnie and I both asked, "Richard, is this so?"

Very slowly he answered, looking alternately at the floor and at me, "Yes, sir."

At this point Bill excused himself and left our family to struggle with this new and devastating situation.

I waited a few minutes and then did the only thing I knew to do: I issued an ultimatum.

"Richard, you must promise to stop this now or you will have to leave home. We are a little society here and we cannot allow you to stay and deliberately break the law of the land, of this house and of God." Both Johnnie and I told him how much we loved him and we promised to do all we could to help him.

It seemed like a lifetime, but only a few minutes passed before Richard replied. "I can't promise you I'll break with my friends and quit drugs," he said, "so I guess I'll leave."

A scene followed that caused as much sorrow as I had ever known to that point in my life. Richard began moving all his belongings into his old car. By this time the whole family knew something very sad was happening. Everyone wept, even little John.

Personally I could not have been any sadder at that moment if an ambulance crew had been taking out my son's dead body. This was a living death. Fears filled my heart, and Johnnie's as well, as our imaginations ran wild.

Where was Richard going?

What would happen next?

What could we do?

As Richard's worn Plymouth pulled out of the drive-way, a new day began at our house.

Johnnie Seeks God

Immediately after Richard left, Johnnie went into our bedroom. As she told me later, she cried out to God, "O Father, my son is gone! What shall I do?"

God is faithful and practical. He answered Johnnie's desperate cry by speaking these words to her heart: *You have a responsibility to teach Sunday school tomorrow. Do that and then come aside on Monday so we can spend time together.*

On Monday Johnnie packed her bags, informing me she would not be back until she had a word from God about the situation. She headed for a motel in Daytona Beach where she could be alone.

Johnnie had had a personal faith-crisis in the mid-1950s. The resulting nervous breakdown, caused by years of trying to live a Christian life beyond reproach in her own strength, had prepared her for this moment. Her encounters with God then and since had taught her that while she was weak, helpless and needy, Jesus Christ was adequate for the situation. She needed to hear from Him in order to know how to respond to Richard's needs. I knew these things, too, but not as experientially as Johnnie did then. She has always been light years ahead of me in this area of listening to—and obeying—the leading of the Holy Spirit. So I knew I could trust what God would say to her.

I will be returning to the details of Richard's story periodically throughout this book, along with stories of our other children, but I would like to stop here to discuss Johnnie's obedient action. It demonstrates several lessons both of us were learning in our personal walks of faith, lessons that are foundational for any parent who longs to hear a word from God about his or her children. We will see how these worked out through the course of this book.

1. She made Jesus her first choice. In times of crisis we need to make the Lord Jesus our first choice and not our last chance. We often try everything and everyone else and then in desperation go to Him. What does that say about the depth of our trust?

God is honored and exalted when we seek His advice and help first, not waiting until we exhaust all human means. Remember, He is the ultimate expert on our children, as well as on everything else in this world. And when we turn first to Him, we avoid the temptation to react out of shock and/or anger, which usually makes a bad situation worse.

2. She gave Him her full attention. Is it always necessary to pull aside as Johnnie did in order to hear God? No, but some situations are so grave they cannot be dealt with casually. We must be prepared to take whatever time and means are required to get a word from God on which to base our faith.

While it is true that we can contact our Lord in the midst of a busy schedule, sometimes we need to get away from it all. When we have crises in the physical and emotional realms we stop all regular activities until they are over. Why not do the same in the vital realm of the spiritual?

3. She didn't rush God.   Sometimes God will not give an answer in fifteen minutes. Johnnie was learning she could not rush God, but must wait until He wanted to speak. Notice that God didn't instruct her to race around frantically, find a substitute for her Sunday school class and throw clothes into a suitcase so she could drive to the motel that Saturday night. And notice also that she did not necessarily expect Him to give her a word of faith regarding Richard within a specified amount of time. That is why she said, "I will not be back until He speaks to me in some way."

Our Father is not reluctant to help, but He knows we have a tendency to use Him, to get what we want and then leave Him until we need Him again. Using people is detrimental to any relationship and will lead ultimately to its deterioration and destruction. God desires fellowship with us. In fact, I believe that sometimes He does not answer right away because He just wants to spend time with us.

4. She let Him work on her, too.   God often wants to deal with our part in a crisis, the things we *did* wrong because we *were* wrong. No situation is ever completely the fault of one person, and the sure way *not* to solve it is to place one hundred percent of the blame on the other party.

Our Lord wants to correct faulty thinking, heal damaged and destructive emotions, refresh our spirits and strengthen faith, hope and love in our lives, as well as answer the requests of our hearts. We will discuss this point more fully in chapter 3.

Getting a Word from God

You have probably noticed that Johnnie and I hear very clear and specific words from the Lord.

How do I get a word from God? How do I know His voice? People ask me these two questions more often than any other. That they even ask demonstrates how much we Christians in the West have to learn.

Why? Because for a Christian to hear God's voice easily and regularly should be a normal and natural occurrence. Jesus' most often repeated statement is "he who has ears to hear let him hear" (Matthew 11:15; Mark 4:9, 23; Luke 8:8). He also said, "My sheep hear My voice, and I know them, and they follow Me" (John 10:27). We can couple these verses with the fact that the Holy Spirit lives in each Christian for the purpose of communicating God's love and guidance. Hearing His voice is natural and normal for His people.

The Christian life is one of faith, but we can have no real faith for a particular parenting crisis until we have heard from God. Ninety percent of the parent-child dilemmas we face are not specifically addressed in Scripture except by way of broad guidelines and principles. It is always necessary, therefore, for us to go to God and ask for a word, a word we can stand on. We need the Holy Spirit to apply those broad guidelines to our individual situations.

It is my greatest joy to teach others to hear His voice. It is very easily done and I want to offer here two guidelines. You will note that they are nearly identical to the two crucial components for a profitable quiet time that we discussed in chapter 1. Just as they apply to our regular, daily times with God, so they apply when we need a word of faith for a specific parenting dilemma.

1. Get ready to hear.   If you believe in Jesus Christ as your Savior and have asked Him to be the Lord of your life, accept by faith the following facts: God is your Father who loves you very much and has sent the Helper, the Holy Spirit, to live in you; as a Christian you have the capacity to hear Him speak to you or, as the Bible puts it, you have spiritual ears to hear (Ezekiel 12:2; Mark 7:16).

Remember: We receive spiritual communication through our minds. Getting ready to hear by meditating on Scripture, alone with God, allows the Holy Spirit to speak.

2. Pray.   Praying includes listening as well as talking. Prayer is really a conversation with your heavenly Father.

We can be sure of this: God knows the pains of our hearts. He is not impressed by vain repetitions or much speaking (Matthew 6:7–8) but He is intensely interested in His children's sincere cries for help.

He wants us to desire Him for *Himself,* however, and not only for His blessings. When we get to the place where we can love and enjoy Him for Himself and not just for what He can do for us, He will give us more than we have sense to ask for.

So start by opening your heart to Him. Tell Him the burden you have for your wandering child and then listen. How can He speak unless you stop talking and give Him a chance?

God will always answer you. His answer may not be what you want or expect, but it will be the right place to begin dealing with your parent-child problem.*

Remember: The Scriptures always lead us to the living Word of God, Jesus, and to the *rhema*, or specific word of encouragement and instruction we need for a particular circumstance. Sometimes the Holy Spirit makes a certain verse of Scripture come alive, as if we had never seen it before. Sometimes He whispers a word based on some principle from the Bible. James writes in his epistle, "If any of you lacks wisdom, let him ask of God, who gives to all men generously and without reproach, and it will be given to him" (1:5). The Holy Spirit, we may be assured, will never lead us astray.

---

* For further reading in the area of communication with God, see *Hearing God* by Peter Lord (Baker Book House).

God's Word to Johnnie

As Johnnie got ready to hear, by going off to that Daytona Beach motel to spend time alone with God, and as she prayed, the Holy Spirit spoke in the quiet of her heart: *Richard is coming back, but I'm not going to tell you when or how.*

With this word of faith our journey began. As we prayed and cooperated with God toward its fulfillment, we faced many difficult days, but we had His promise to cling to.

Having received the word of faith, it was now time to enter the walk of faith. This means allowing Him to work with us as parents and is the subject of the next chapter.

3

The Walk of Faith

Principle: In the walk of faith God cleans up parents' lives as they wait and pray for His promises for their children to be fulfilled.

Scripture: Jeremiah 7:23; Psalm 138:7; Romans 4:12; 2 Corinthians 5:7

Faith always has a walk Even though faith for our children's total well-being—physical, emotional, spiritual and mental—begins with a promise from God, there comes a time when we must act and react on the basis of that promise, and not on what we see happening in their lives.

Many parents, including me, find this difficult. We are impatient. We get discouraged by our children's behavior and the circumstances surrounding them and we want results from our prayers. But in the walk of faith, God teaches us patiently, situation by situation, that we have much to learn, too.

In his bestselling book *The Road Less Traveled*, M. Scott Peck makes the following statement:

The neurotic assumes too much responsibility; the person with the character disorder not enough. When neurotics are in conflict with the world they automatically assume they are at fault. When those with character disorders are in conflict with the world they automatically assume that the world is at fault.

Most of us probably fit somewhere in the middle of these extremes. Sometimes we fall under the weight of our own guilt, feeling we have done everything wrong. Sometimes we strike out at the other person, blaming him or her entirely for causing so much pain.

From my own experience and observation I would say that in any conflict or trouble, including the heartbreak of having a child leave God, some of the problem lies on both sides. There is not much we can do about the other person: Trying to make someone over is an exercise in futility for anyone but God. But we can work with God to change ourselves. Here are two principles to help us.

God Gets Our Attention

Have you noticed that when the physical and material matters of life are going well, it is harder to stay in communion with God? The unfortunate reason for this is that Christians' value systems often differ little from those of non-Christians: We place far too much emphasis on the blessings of this world, and far too little on the richness of conforming to the image of Jesus Christ.

When problems come we turn to Him, true enough,

but if we could only realize that when we make our relationship with God our number one priority at all times, we have far fewer troubles.

There are two reasons for this. First, when we are meditating on Scripture and praying conversationally with God, He becomes our "high tower" (see 2 Samuel 22:3; Psalm 18:2; 144:2, KJV). He helps us see the enemy coming so that we can head off the attack. Second, our regular times alone with God keep us tuned to the voice of the Helper, the Holy Spirit. This means that we make far fewer errors of omission and commission.

We have a tendency, however, to take God for granted. And so, as a parent and through forty years of pastoring, I have learned this first principle: Our Lord often uses children's problems to get the attention of their busy, preoccupied parents. He desires good for us as well as for our children and He is working on us as well as on them.

By now Johnnie and I have learned, when our children are troubled or in trouble, to ask God if He is trying to teach us something in the process. Since He has our full attention when we are concerned about a child, He is able to deal with us in any way He desires. If there is nothing in our attitudes, actions or reactions that needs correcting, He will tell us so. If there is, He can show us what to do about it.

Often we do not understand His ways any more than our children understand ours. Someone once said, "God is willing to look bad for the moment in order that over the long haul He may do good." And God Himself reminds us in Isaiah 55:8–9, " 'My thoughts are not your thoughts, neither are your ways My ways,' declares the Lord. 'For as the heavens are higher than the earth, so are My ways higher than your ways, and My thoughts than your thoughts ' "

God, What Are You Saying to Me?

Early one morning more than a dozen years ago, I was in my small study in our church where I go in the early hours to have my quiet time. While meditating on Scripture and praying for our nine-year-old, John, I learned a major lesson about God's using children's difficulties to accomplish His purposes in their parents' lives.

At this particular time I was spending two hours each day alone with God. One of my disciplines and joys was to read five Psalms a day.

But I had developed a bad habit from the period when I had simply studied God's Word and knew little about meditating on it: I skipped over portions of Scripture that seemed to hold no meaning for me or for anyone else I knew.

One verse that I skipped over easily appears twice in the Psalms. This means I came across it twice a month or 24 times a year. Found in Psalm 60:8 and again in Psalm 108:9, it says, "Moab is My washbowl; over Edom I shall throw My shoe; over Philistia I will shout aloud."

This is not a verse we normally decoupage for our refrigerator doors!

That morning I saw this text coming up and was gaining speed to jump over it, when the Holy Spirit said to me, *Stop!*

Well, I did—right on "Moab is my washbowl"

Then the Holy Spirit said to me, *Get your Bible dictionary and look up Moab.* I learned that the Moabites were Israel's kinfolk who lived next door.

Then the Holy Spirit said, *Let Me explain this Scripture to you. When My people, Israel, got dirty, I used their wicked kinfolk to wash them up.*

I still remember my excitement at understanding an obscure verse that had been like a foreign language to me.

The Holy Spirit is much more, of course, than a history teacher. He is interested in our lives and wants to help us live them to the fullest. So He said to me, *Here is the application of this truth for you. You have been praying, asking Me to clean John up, but I am using him to clean you up.*

Wow! I had been handing God a list of things I wanted Him to do in John's life, but He was using John to clean *me* up, and still is, even though John has now been redeemed.

I like to compare this process to what happens when you shake a full glass of water. What comes out? Splashes of water. But the water does not slosh out just because we shake the glass; it comes out because it was already in there to begin with.

The same is true as our children's behavior and attitudes shake us. Out slosh our worry, fear, rejection, resentment, sarcasm and insecurity. That is not the children's fault: Those flaws were in there to begin with. God's cleansing happens when we acknowledge our need for Him to clean out our sin and inadequacies and replace them with the power and wisdom of His Holy Spirit.

This can take some time. Johnnie sometimes says to me, "Are we going to have to take this course again?" meaning, "When are we going to learn the lessons God is trying to teach us?"

You see, God does not give social promotions. He does not say, "Let's just forget about trying to teach Peter this lesson. It doesn't look like he wants to learn it, so let's just move him up to the next grade."

He loves us too much to do that. He is not content to leave those things in us that hurt us and prevent us from receiving and returning His love. When we fail to learn the lessons He tries to teach us, He works on us just that much longer.

As I reflected on the Holy Spirit's words to me that morning, I realized I needed to pray differently. I needed to ask Him not only for John's redemption, but also to help me cooperate as He did His work in me.

I went home that day singing and praising, as I always do when God speaks, because He is the great encourager.

Another Lesson

But God had another lesson to teach me about the walk of faith from this experience. Just a few minutes after I arrived back home that morning I was standing in front of the bathroom mirror shaving and getting ready for the day. I still felt as though I were bouncing on six inches of joy. Then a terrible thought flashed through my mind.

"Yes, John is going to be used to clean you up, but just as Moab went to hell, so will John."

That is not fair! I shouted in my heart. *That is not fair!*

Despite the many hours I had spent learning to hear God's voice, I assumed wrongly that God was speaking again. But that was not His voice. I did not realize then that when God speaks, the devil will often come and say something to distort what God has just said. He may challenge God's word to us, or deny it.

Then God really did speak again, and my heart responded with warm recognition, because this time the message was one of help and comfort, as God's messages always are. Even more thrilling, this time God had a word of faith for me—the first ever—about John's future salvation and relationship with Him.

God said, *Ruth was a Moabitess.* With those few words God refuted the enemy's lie in comparing our John's ultimate fate to that of the wicked Moabites. Ruth *was* a Moabitess, but God worked mightily in her life, and eventually she became a member of the house and lineage of David, a link in the ancestry of Jesus Christ.

Hallelujah! God had given me a strong promise to stand on! Not only would John be redeemed to be His child, but he would also be used in God's redemptive purposes, just as Ruth was.

But He had also taught me that morning that I need to be sure I am hearing *His* voice as we continue on the walk of faith.

Standing on the Promises

The second major principle God teaches us in the walk of faith is to stand on the promises He gives for our children, and not to stand (or base our feelings, attitudes and actions) on what they are doing and saying.

I wish I could tell you that I have learned this lesson once and for all, that I now stand consistently on God's promises despite what my children's outward behavior indicates, but I can't. When I take my eyes of faith off of God's promises and place them on individual behaviors I usually react out of anger and fear. Neither anger nor fear is of God. Both come from the evil one.

I am grateful that our heavenly Father is continuing to cleanse me of worry and fear in my life. He is teaching me to live by faith, to trust Him. He is showing me that faith is a walk based not on what I see, but on what He has said.

I recently read this statement of David Grant's: "If I treat you as though you were what you could become, that is what you *will* become."

What a powerful beacon of hope and truth for the parent trying to act on God's promise for a child!

The other day God asked me in my quiet time, *How do you see John today? Are you looking at his present, stabilized, but still uncommitted behavior? Or do you see him through the eyes of faith, as he will be when I completely fulfill the word of faith I gave you about him?*

Can you think how you would answer that question if the Holy Spirit asked you about your child? Can you trust Him to keep His word even when you can't see any changes? This is a critical challenge.

You see, one of God's methods in dealing with human beings is to work from the inside out. He may be working on the inside of your child or mine—in his character, in her heart. Since these are places and works we cannot see, we have no idea what is going on. In fact, there may be times when we see no outward conflict or rebellion and assume that all is well. We drop our guard and become careless about trusting God to continue His work. We forget that attitudes go bad inside before they show up on the outside.

If we concentrate on the outward appearance (see 1 Samuel 16:7), we will have wrong reactions. It follows that we will try to take matters into our own hands. This will hinder God's work.

It may help to remember that until there is a fundamental change on the inside there is really no change at all. Inside changes bring about a permanent work. The condition of the inner life always precedes the expression of the outer life.

But what do you do in the meantime when the outward behavior is appalling? I can just hear you asking the question! After all, you say, parents can't just ignore attitudes and actions while they wait for God to keep His promises!

No, but you can take them to God in prayer. You can ask God to help you learn what it is He wants to show you. In short, you can be patient. This is the walk of faith in which God deals with us. In the *work* of faith, which we will discuss in the next chapter, we will see how He helps us deal with the need for correction, discipline and instruction.

Some Tips for the Journey

God has individual lessons to teach each parent on the walk of faith. Johnnie's lessons were not for me, nor were mine for Johnnie. But we did pick up several tips that can apply to everyone.

1. Keep relationships strong.   The devil likes to lure us into neglecting our relationships with God and our families. His plan is to separate us from God and each other and to make us spiritually weak. Then when he launches a major attack, we are unable to resist in a Christlike way. Our ungodly reactions and/or strained relations make bad situations worse. Estranged from grace, and weak in faith and love, we do not respond as a follower of Jesus should.

I remember hearing Pastor Paul Yonggi Cho, of the famous Full Gospel church in Korea, tell how he became so involved in ministry that his personal relationship with God deteriorated. One day during a meeting he received a message that his son was dying of food poisoning. He rushed home and began to pray, only to find how far he had drifted from a close and dynamic relationship with God. It took him six hours of concentration and confession to get back in tune with the Lord Jesus and be able to pray effectively for his son.

So beware! When you sense in your spirit that you are drifting from God or your family, take action. Restore the "ties that bind" no matter what it takes so that the devil cannot capitalize on your weakness.

2. Pray out of faith, not fear.   Fear drives us, and driven people are too caught up in their own inner turmoil to relate to God.

When we confronted Richard about his drug use and he chose to move out of our home, we were scared, scared stiff about what could happen to him. He was gone: That was bad. *Where* he had gone—to live with a group of hippies—was worse!

But once Johnnie received the word of faith about Richard, we had to learn to pray out of faith, not fear.

I remember, for example, that after Richard left home I prayed repeatedly, "Father, do anything to Richard to bring him back except put him in jail."

One day, when I let Him, God said to me, *Why don't you want him in jail?*

I gave what I thought was the obvious answer. "Father, it would ruin his life!"

To my surprise God asked again, *Why don't you want him in jail?*

Now I know that when God asks a question a second time it is not because He did not hear my first answer, but because my first answer was a lie. So I examined my response and said, "Well, to tell You the truth, if Richard ended up in jail his name would be in the papers. We live in a small town and people in the world love to publish anything bad about ministers and the Church. Then what would they think about us?"

God answered kindly, *You see, your problem is one of pride.* And I realized that I was less concerned about how jail would affect Richard's life than I was fearful of having my name dragged through the dust.

Fear blocks us from seeing the root issues God needs to deal with. When we learn to abandon fear and pray out of faith, the Holy Spirit is able to deal with the root issues, and His work can continue.

3. Don't hide your problems out of pride.   In years of helping people with family problems I have observed that one of the first things they want a pastor to promise is that he or she won't "tell anybody." Well-trained pastors, of course, always maintain confidentiality; that is not the issue here. The issue is that we humans like to hide our problems to protect our pride. And pride, like fear, always blocks relationships.

Johnnie and I are fortunate because God has given us a congregation that allows us to take off our masks. We can tell them when and where and how we are hurting, and know that they will not use our problem against us, but rather will pray and support us.

This is not to say you should broadcast your difficulties with your children to anyone and everyone. But sharing with a pastor and close friends at church, or a support group, opens the way for the Holy Spirit to speak through them to you. In addition, the lessons the Holy Spirit teaches you may bless someone else.

The principles that help light the walk of faith are not always easy, but that does not negate the fact that God loves both parents and children with a tender, patient love. And He helps us express that love to others. too.

Throughout that spring of 1971 and on into 1972, Richard was on drugs and not giving a single indication that he wanted to change. But Johnnie and I had received a word of faith from our heavenly Father that someday Richard would be fine—fine from God's viewpoint and value system—and we would not let go.

God was also using the situation to get our attention and bring us to greater Christian maturity, correcting our faults and giving us a deeper understanding of Himself and how to relate to Him. As we trusted Him on the walk of faith, His presence and teaching sweetened even the bitter pill of watching our child stray.

Now it was time to enter the work of faith.

4

The Work of Faith

Principle: In the work of faith, God asks us to cooperate with Him, step by step, as He deals with our children's sins, problems and potential.

Scripture: James 2:14, 17, 18

In the first chapter of this book we talked about two building blocks on which the whole volume rests— *relating intimately to God* through prayer and meditation and *cooperating with God.*

Johnnie and I were accepting the *word* of faith and attempting the *walk* of faith. But we were also learning that God usually asks parents to cooperate with Him in solving difficult parent-child situations, and that is the *work* of faith. So we were asking for and receiving instructions from Him about what He wanted us to do with Richard.

This has a sound biblical basis. There are numerous stories in the Bible in which men and women were required to cooperate with God in order to see His promises come true.

Remember, after receiving God's promise:

• by faith Noah obeyed God and built an ark (Genesis 6);

• by faith Abram obeyed God and left his hometown of Haran, moving to a land he did not know (Genesis 12);

• by faith Naaman, afflicted with leprosy, obeyed Elisha and dipped in the Jordan River seven times (2 Kings 5);

• by faith the blind man obeyed Jesus and washed in the pool of Siloam (John 9:1–7).

I could go on and on, listing incident after incident in which God asked His children to act on His instructions in order to receive the fulfillment of His promise. We are His children in this generation, and the principle is just as true for us today as it was in Bible times.

There may be times when you wish God would just do an overnight miracle. Believe it or not, that might not draw you closer to Him. We are quick to forget God's goodness, or to take it for granted. In asking us to cooperate with Him, God leads us into more intimate dependency on and fellowship with Himself, and also grants us the joy and satisfaction of being part of the solution.

Let's look now at ten principles God taught Johnnie and me about the work of faith.

1. Faith is always a choice.   I often hear a person say, "Well, I have no choice but to believe," and think that is faith. It isn't. Faith always involves the choice to trust God and His Word or something or someone else—including yourself.

Wait a minute, Peter! you say. We've already received the word of faith for our wandering child, and we're trying to allow God to deal with our own problems on the walk of faith as we wait for the promise to be fulfilled. Why this reminder that faith is a choice? We *have* faith!

For some reason God doesn't seem to give His children a lifelong dose of faith all at once. He could. He could say, "Here, Peter, you'll need this much. Here, Johnnie, you'll need this much. That ought to last you until you get to heaven."

No, God seems instead to want us to choose to appropriate the faith we need for each new situation. When we do, He's not stingy; He comes more than halfway to meet us.

"Lord, I believe; help my unbelief," the father of a tormented child once said to Jesus. Did Jesus scold him for his unbelief? No, He tenderly fulfilled His promise and healed the child (Mark 9:14–27).

God is pleased when we choose to exercise our faith. And since our faith grows each time we do, it becomes a little bit easier to appropriate it the next time.

We need to reaffirm our trust in God during each encounter with our children because then we are admitting that He is the One who acts on our behalf, and we are less tempted to take credit ourselves for His work. When we choose, by faith, to believe that He knows best and try to cooperate with Him, each victory, no matter how small, belongs to Him.

2. We need to take it step by step.   This business of cooperating with God in the work of faith is a step-by-step procedure. Leading us one step at a time seems to be God's normal method, even though we often wish He would unfold His entire plan at once.

There are at least two reasons for His dealing with us this way. First, it is our human tendency to take His blessings for granted. If we know only one step at a time, we are forced to depend on Him, to relate intimately to Him, to go back to Him day after day to give thanks for what has occurred in the lives of our children, and to receive encouragement and instruction to go on.

Second, if God showed us a blueprint of the future, we would do one of two things. We might take it and run, trying to accomplish our children's salvation and deeper walk with God all on our own. Or we might shrink in fear from what is ahead for our children, our families and ourselves before the promise is fulfilled, and refuse to keep walking in faith.

3. We need to remember that we are not responsible for changing our children.   Only God can change a person—fundamentally, deep down, restructuring even his or her natural inclinations. This is another way of saying what I said earlier: Our *actions* cannot make a child godly; only *God* can make a child godly.

You see, we function best when we are doing what comes naturally. The Christian life is not meant to be a continual struggle to be something we are not. God alone can give each of us a new quality of life—through salvation and redemption by Jesus Christ and by the power of the indwelling Holy Spirit—and develop it so that it flows naturally.

Our responsibility to our children, therefore, is not to change them, but to train them to live in the world. We will develop this point in more detail in chapter 8.

4. We can adopt an open-door policy.   One of the ways God told us to cooperate with Him about Richard was to tell our son that our door was always open to him: He could come home and visit as often as he liked. And he did—to wash clothes and eat! Naturally, these visits gave us opportunities to talk with him.

We soon realized—and this is why I include the open-door policy as a principle—that since Richard wanted nothing to do with Christians or the Church, we were the only direct and personal contact God would have with him through people. It was important for us to make the most of these contacts by allowing him to see Christ in us. The open-door policy showed him that while we did not approve of his lifestyle, we loved him and had not rejected him.

I know from our own experiences that it is easy in the strain of parent-child confrontations to move in anger or hopelessness and decide to wash your hands of the whole matter: "Just get out and leave this family in peace!"

Remember two things: 1) Both temper and hopelessness are not from God. They are from the devil. Leash your anger and go to God in your quiet time for instructions before acting. 2) You may be the last human contact through whom God can manifest His love to your child. Don't shut the door unless the Lord gives specific directives to do so—and this would be the exception, not the rule.

5. We need to make our children responsible for the consequences of their choices. We do our children no favors when we soften the consequences of their rebellious behavior. If we have cooperated with God (acting on the Holy Spirit's directions or impressions) by setting consequences for a certain act, we must continue to cooperate by following through, whether the child is age two or twenty In fact, the earlier we parents learn this principle, and the earlier the child knows we have learned it and sees us acting on it, the easier life will be for everyone!

As I indicated in chapter 1, I had told Richard that if he got arrested for his drug use we were not going to bail him out. "Make sure you are prepared to live with the consequences of your choices," I had said.

Soon after our conversation came the telephone call telling us Richard had, indeed, been arrested for possession of narcotics and was being held in Orlando until he could be arraigned. As you can imagine, cooperating with God was not easy for either Johnnie or me God had to strengthen our backbones to enable us to leave

Richard in that jail—and He did. It was probably one of the best, and toughest, learning experiences Richard had. It certainly made a memorable impression on us.* We will address this topic further in chapter 15, "Knowing Where to Draw the Lines."

6. We must not react to our children's behavior but should allow the Holy Spirit to determine our responses. I have touched on this idea briefly, but it is important to look at it further. Some of my greatest mistakes as a parent have come from reacting to my children's actions. I have allowed their behavior to determine my response—and my response was usually anger.

Here is an important distinction to help you understand this principle of cooperating with God: Reactive behavior responds instantly, like a knee-jerk reflex, rather than taking the time to consider the matter from a deep, internal value system.

What if God had responded reactively to man's sin and rebellion in Noah's time? Rather than take elaborate measures to save Noah and his family from the flood in order to repopulate the earth, He could have wiped out humankind forever in one angry stroke. He chose instead to give us a second chance, and sent Jesus to redeem and reconcile willing members of the human race to intimate relationship with Him. He did that out

* For further ideas in this area I recommend *Dare to Discipline* and *The Strong-Willed Child*, both by Dr. James Dobson, and *How to Make Your Children Mind Without Losing Yours* by Dr. Kevin Leman.

of His deep, internal value system of love and compassion and commitment.

If, by the grace of God, we hear from Him regularly and live by His principles and His value system, we, too, can respond to our children's behavior out of love, compassion and commitment.

We need to acknowledge that our knee-jerk reactions often arise out of fear. "Why in the world did you *do* that? Don't you realize how seriously you could have been hurt?"

When we forget to exercise our faith for each situation, fear takes over. And fear always brings a reactive response. But when we choose to trust God with the details of our response, He helps us to avoid the internally and externally destructive consequences of fear.

7. It is important to be honest, not devious, about our labors. Christians are tempted far too often to use deceptive methods in order to get someone to hear the Gospel.

You would be surprised how many times a Christian husband or wife or mother or father with an unbelieving loved one has said to me, "My spouse/child is home tonight. Why don't you just drop in? He will never invite you or let me invite you."

I do not agree with this method. The end does not justify the means. We need to be open—not obnoxiously, but courteously—about our spiritual concern for a loved one.

Johnnie and I discovered how God will bless our use

of this principle. After Richard got out of jail we felt our Father instructing us to invite Richard and all his friends to our house for a meal with the express purpose of sharing with them a different way of life—God's way.

So I went to the house where about eight of them were living. I remember standing on the front porch and saying to them, "You fellows can see from your recent arrest that you are heading for trouble. We would like to have you over for a meal and explain to you about an alternate lifestyle."

Miraculously, they accepted. I use the word *miraculous* because that was how it seemed from our perspective. Why were they willing to visit us when they knew that Richard's father was a Christian pastor and that the alternate lifestyle he was proposing was undoubtedly Christianity?

But when we ask God for instructions and He gives them, we can be sure He has a plan. One of the obvious reasons they accepted, of course, was the prospect of a free meal! Richard had shared with us on one of his visits that all of their money went for drugs, and food was scarce. God wasn't reluctant to use their need to draw them toward Him. So their acceptance wasn't any miracle from His viewpoint; it was just His way of accomplishing His work.

After the boys had eaten the lovely dinner Johnnie prepared for them, I shared the Gospel. They listened politely. Then I said, "Would any of you like to receive Jesus as Lord and Savior and start a new life?" Much to my surprise a young man sitting at the end of the table said, "I would." Then and there Buzzy prayed to receive Christ and become one of His followers. Shortly afterward the boys left.

Devious methods to "corner" our children with the Gospel may backfire, appearing to them not as acts of genuine love and commitment, but as a desire to "add scalps" to our belts. But if we cooperate with the Holy Spirit in expressing our spiritual concerns for them *as He directs us to*, our Father will continue to work in them.

8. We need to give of ourselves generously. You may be sure that God is working out His plan to fulfill the word of faith He gave concerning your child. But watch out! It is far too easy to want God to do all of the work while we just continue on as before. In many instances He wants to use us, His servants, to perform His will.

We found this out in a surprising way. A few days after Richard and his friends ate dinner with us there was a knock at our front door. I answered it and there was Buzzy.

"Mr. Lord," he said, "I can't live the Christian life in the place where I am staying now. Can I come and live with you?"

Wow! This would require quite a commitment from Johnnie and me. But as soon as we considered Buzzy's request we realized his dilemma, and agreed gladly to take him in and disciple him in the ways of the Lord Jesus.

It was not an easy commitment for a busy pastor's family to make. But we were soon doubly glad we had: When Buzzy moved in with us, Richard came, too. We had never known they were best friends.

Buzzy kept growing in the Spirit and continued to follow Jesus, active in a church and in Kingdom work until his untimely death in a construction accident. How grateful we were to know that God had used us to bring that young man into the Kingdom! We were thankful that we had been willing to cooperate with God in sharing ourselves, our home and our family time with Buzzy.

Richard remained unchanged at this point except that he did not use drugs at home. He lied about his drug use elsewhere, but he was home, and exposed to a Christian atmosphere. Praise God! He works all things together for good—even our rebellious children's "unsavory" friends!

9. We must uphold Christian standards and practices in the home as "givens." It is my firm conviction that God has given parents the privilege and responsibility of educating our children in the Christian faith. That task does not belong to the local church or the Christian school, although they may serve supportive roles. (There are times, however, when God allows a church or Christian school to play a major role in a child's life, such as when the parents are not Christians.)

When we do our part by modeling a Christian lifestyle and educating our children in the faith—through devotional times or "family altar," Christian music, books and exposure to other Christians and Christian experiences—we release God to change their hearts and form them into godly people.

It is important for children to understand that certain of these practices are "givens" in the home. They are non-negotiable: Everyone is to participate. (Parents may need, as the children grow older, to make individual judgment calls as to which practices are negotiable, and at what ages. Here is another area where the Holy Spirit can give you discernment.)

Naturally we need to do our best to be somewhat flexible in planning the schedule, so as to make it possible for family members to take part, and to make the activities enjoyable and oriented to the age levels and abilities of the children involved.

We always had family altar times with our children as they were growing up. Since John was younger than the last of our other four youngsters by about nine years, there were several years after the older ones left when he was virtually an only child. Morning after morning Johnnie and I had devotions with him, but it was one of the hardest things I have ever done. Even before his time of rebellion he was not really interested. During his rebellion he said, "I do not want anything to do with God or the Church. I do not care about any of that stuff." I persisted in having devotions with him, but it was terrible. He seldom paid attention, and frequently fell asleep.

But what I did, I did by the firm conviction that God wanted me to do it. I knew He could and would use the facts and principles I was teaching during those devotional times as soon as John was ready to incorporate them into his life.*

10. We need to be willing, as God directs, to ask for our children's forgiveness.   I have become a professional in asking forgiveness from my children! I have failed them often, usually because I didn't seek God's direction for my responses, and reacted emotionally on the spot.

I just described how John often acted during our devotional times together. Can you guess how I reacted? By getting angry, over and over again. What a shame: Getting angry while seeking to impart the things of God! I learned, of course, that this was counterproductive; as James tells us, "The anger of man does not achieve the righteousness of God" (1:20). And so I would always apologize for the anger and its expressions.

Clearing the decks of hurts and wounds, both real and imagined, shows our children that we are still learners in the faith, too, and demonstrates our sincerity about living the walk we talk about so much.

I hope that these ten points will help you if you are

---

* For an excellent resource on Christian parents' responsibility to educate their children in the faith, see Sally Leman Chall's book *Making God Real to Your Children* (Fleming H. Revell Company).

currently struggling through the work of faith. My experience has been and still is that God rewards our faithful efforts. And even if we make many mistakes He can redeem them, for He remembers our frame, that we are but dust (Psalm 103:14).

5

The Wait of Faith

Principle: The time between receiving the word of faith about a wandering child (a promise) and receiving its fulfillment is the wait of faith.

Scripture: Hebrews 11:1; Philippians 1:6

Faith always has a wait! That is the very nature of faith: If there were nothing to wait for, then we would have the fulfillment in our hands already. Hebrews 11:1 is, of course, the "classic" statement of this truth: "Faith is the assurance of things *hoped for*, the evidence of things *not seen*" (italics mine).

When the word of faith comes, it is usually a mountaintop experience. We sing and praise God because He has reassured us that He will answer our prayers and draw our erring children back to Himself.

But the wait of faith is done in the valleys of life, where the demoniacs live, as Jesus' disciples discovered when they came off the Mount of Transfiguration (Matthew 17; Mark 9). The wait of faith occurs as we live our everyday lives—with or without our children.

Personally I have found this to be the most difficult of all the aspects of faith. My fleshly nature is very impatient. It is a besetting sin of mine, an area of real weakness, one that I am working on, and in which God is working on me.

But most of us have only to look down the street or in our local newspapers to realize that our society as a whole is impatient. We demand "instant everything," from food to sex to money. A young mother from the city recently took her little girl to a Christian camp for a mother-daughter retreat. En route to the camp's rural location the mother was heard to exclaim, "I haven't seen a McDonald's for miles. My kids couldn't *live* without McDonald's!"

Her kids aren't alone. And our Western preoccupation with "having it all" and having it now has a drastic impact on our Christian faith.

Why Is God So Slow?

The wait of faith has been difficult to bear as God has worked on each of our children, but it has been longest (over eight years) and perhaps most difficult (who can qualify this type of thing?) in the life of our youngest son, John, whom I mentioned in the last chapter.

It almost never seems to fail that after you get a word from God about your child, a word on which to stand, a word of hope, the situation seems to get worse. In her absolutely delightful book *Pain Is Inevitable, Misery Is*

Optional, So Stick a Geranium in Your Hat and Be Happy,
Barbara Johnson has entitled one chapter "It Is Always
Darkest Just Before It Goes Totally Black."

In our parental experience, especially with John, this
has been par for the course. It has seemed as if when
things could not get worse, they did. We would think,
This is the fulfillment, and then John would have a setback.

After a major turnaround in his spiritual life, John
went off to college. This victory was followed, however,
by a crisis in which he spent six months in a drug and
alcohol recovery center and then six more months in a
halfway house in Orlando. At this writing he is attend-
ing a Christian college. He is on the right track, more
stabilized, but still with much to learn (like all of us!) in
his personal relationship with Jesus.

Why is God so slow? Why does He take so long to
fulfill His promises? Why, since He has the power to do
anything, does He not do it right away, or at least more
quickly, and save us all the pain and trouble?

Let me share with you four principles I believe God
wants us to learn in the wait of faith.

1. God's concept of time is different from ours.   I'll
go even further: God's concept of time differs from ours
completely! Peter's second letter tells us, "With the Lord
one day is as a thousand years, and a thousand years as
one day" (3:8).

Dr. Edward J. Willett, now retired after teaching eco-
nomics at Houghton College for more than twenty

years, uses an analogy from the days of the lower-flying piston-engine planes to explain God's concept of time. It was easy, back then, to see what was happening on the ground below.

One day as he was flying to Syracuse, New York, Dr. Willett saw a winding two-lane road below the plane, with two lines of cars heading toward each other, about a mile or so apart. The driver of a sports car, impatient to pass the leader of his line, kept pulling out to pass and dropping back, pulling out and dropping back. Apparently the road was so curvy he didn't dare go around the cars ahead of him.

"The thing that struck me," Dr. Willett says, "was that from my position in the plane, three thousand feet up, I could tell that if that sports car driver *did* pull out to pass he would almost certainly crash head-on into a car in the opposing lane. And that's how God must feel about me. Just as I could see the entire span of that highway and all the traffic on it, God can see the entire span of my life, past, present and future. But like the sports car driver, I can only see a short way ahead—a few days or weeks, at most. Once we begin to figure out that God sees the whole picture, and have faith that He is operating according to His perspective, we can better handle what life throws at us."

When God speaks a promise, He is speaking from His time perspective, not ours. The Bible says that "God is . . . a very present help in trouble" (Psalm 46:1). Not a past help, not a future help—a *present* help. I have learned that God may be very, very slow, but He is never, ever late!

2. God has bigger, better plans than we know enough to ask for.   Remember Isaiah 55:8–9? " 'For My thoughts are not your thoughts, neither are your ways My ways,' declares the Lord. 'For as the heavens are higher than the earth, so are My ways higher than your ways, and My thoughts than your thoughts.' "

God's purposes in the wait of faith include much more than our requests that He redeem our children and draw them closer to Himself. (And even in fulfilling those requests, He outdoes Himself, going "exceeding abundantly beyond all that we ask or think" (Ephesians 3:20).) Our experience with Buzzy, told in the last chapter, is one example.

In our bedroom, where Johnnie and I pray together, hangs a banner of what we call the mission statement for our lives, our common goal: *Come worship the Lord with me and let us exalt His name together*. We also have a well-established family tradition that when we finish our prayer times we raise our hands over our heads and say, "The only reason we are alive is to glorify God."

It took me some time to see that God was not only allowing the trials with our children, but was using them, as a means to accomplish this desire in our lives.

Now we really hoped and prayed, of course, that God would conform us to His image painlessly, instantly, without cost to us. This has not happened and I don't think it will for us or for any of His children.

Through our children God has gained our attention and enabled us to make the character changes necessary in order for our lives to glorify Him.

Remember: It is always God's purpose to enlarge us so He can give us more, to develop us so He can trust us with more. If we cooperate with Him in the walk and wait of faith, acknowledging that His ways and thoughts are higher and wiser and better than ours. we will see someday just what He was trying to do.

3. The wait teaches us that we need others in the Body of Christ to support us. The wait of faith is best done in conjunction with other Christians. We need close friends to help us through those difficult times when things seem to be getting worse from every conceivable viewpoint.

As I mentioned earlier, most of us are tempted to hide our family problems in order to preserve an image of religious integrity. Such pride, plain and simple, not only displeases God because it denies our need for Him, but also robs us of the tremendous caring, camaraderie and lessons to be learned from other Christians who have themselves ached over wandering children.

If it were not for the wait of faith, we might never know the comfort that comes from feeling our burdens lift as our brothers and sisters in the Body join us in loving, praying and believing for our children.

4. The wait purifies our faith. It is easy to think that our faith is solid when we are talking about it or singing about it at church, but in the walk and wait of everyday life, in the valleys, we see how strong or weak, pure or flawed our faith really is.

You see, the plain teaching of Scripture is that faith pleases God and releases Him to act on our behalf (Hebrews 11:6). And a strong, pure faith carries with it an absolute assurance that God will keep His word (Hebrews 10:35; 11:1). So having faith is like knowing beyond the shadow of a doubt that your team is going to win. Even if you are so far behind at half time that a win seems impossible, you rejoice anyway.

But sometimes it seems we just can't. In those cases our faith in His promise is flawed. Adrian Rogers once said, "The faith that falters before the finish had a flaw in it from the first."

Among the many signs of flawed faith are despondency, worry, anger and depression. The best way to detect flawed faith is to listen to your own words. Make a list of all the things you say regularly about the problem (or the problem child) for whom God has given you a word of faith. Words are always indicators of the true heart condition because Jesus said, "Out of the abundance of the heart the mouth speaks" (Matthew 12:34; Luke 6:45).

Some time ago I went out to lunch with one of my children for whom I was at the time in the wait of faith. In the course of our conversation I asked him several questions. His answers indicated no change in some fundamental areas of his life, areas necessary not only for walking with God but for living life successfully on this planet.

Instead of turning to the Lord and asking Him to

reconfirm His promise and give me encouragement, I centered on the appearance of things and became discouraged and depressed. I did not respond to my son as a father with a strong, pure faith in God, but as a father who had no faith that his child was going to be redeemed. A meeting that should have been a positive encounter of love, mercy and grace turned instead into a temporary setback in our relationship. The experience left me in total despair and frustration.

When I got home I heard myself saying to Johnnie, "What's the use? I give up; I'm tired of trying. That child will never change. If God wants to act then He will, but our child shows no visible interest. I refuse to do any more; I wash my hands of this situation."

Later, as I rehearsed both my conversations with my child and with Johnnie, listening particularly to my own words of unbelief in God and His promise, I was appalled that I could have uttered such things. They were blasphemous expressions attacks on the character of God. You can be sure I repented, but I also saw how flawed and imperfect my trust in God for this situation really was.

Even as our faith's flaws can be seen most easily in the way we talk, so can its strengths. True faith speaks confidently, joyously, thankfully. It sees and knows the end and is fully persuaded that what God has promised, He is able to perform. The repeated admonition from Scripture, ' Let us not lose heart in doing good, for in due time we shall reap if we do not grow weary,"

(Galatians 6:9; 2 Thessalonians 3:13), is applicable both for the walk of faith and the wait of faith. God will fulfill the promises He has given concerning your children and mine. In the process He shows us how much refining our faith really needs.

6

The Fulfillment of Faith

Principle: The fulfillment of faith is when the word of faith—God's promise for the salvation and redemption of the wandering child—becomes flesh and blood reality.

Scripture: Hebrews 6:11–20

Suddenly . . . One Sunday night Richard was tripping out on LSD. The next Sunday night he was turned around and headed in a new direction—God's direction. The fulfillment of faith had come in Richard's life, and he has stayed on God's course now for twenty years.

Suddenly . . . One week John was in active rebellion, away from home, doing his own thing. By the next Sunday he was back home after giving his life to Christ, confessing to and making restitution for crimes he had helped commit.

Suddenly . . . One week your son or daughter is wandering far from God, angry and disrespectful and selfish. The next week he or she has repented, received Christ as Savior and Lord, and is eagerly telling others about God's goodness.

Over and over again in this walk of faith, the fulfillment comes suddenly. Suddenly from our viewpoint and perspective, that is, but not from God's. It's all a part of the plan He has worked on all along. Through all of what *we* saw as ups and downs, starts and stops, progress and setbacks, He has been setting the stage for a visible manifestation of His work, the fulfillment of His word of faith to us.

God's ways are *not* our ways (Isaiah 55:8–9), a marvelous truth of which we need to be reminded over and over. So often we are like the children of Israel, who, according to the psalmist, "saw His works, but [did] not understand His ways" and therefore were unable to cooperate with Him. Sooner or later, in the walk and wait and through the work of faith, we discover the enormity of God's ways and plans and are glad to accept them as best.

I remember saying to Him, "God, if I were You I would do things much differently!"

He replied, *Look at the way you have done them. That's why they're in the mess they are now!* That was enough to stop my complaining!

As our years of parenting continue (for we never stop being parents) I keep on learning about the processes we have discussed in the last five chapters. I know now to seek a word of faith from Him for each of my children's difficulties. I try to allow Him freedom to deal with my sins on the walk of faith. I yield, sometimes fearfully, to His plan for correcting and redeeming my children for Himself in the work of faith. And I allow Him, sometimes hesitantly and unwillingly, to purify my trust in Him in the wait of faith.

Though I am stubborn and impatient and sometimes slow to learn, the process has always been sweetened by His love and mercy. And when the fulfillment of faith comes, that is truly a time of excitement. When God's word becomes reality and we see tangible answers to our heart's cries for our children, then we experience worship and wonder. Kneeling before our Lord and God, our Maker, we offer Him our thanksgiving, love, adoration and praise.

Thus far we have looked at the overall process through which we pass on the parent-child journey, from grieving parent and wandering child to rejoicing parent and redeemed child. Now, by studying the Fatherhood of God and His patterns for parenting, we can cultivate many attitudes and actions along the way that will help us cooperate more fully with God. Those patterns will be our focus in Section 2.

Section 2

God's Patterns for Parenting

7

The Heavenly Father, Our Model

The Bible refers over and over again to the tremendous Fatherhood of God, and to His watchcare over His children. I cannot say strongly enough that this is an area in which we need to study and meditate carefully, both as individuals and as the Church at large.

Students of human behavior—psychologists, teachers, psychiatrists, social workers, ministers, sociologists, to name just a few—have known for a long time that parental behavior affects children. In the last few years more and more books and articles have explored just how strongly those beliefs and attitudes shape children's feelings, actions and personalities.

And, yes, in Christian circles many sermons have been preached and some articles and books written, especially in recent years, on the connection between a child's relationship with his earthly father and his relationship with his heavenly Father. But not nearly enough thought has been given to just what kind of heavenly Father we have, or to the implications of His Fatherhood in straightening out the damaged places in our lives, or to the fact that He means for us to model ourselves as parents after Him.

Certainly neither Christians nor non-Christians have, by and large, taken seriously the knowledge and information now available about the crucial effect of parental modeling. If we were incorporating these understandings into our personal lives in any significant way, the impact on society—on crime rates and domestic satisfaction and educational statistics alone, not to mention on church life—would be noticeable within a few years. But such personal application requires changes in lifestyle and attitudes few of us are willing to make.*

Walter Brown Knight writes, "A father was one day teaching his little boy what manner of man a Christian is. When the lesson was finished, the father got the stab of his life when the boy asked, "Father, have I ever seen a Christian?"

Have our children ever seen Christians? Christian fathers and mothers whose parenting consistently resembles God's?

Hundreds of biblical passages show us the principles by which God operates as our Father, as you can see by

* For helpful reading about the earthly father/heavenly Father connection, see Donald Joy's *Becoming a Man* (Regal Books). Also, *Always Daddy's Girl* by H. Norman Wright (Regal Books).

checking any good-sized concordance. Just as an earthly parent has many roles to play in the lives of his children, so our heavenly Father plays many roles in our lives, including protector, nourisher, chastener, comforter, deliverer. We need to study and meditate on how God acted with and spoke to His children in the past, and how He continues to model the same fatherly attributes toward us, His children in this generation.

Just follow the Israelites on their journey to the Promised Land, for example, as told in the book of Exodus. God *heard* His children's cries of distress as they endured slavery (Exodus 2:24; 3:7–10). He promised to *be* with them (3:12–22). He *protected* them (11:5–7; 14). He *instructed* and *encouraged* them (14:2, 13–14). He *provided* for their physical nourishment (15:22–27; 16:11–21). He *rebuked* them (16:28). And all of this before they had been on the road two months!

Surely the God who inspired His servants to record such a wealth of interaction between Himself and His children wanted us to learn how to parent from His example.

The following chapters are an attempt to share several of God's patterns for parenting that Johnnie and I have discerned through trial and error, experience and the study of God's Word, our years of child-rearing and continuing to relate to our grown children. Again, it is important to remember that the Holy Spirit must interpret the application of these patterns to each of us individually for use with each of our children.

As we begin this all-too-brief study of how our Father's attributes need to be lived out in our dealings with our children, let us do so in the attitude of Walter Russell Bowie's thoughtful prayer, taken from his book *Lift Up Your Hearts*:

O God, who art our Father, take my human fatherhood and bless it with Thy Spirit. Let me not fail this little son of mine. Help me to know what Thou wouldst make of him, and use me to help and bless him. Make me loving and understanding, cheerful and patient and sensitive to all his needs so that he may trust me enough to come close to me and let me come very close to him. Make me ashamed to demand of him what I do not demand of myself; but help me more and more to try to be the kind of man that he might pattern himself after. And this I ask in the name and by the grace of Christ. Amen.

8

Cooperating with God

In the very first chapter of this book we concluded that the process of child-rearing is not applying a formula in order to build a product, but rather participating in the growth of a life that already contains predetermined qualities.

Now, as we work and pray our way through the five faith steps outlined in the first section of this book and learn more about God as our example of what a parent should be, we will find that He is changing our attitudes. He is shifting our gaze off the problem child and onto Himself as the solution. He is taking away our unrealistic expectations and helping us put our hope in Him. In other words, He is teaching us to cooperate with Him.

We know the concept of cooperation; now let's see how to put it into action. In this chapter we will study the patterns behind three key areas of cooperation: development, leaving change to God and training. The better our ability to apply ourselves to them, the better we will fall in step with God as He does the work of faith in a wayward child.

Development

For any living thing to develop, it must have two things: cooperation from the grower (provision of food, water and cultivation) and time.

When our first child was born, I was plowing and cultivating peanuts for a living on a farm in central Florida. It was long, hard work—especially the cultivating. I worked for ten to twelve hours a day on a tractor and could weed four rows at a time.

Eighteen years later, after our youngest was born, we revisited the same farm. The owners were still growing peanuts on the same property, but they were harvesting twice as many peanuts with about half the effort.

What had happened? The owners of that farm had learned better methods of cooperating with the life and growth process of the peanut plant.

Just as the farmer does not create the peanuts, so parents do not create a child's life; through the act of procreation we, the developers or growers, cooperate with God in creating it. Then we work to bring it to adulthood. Proper development encourages the child's greatest potential. A lack in this area can inhibit or even destroy life.

Any counselor, secular or religious, can tell you that a great number of the people he or she sees are unhappy in their vocations. They spend their lives doing what they are not fitted for, emotionally, physically or mentally, and therefore do not enjoy it.

This problem could have innumerable roots, but I would venture to say that a good portion of them are traceable to parents who did not cooperate with the child's natural development.

Take, for just one instance, the parents who ship children off to college who are totally ill-equipped for that experience. Perhaps they are gifted in working with their hands and would find personal satisfaction in studying at a trade school.

It isn't hard to see that the children's inevitable unhappiness has been caused by parents who tried to get them to do things they were not designed to do. In other words, the parents tried to build certain traits into their children, rather than helping develop what was there inherently.

A story in the popular children's book series *Frog and Toad* illustrates the concept of time. It tells how Toad wanted to have a garden. He planted seeds and watered them but was dismayed when they didn't sprout within a few hours!

As ridiculous as Toad's ignorance may seem to us, that is sometimes how we parents treat our children's development process. We want instant results. We overlook the fact that each life-form has a time for growth scheduled into its being at conception.

This is true in the natural realm; children develop different abilities at different stages and at their own paces. One perfectly normal ten-month-old may be able to walk. His equally normal cousin, born the same week, may not. Neither is "right" or "wrong," "slow" or "fast." Each is growing according to his or her predetermined schedule, and for the parents to force a child to "perform" before he or she is ready may actually stunt his or her development.

Our children's spiritual development takes time, too, as we have already mentioned in our discussion of the wait of faith. It is important here, too, that parents not force growth. Imagine what happens when parents insist on making a child spiritual! They know what good Christians do and don't do and are determined to build these traits into the lives of their children. I assure you, this is futile!

Parents need to remember three important points in this matter of spiritual development:

1. Allow for a spiritual pregnancy in your child's heart before the new birth can take place.   It takes time for a developing child to be born. Allow God to germinate His thoughts in your child and bring new spiritual life into the world *in His time*. Parents can cooperate in this process by training a child, that is, offering proper spiritual food in the form of family worship times, Sunday school and church attendance and so on. We will discuss this further in the section on training.

Sincere evangelicals have a tremendous tendency to push their children into decisions for Christ. This is very easy to do with small, vulnerable, eager-to-please youngsters. While a child in a strong Christian home should not be discouraged from spiritual developments, parents need to make sure he is not pushed or manipulated into a profession of faith that is no more than that—a profession. If such "decisions" are made before God's time, they will not represent true salvation and regeneration.

In fact, there is a danger in pushing a child to "pray the sinner's prayer." He or she may be deceived or fooled into thinking he or she has been born again when that may not have happened at all. Many people have been inoculated against genuine Christianity by a false version of it. They may think, "I prayed that prayer, so I must be O.K.," or, "I prayed that prayer and it didn't work for me." Only the touch of the Holy Spirit in His own time and His own way will awaken a child to the gift of eternal life and a personal relationship with Jesus.

2. Parents cannot cooperate with life that isn't there. Before we can expect a child to manifest godly traits he or she needs God's life within. Only God can give this. We can offer training and education, but all of our efforts to develop spiritual life when none is present may bring detrimental results.

Author Eugenia Price once suggested that people who don't know Christ have *no* reason *not* to swear! The same is true for smaller people—children who have not yet received Jesus as Savior and Lord. Lacking God's life within, they have no reason *not* to manifest worldly actions and attitudes; but these are only symptoms of the root problem: sin.

This does not mean that parents need to tolerate unacceptable behavior in the home. It does mean we shouldn't use God as a club to beat non-Christian children over the head: "It makes God really angry when you do that" or "You know Christians don't act that way!" Such statements merely reinforce a child's feeling that God is a demanding ogre to be avoided at all costs.

If we must object to a particular behavior we need a valid reason: "Smoking is not acceptable in our home because it is an unhealthy habit, and it is discourteous to expose others to unwanted smoke" or "When you swear you offend my Christian beliefs; I am willing to be tolerant and courteous *toward* you, and I expect the same courtesy *from* you, especially when you are living in this house."

3. Once a child becomes a Christian, parents must be ready, in attitude, action and lifestyle, to help him or her cooperate with the new life God has given. Remember: Full maximization of the life of God in any person—in other words, what that life should represent at its fully developed potential—is the stature of the fullness of Christ, His life living in that person.

From birth to the age of thirty Jesus was developing. Then He was able to go out and do a marvelous ministry. One of our weaknesses in the Body of Christ is that we do not allow new Christians time to grow.

Cooperation with a developing Christian's new life will vary, depending on the age at which the person receives the life of God. You cannot treat a seventeen-year-old who has accepted Christ the same as you would treat a seven-year-old who has accepted Christ.

No matter what the age, it is important that you have been a godly parent up to that time so that there will be openness between you and your child and you will be able to help him or her. When children become Christians later in life, any barriers between them and their parents will make their spiritual growth difficult, and will hinder the parents from cooperating with the life of God in their children.

We're ready now to discuss what it means to try to change a child.

Leaving Change to God

Johnnie and I were determined to change the behavior of one of our daughters, particularly the strong will with which she used to pin us to the wall and leave us hanging there! If we told her to go and clean her room, for example, she came up with strong arguments as to why she should not do so, and she continued to argue until she had worn us down. Eventually we would just give up.

Day after day we tried to change her by "picking off the bad fruit," telling her not to argue with us. We insisted she should start behaving "correctly." But the harder we tried, the worse she seemed to get and the deeper the gap between us grew.

Finally we realized that no matter how good our motives were, no matter how sincere we were, we could not change her. Not only was it an impossibility, it was not our God-given responsibility.

Change, or Behavior Modification?

Change, as we use the term here, means a basic and fundamental turnaround in the quality and character of life that results in different behavior patterns.

Now, parents can cause a child to *act* differently, usually by using the threat of punishment or the promise of reward. But there is no fundamental change in the child's character. If there were no form of manipulation, the child would not perform in the desired manner. No change has occurred; the child's behavior has simply been modified.

You have seen this in action. At the circus, for instance, you will see many illustrations of behavior modification. A dog may stand on his hind legs pushing a doll carriage, a monkey dressed in a cowboy outfit may ride horseback, leopards and tigers may leap through flaming circles. These animals are not changed; their behavior has merely been modified. All of them go back to their normal and natural behavior as soon as the show is over.

When we try to change our children spiritually we generally end up producing one of two types of people: hypocrites or rebels.

Hypocrites are playactors, people pretending to be something they are not, acting a certain way without their hearts in it. Hypocrites are joyless people; they cannot be joyful when they have to act in ways inconsistent with their true natures. Pretension causes their religion to be a burden rather than a joy, a set of rules to follow (rules determined, of course, by the group to which they belong). Rules can modify behavior but produce no inner change.

Rebels refuse, either passively (inwardly) or actively (outwardly), to conform to the behavior patterns we are trying to impose upon them. Passive rebellion is much harder to detect in a child than active rebellion.

Both passive and active rebellion are reasons why so many children give up every bit of their religious training the minute they leave home. They go off to work or college and abandon church, God and all religious practices because parents and other well-meaning people have tried to change them.

Behavior modification is not what we are after in rearing our children. But until they are radically changed from within, the best we can hope for is a performance. Until they are new creations in Christ Jesus they may perform for the hope of some reward or the avoidance of some punishment, like hell.

According to a recent article in *Christianity Today* magazine, the number one reason people claim the Christian faith is fear. This is totally inconsistent with the Christian Gospel and completely opposed to God's way of doing things. What has caused this? People have professed the Christian faith without experiencing the transforming change God can make in their lives.

Real Christians are people who are fundamentally changed, and not just trained to act in a certain way. When we are truly changed on the inside, the Christian life is no longer a continual struggle to act in ways inconsistent with our inner being. It is, instead, the spontaneous action of what we are on the inside coming out.

This is what we long for in our children, a change so radical that they do not have to spend the rest of their lives struggling against their natural inclinations.

How does this fundamental change take place in a child's life? It can happen only through Jesus. But we can cooperate with Him in several ways by following these patterns.

1. We need to repent.   Repentance is a change of heart that will eventually result in a change of action. Repentance, in one sense, is a gift of God: He shows us where we are wrong. Our part is to agree with Him and accept the truth. When we are able to say, "I am wrong," and not attempt to justify our thinking, then we are ninety percent on the way home to allowing God to change us in the way only He can.

For what do we need to repent? For our failures as Christians and as Christian parents, for our attempts to do what only God can do in drawing our children back to Himself, for our lack of faith in the promises He has given for their eventual redemption.

2. We need to ask God to give our children the gifts of repentance and new life in Him.   The Gospel of John tells us that the Holy Spirit comes, in part, to convict the world of sin and of righteousness (16:8–10). We are helpless even to repent without His assistance. We need to ask God to grant our children the conviction of the Holy Spirit that leads to true repentance.

This kind of repentance and change happens within the realm of the spirit, unlike the education we offer in the realm of the soul and body.

To live and minister as Christians and Christian parents we need to understand the difference between the realms of the soul and the spirit.

The soul refers to our personalities and intellects— those traits and characteristics that make us uniquely recognizable individuals. At all levels of life and in all professions or vocations we meet nice, decent, thoughtful, intelligent, well-read but ungodly people. They have characteristics that make them easy to relate to on a human level, and some of those characteristics are even characteristics of God. But those do not make a person a Christian. Any individual can be trained to learn these characteristics to his advantage.

But a Christian is more than just a well-trained human being. He or she has the life of God, which is a gift God gives us through Jesus Christ our Lord. It is a gift we can receive only when the Holy Spirit causes our spirit—that part of us designed to communicate with God—to be open to genuine change, repentance and intimate relationship with Himself. Until God touches each of our children in the spirit they will experience no change.

So our responsibility is not to get them to pray a certain prayer but to pray that they will be touched by God with His life.

3. We need, by the grace of God, to live supernatural lives that will make our children see Jesus in us. Unless we are godly, loving, Spirit-filled, joyous people of faith who demonstrate the life of God consistently in the drudgery and relationships of everyday living, all the talking in the world, all the churchgoing, all the Bible-reading, all the tithing we do will mean nothing to our children. It will be religion, but it will not be Christianity. Joyless, struggle-filled religion will not attract our non-Christian children to our Lord, and it will not draw our wandering children back to Him, either.

The more we rejoice in Him, rather than being negative about any unhappiness in the home, the more successful we will be in the third area of cooperation with God: training.

Training

To train a child means to shape an existing life. It means to educate him or her in all the relational and personal and physical skills he or she will need to get along in the world. Manners, responsibility, pleasant attitudes, morals, the ability to stand up for what is true and honest and right—we are responsible as parents to do our best to instill these in our children, under the guidance and teaching of the Holy Spirit.

God worked hard at training the Israelites, His chosen children. A loving, fair, sometimes stern Father, He gave them the Ten Commandments for successful God-human and human-human interaction. He tried repeatedly to teach them an "attitude of gratitude." He placed enormous responsibility on their shoulders, when He as a Father knew the time was appropriate. And He didn't stop there. He trained His children to know and understand Him and His Law.

We can expose our children to the truth about God and the marvelous stories found in the Bible, and then trust the Holy Spirit to do His work. We do this by means of the family altar, Christian books, music and art in our homes, contact with our own Christian friends from all walks of life, youth outings, exposure to Christian role models, Sunday school and church attendance. (Constant exposure to a dead church, by the way, is one of the worst things we can do to a young person. Parents need to consider moving to a church where the life of God is, no matter how comfortable they are, or in spite of the fact that "we have always been Baptists, or Methodists, or whatever.")

By training our children we accomplish two purposes. One, we give them, early on, when it's easier to learn, the basic skills and abilities they need to get along with others and provide for themselves. The "elementary required courses," so to speak, are then out of the way. Now they can concentrate on learning the refining lessons of the Holy Spirit, which are sufficiently challenging! Young people who come to Christ later in life and

have no background in common courtesy, money man-
agement and responsible work habits, to name a few,
have a huge "course load" to carry all at once. And two,
we instill in them the knowledge of God's Word and
Christian truths and principles, so that the Holy Spirit
can call it to their remembrance (John 14:26) and apply
it to their personal needs.

Development, letting God do the changing, and training are three of God's fundamental patterns for parenting. We must understand them in order to cooperate
with God in the work of faith. Let's move on, now, to
some further parenting tips, or patterns, from our heavenly Father.

9

The Importance of Nurture

In the summer of 1990 I had a "spiritual"—the spiritual counterpart of a physical. For six hours I was examined thoroughly by three godly men in the areas of my soul and spirit.

You might ask, "Why get a spiritual? Did you have some pressing problem that needed to be fixed?" No, but I had a burning desire to be all I can for the glory of Jesus Christ. As a sixty-year-old man I know I am running my last lap on the race course God has laid out for me, and I want it to be the best lap I've ever run. I want to maximize my life. I want to finish well.

I went into my spiritual with two determinations. First, I wanted to answer every question my peers asked as honestly as possible. Second, I wanted to trust the

Lord to reveal any hidden areas that needed to be brought into the open.

A spiritual is not a cure-all. It is a time for insight, a time to deal with the past, set new goals for the future or discover new direction from God to better utilize a person's aptitude and skills.

My spiritual was profitable because all these things happened to some degree. But the major disclosure that came out of it was that as a child I had not been nurtured. I will say more about that later, but first. . . .

What Is Nurture?

Nurturing consists of two basic functions: nourishing and cherishing. Both are essential in rearing children. Both are biblical and, of course, both are qualities God manifests toward us, His children.

Nourishing

To nourish is to feed, and not just with physical food. As people made in the image of God we need nourishment on all three levels of our lives: body, soul and spirit.

The Bible is clear about our responsibility as parents to provide such nourishment for our children, as well. First Timothy 5:8 says, "If anyone does not provide for his own, and especially for those of his household, he has denied the faith, and is worse than an unbeliever." And 1 Thessalonians 2:11 explains how natural it is for a father to provide nourishment for the soul and spirit—"exhorting and encouraging and imploring . . . as a father would his own children."

Few good Christian parents could be accused of failing to provide food, clothing, shelter and health care for their children. Within reason, and within our budgets, we do the best we can to ensure our children's bodily comfort, safety and welfare.

The same cannot be said regarding our children's souls and spirits. Unfortunately, very few homes today offer adequate nourishment in these two areas. Instead, we all too often expect the school, church or outside programs to feed our children.

Scouting programs may do a wonderful job of sharing the importance of patriotism and good citizenship, for example, especially in the cases of children whose backgrounds do not include those values. But a child who sees patriotism manifested in the lives of the two most important people in his life—his parents—is much more likely to grow up loving his country.

In the matter of sex education, parents often neglect totally the need to provide nurture. Many Christian parents fiercely oppose the sex education programs offered by the public schools, but then never give their children any sex education at home. It is no wonder that the statistics for premarital sex and teenage pregnancy among Christian young people are nearly as high as those among secular teens.*

* See *Why Wait?* by Josh McDowell and Dick Day (Here's Life Publishers).

Another soul need: In how many Christian homes do stimulating discussions of current issues take place around the dinner table, offering our young people Christian perspectives on local, domestic and world events? We're more likely to plan the evening's TV watching between mouthfuls!

If we think Sunday school is enough to furnish our children with spiritual food we are in for a great disappointment.

First of all, it was never intended to so do. Sunday school was designed to *supplement* the Christian education given by parents in the home.

Secondly, what is offered in Sunday school is not enough. Most Sunday school teachers are sincere and dedicated, but they are not necessarily good teachers, nor do they always know a whole lot about the subjects they are teaching. And even those who are good teachers and have studied their topics carefully cannot spend enough time with their students to offer much more than information.

Please hear me: I praise God for those Sunday school teachers who give of themselves as role models and nurturers on Sunday morning and beyond! God has certainly used them mightily to affect the lives of children. But no matter how well the good teachers teach and how relevant their material, nothing can take the place of what children see and experience in the home.

The book of Deuteronomy offers a clear directive to parents about this matter of spiritual nurture. Look at chapter 6, verses 5–9:

"And you shall love the Lord your God with all your heart and with all your soul and with all your might. And these words, which I am commanding you today, shall be on your heart; and you shall teach them diligently to your sons and shall talk of them when you sit in your house and when you walk by the way and when you lie down and when you rise up. And you shall bind them as a sign on your hand and they shall be as frontals on your forehead. And you shall write them on the doorposts of your house and on your gates."

The spiritual nurture of our children is to be a daily, natural part of our lives. Think back on an average week in your home. Did any spiritual nurturing, any natural conversations about the things of God, take place? Once? Twice? Frequently?

It is not my purpose here to give exhaustive instructions about the how-to of spiritual nurture. Many fine books have been written in that field. Take time to visit the family section of your local Christian bookstore to discover the excellent resources available. We need to research the best ways to nurture our children's soul and spirit needs, taking into account their personalities and interests and the schedules and habits of our families. Then we must do it.

Cherishing

To cherish someone is to handle him or her gently and lovingly, especially in the early stages of life when he or she is very weak and tender. All children need to be cherished.

Why? First of all, young children are tender by nature. If you know a child whom you would not call tender, look at his or her environment. The child is probably surrounded by callousness, cruelty, harshness or even just a lack of general good manners and unselfishness. Children normally begin life with very gentle natures.

Secondly, we know that children need to be treated tenderly just by looking at the majority of adults. Most people have been beaten up at some point in their lives and have sore spots. Some are raw all over; some are sore only in certain areas where they have been hurt repeatedly.

Again, the Bible has much to say about cherishing. Isaiah 40:11 is one of many references in which God is pictured as caring gently for us. First Thessalonians 2:7 speaks of the tenderness of a nursing mother for her children, and suggests that Christians need to be equally loving with each other. Ephesians 5:29 mentions the importance of cherishing in the marriage relationship and declares Christ's cherishing love for the Church. Earlier in the same book (4:32) Christians are directed to offer tenderhearted forgiveness and kindness to each other.

Cherishing is a Christian value and practice, yet we have failed miserably. We do not show love and special attention to those who are newborns in body, soul and spirit.

Dudley Hall, a superb minister of God, told me of an astonishing incident that occurred while he was leading a men's retreat in Texas. During one of the sessions he asked the men who had never sat in their fathers' laps and been hugged to come to the front of the room, sit in his lap and allow him to hold them as their fathers should have.

Dudley said the men lined up to do this, and each one who sat in his lap cried his heart out. Here were men who had not been cherished by their fathers.

All forms of life are fragile in their infancy and need special care. We must not deprive our children any longer of their need to be hugged and treated gently and tenderly.

My Own Experience

I mentioned earlier my discovery, in the course of my spiritual, that as a child I had not been nurtured properly. It was a revelation about many of my personality and spiritual lacks, and also about my behavior toward my family.

Several factors contributed to the lack of nurture in my early years. First, since I grew up in a wealthy home in Jamaica in the 1930s I was partially reared by a nanny, a servant whose chief responsibility was to take care of me. She was a good woman; I remember her pushing me around in a "pram," the British word for a baby carriage.

It was not that my parents did not love me; I know they did. The fact that my primary care was given by an employee in our home was simply part of our culture. Added to this was my mother's insecurity (she was an unwanted child) and her poor health. When I was about two years old she had to leave Jamaica and go by boat to England for surgery. Back in those days it took a long time to make this trip, so my nanny probably gave me more time and care than did any other adult.

Then, at the ripe old age of seven, I went away to a boarding school. (This, too, was a fairly routine practice in the Jamaican upper class.) Run much like a military academy by the teachers and school administrators, the school left the boys to themselves in their dormitories, and you can be sure they did not treat each other with parental gentleness and love. It was more like survival of the fittest.

I was very lonesome for the first month; I remember crying myself to sleep during the opening week. But you don't cry in front of other boys. I had to live with my peers, so after the first four weeks I pretended I didn't care anymore and learned to stop crying. It is hard to imagine now, but after that year I never spent more than three months of any year in my parents' home.

My other school experiences were equally militaristic, with everything run by a bell, life fenced in on every corner and educational techniques intense. Each was a religious school, but I can remember only one teacher and one student who even vaguely resembled what I know now it means to be Christian. This, of course, turned me off to the faith; bad religion in the name of Christ is damaging to one's concept of Christianity.

The point I am trying to make is that in my early childhood my physical and to some extent my soul needs were nourished. But during my school years I received nourishment only in the areas of books and manners. And the tender loving care from being cherished was an unknown quantity.

As I look back on my own parenting years I realize that, in turn, I did not properly nurture my children. I did provide enough nourishment, both physical and spiritual, but I was not tender. I did not know how to cherish. I was never told the need for it and so did not do it.

To my upbringing was added the matter of living up to the image of a macho American man—an idea full of nonsense. We need to rid ourselves of it. It comes nowhere near to the image of God, in all His tenderness, gentleness, firmness, fairness, forgiveness, holiness, lovingkindness and wisdom.

So many times I was rough and hard with my children. I can remember spanking John too harshly. I did not empathize with him or ask his forgiveness. Many times when I said the right things I said them in the wrong way. There was no tenderness in what I said, no kindness, only harshness, contempt and anger.

By the grace of God I have realized, admitted to and sought forgiveness for failing, particularly, to cherish my children. Now I am seeking to make amends for it. Just before I wrote these words I called one of my daughters to see how she was doing since she and her husband are going through a rough time vocationally. In the past I would not have done this, thinking a phone call in the middle of the day a waste of good money. Now that I know the importance of cherishing, I see it as an investment in the nurture of my children's souls and spirits.

Oh, how much we fathers have to learn about fatherhood! And we who are Christians can learn so much from our heavenly Father, if we will, as well as from God-inspired books and from other fathers. We don't know much about golf or woodworking or other such subjects until we study them. We talk about them with other men, read, practice and become knowledgeable. We can do the same with fathering.

Mothers, you see, bond with their children before birth to some extent because they carry them in their wombs for nine months. But other than the act of conception fathers have little to do with their children until they come into the world. So fathers need to make special efforts in the whole area of nurturing. What a difference we could make in our families, our churches and our world if we took seriously this vastly important role!

My childhood in a rich Jamaican home was strongly influenced by Jamaican upper-class culture, just as my children's childhoods were influenced by Southern American culture, and yours are influenced by the culture that predominates where you live. We must remember that because something is culturally acceptable does not mean it is necessarily the best or necessarily Christian. We need to see the difference.

It would be easy to look at my upbringing and say, "That poor neglected child! Nobody cared about him! What kind of society does that to its children?"

Yet we have only to look around us to see that there are millions of children in America today who are not receiving nourishment or cherishing either. In many cases both parents work outside the home in order to uphold a certain standard of living and come home too tired and concerned about household chores to make any investment in the children, except to order them around.

Low-income couples and single parents are under a double burden in this regard. They need to work, sometimes even at two or three jobs, they cannot hire help for household repairs and they are exhausted when their children need special attention.

Other single- or double-income couples may spend plenty of time at home, but are so busy with their hobbies and clubs and friends that the children still lack the nurture they need and might be better off in a good daycare center!

We do not have to do anything God disapproves of, even if it is culturally acceptable. We need the Holy Spirit's direction and discernment as we examine our hearts and lifestyles to make sure our families are taking their proper place on our list of priorities. That proper place is *after* our relationship with God, but *before* ministry opportunities, work, friends and recreation.

Nurturing—nourishing and cherishing—is part of godly parenting, part of cooperating with God as He deals with our children in the work of faith. Our nurturing Father God is our model, our teacher in this important task.

In the next three chapters we will look at ways in which we can use—and control—our tongues to nurture our children's souls and spirits.

10

Mastering the Indicative Mood, or Establishing Relationships God's Way

For a few years I have discipled a group of single men ranging in age from 25 to 35 years. Several months ago I asked them a series of questions about their fathers, including:

- Did your father love you?
- Can you describe your father in one sentence?
- How do you view your father?

Only one of these men was absolutely sure his father loved him. The others *did not know*. Their fathers had not communicated their love clearly—the most important and vital truth in the relationship between father and son.

I made the same mistake with my own children. I communicated plenty of imperatives, or commands, and not nearly enough indicatives, or statements.

To understand this important principle for establishing successful relationships with our children, we need to turn briefly to the Greek language. The New Testament was written in Greek and its usage of Greek verbs offers a vital key to modern-day disciples. Bear with me for a brief explanation, and then we'll apply it to dealing with our children.

A verb is the part of a sentence that affirms action or state of being. This is done in the Greek through voice, tense and mood.

The mood, with which we are interested here, takes either the indicative or imperative form. It defines the action's relationship to reality.

The indicative mood denotes fact or possibility. To say, "He ate" states the fact. To say, "If he eats" states the possibility that he will. Dana and Mantley's *A Manual of Greek New Testament* defines the indicative this way: "The indicative is . . . the mood of certainty. . . . [It] states a thing as true." If I say, "I am a man, sixty years old. I live on Keiser Court and Johnnie is my wife," I am using the indicative mood. These are simple factual statements.

The imperative mood, on the other hand, is used to give a command. When a parent says, "Pick up your clothes," "Clean the garage" or "Take out the garbage," he or she is using the imperative mood. The parent is expressing his or her will, addressing the child's will and expecting a response.

In rearing children parents have to use the imperative mood frequently. It is impossible to do the task of parenting without giving orders and prohibitions:

"Stop hitting your sister."
"Brush your teeth every morning."
"You may not smoke in the house."

Remember: When a parent uses the imperative mood, his or her will is expressed, and the child must decide whether or not to obey. In essence, the use of the imperative sets up a potential confrontation. The indicative mood does not depend on anything the child does. It is simply a statement of fact.

The Way God Did It

A few years ago someone said to me, "Did you know that in the first eight chapters of Romans there is only one verb in the imperative (command) mood?"

I had to admit I did not. Curious, I decided to count the number of times the indicative mood is used in those same eight chapters. To my surprise I found 295 indicative mood verbs. One command to 295 statements of fact! And in the book of Ephesians there are 1101 indicatives as compared with 37 imperatives.

Now here is where an understanding of the Greek moods is important because we gain a new, key truth about God's parenting style. God, in His Word, written by men under the inspiration of the Holy Spirit, wanted to establish certain definite facts *before* He issued commands.

Do you know why?

Read carefully, because when you understand this concept it will enable you not only to live the Christian life in a fuller way, but also to be a better parent as you establish meaningful relationships with your children.

God, our Father, wishes to establish His relationship with each of us based on certain unquestionable realities.

You see, before God tells us to *do* anything He desires that we *know* some things for certain—things that establish His relationship with us, our relationship with Him, the resources available to us and many more certainties. By naming just a few of the 29 indicatives, absolute facts, to be found in Romans 5, for instance, we learn that:

- we have peace with God;
- we have access by faith into this grace;
- we exult in the hope of the glory of God;
- the love of God has been poured out into our hearts;
- we shall be saved from the wrath of God through Christ;
- grace abounds.

These certainties do not depend upon our doing anything, but only on God's grace extended to us in Jesus.

For any relationship to be happy and meaningful both parties must understand what the relationship is (Father God to son or daughter, human parent to human child, employer to employee) and feel assured of the relationship's strength and permanence. Then, and only then, can one party accept commands from the other, because he or she feels secure in the relationship and in the reason for those commands.

I had not seen the Christian life in this light before— as first of all an *absolutely secure relationship*, one of a loving Father committed to me. I had seen it rather as a Master-servant relationship, with the Master (God) giving commands and the servant (me) taking orders. But a relationship built and maintained on performance is never secure and satisfying because both parties know that performances may not always meet expectations.

Here we see the fundamental difference between imperatives and indicatives—a difference with deep implications for parenting. It is the difference between law and love.

Law works primarily in the imperative mood. It says you earn the indicatives—the positive statements—by obeying the imperatives—the commands. "Be a good boy or girl [imperative] so God [or Mommy or Daddy] will love you [indicative]."

Love works primarily in the indicative mood. It says, "Know these things for certain, and then it will be easy to obey: God loves you now, just as you are [indicative]; therefore do good [imperative] as a means of expressing your love back to Him '

If the imperatives (commands) are not *preceded* and *exceeded* by positive indicatives (statements of fact) they

will produce adverse reactions in our children—
reactions ranging from dislike to insecurity to doubt
about the relationship to outright rebellion.

Most parents would be surprised if at the end of a day
they could see the number of commands they have issued as compared with the number of assurances. In
many cases our use of the imperative far outweighs our
use of the indicative.

It is essential to establish certain indicatives with our
children before we give them imperatives. And we must
continually reinforce and strengthen the indicatives.

Under ideal conditions this should be a fairly easy
task. Parents have many opportunities to give small
children indicatives before they must begin giving imperatives.

"What a special girl you are!" "Mommy and Daddy
are so happy to have you in our family!" "We think
you're great!" Sincere, positive actions and words of
love and commitment can help a child establish a secure
basis from which he or she can receive commands and
know they are given in love for the child's own good,
and not out of harshness or demand.

Marriage and parenting are about the only major,
complicated relational tasks a person can attempt in this
life without knowing anything about them! Almost anyone can get a marriage license for a few dollars; no
special knowledge is required. And a person can have
children and know absolutely nothing about being a
parent.

Because we blunder into these complicated relationships and learn the ropes as we go, many of us do not realize we have done a bad or inadequate job of parenting until the children become teenagers. By then many dynamics have been set in motion, and we discover we cannot order our children around in the same way we could when they were small. Having made many mistakes both of omission and commission, we have to develop a different strategy. Unfortunately too many parenting books and seminars offer push-these-buttons-and-you-can-have-wonderful-children formulas, and only involve more imperatives.

It's Never Too Late to Start!

Our children need to know we love them just because we love them, and what this love means in practical terms. And the good news about establishing relationships God's way is that it's never too late to start! You can do it even if your child is in outright rebellion. I am doing it now with my grown children by affirming their worth in my eyes and building them up, indicatives I should have established long ago.

How do we do it? Indicatives need to be established and maintained. We do this in two ways.

First, we employ *verbal repetition*. Just as the Scriptures repeat certain facts about God over and over again, so we need to repeat truths about our relationships with our children frequently. They need to hear us affirm:

1) our unconditional love for them (I will love you regardless);

2) our unqualified acceptance (you are mine and I am yours, period);

3) our reliability and availability (I will be there when you need me);

4) their importance in God's eyes and ours (you were created for a purpose);

5) their worth as individuals (you are unique);

6) their competence and adequacy (I know you can do it!).

This repetition is a never-ending process, but so is the parent-child relationship. And once the indicatives are established in our children's lives they are easier to maintain.

Second, we act in ways that support the truths we have been declaring. Telling a child "I love you regardless" and then screaming because he or she bats a home run through the living room window doesn't strengthen a relationship. Promising to "be there" for a child and then consistently placing other activities (however noble) before family times undermines our credibility.

It is tremendously important to communicate to our children our unconditional love, acceptance and support, as well as vital truths about their worth and adequacy. Then when we give imperatives (as we will have to), our children can receive them on the basis of a healthy, secure relationship.

Our heavenly Father has established indicatives for

us and given us a marvelous pattern for relating to our children. But He has taught and demonstrated another principle as well: He is our *listening* Father. We will discuss His example and how we can model it for our children in the next chapter.

11

The Listening Parent

If your son experimented with drugs last week, would he sit down and share his experience with you? If not, why not? If so, what response would you give him?

If your daughter had a sexual encounter last week, would she feel free to talk with you about it? If not, why not? If so, how would you respond or react?

At the close of our first Sunday morning worship service on January 20, 1991, I received a revelation from God that drastically changed both my conception of Him as my Father and my understanding of what it means to be a listening, accepting, godly parent. It happened this way.

After preaching on our Father's desire for our worship to be in spirit and in truth (John 4:24), I suggested that He wants us to tell Him the way we feel about Him and about what He has done, is doing or is not doing in our lives. I urged the congregation to tell God any "beefs" they had with Him, knowing He would hear them not out of condemnation or judgment, but out of His love. Then they were to listen for His response.

Whatever I ask the congregation to do, I always do myself. So I began to talk to God, telling Him that for a long time I had observed a lack of action on His part with regard to something I considered to be a reasonable request.

I heard Him speak to my heart and say that He was not upset by what I had expressed. In fact, He seemed glad I was being transparent about my feelings, and He wanted me to listen to His explanation of the situation.

I agreed.

Then He said how glad He was I had shared my heart with Him because my honesty allowed Him to teach me in a new area. He was sorry I had not discovered this before, as it would have solved many of my problems.

The teaching was this: My perception of Him as a Father who would not allow me to express my true feelings was living itself out in the type of father I had become to my own children. Not only had I not encouraged them to share their feelings, I had actually *discouraged* them by responding with disappointment, disgust, blame and censure when they did. This was especially true when they had tried to share their feelings of frustration or anger with me as a parent.

As small children, then, our sons and daughters

quickly learned what to share and what not to share with me. But their feelings, though throttled and stuffed deep inside, did not go away. These became the breeding ground for anger, bitterness, resentment, low self-esteem and rebellion.

Not only had I left the children with bad feelings toward me, but I had lost the opportunity to help them know how to handle feelings.

Thoughts tumbled through my head quickly. Where had my misconception of my heavenly Father come from?

While I believe we are all responsible for our own actions, we do model our behavior and thinking on our background and upbringing. I do not wish to place blame on my parents, but two factors from my childhood undoubtedly accentuated my lack of good listening skills. Perhaps these will sound familiar to you, or will help you identify some other factors in your background that affect the way you listen to and communicate with your children.

First, I remembered the philosophy of most of my parents' adult friends, one that was common for that generation: "Children should be seen and not heard." In fact, I can recall clearly being patted on the head while some adult on the tennis court repeated this saying.

Second, since religion in our home was of a very legalistic nature, especially as expressed by my mother, I would never have thought of sharing my feelings about certain failures. The way I heard the adults in my home talk about those who drank or committed adultery was absolute insurance I would not admit to such sins if I did commit them!

For the first time in my life, that morning in January, I saw clearly that our God of truth wants me to share the truth of what is going on inside of me. Then I can listen for His explanation, response and help. This was an awesome revelation. It was as if a 500-watt lightbulb had been turned on inside my head. I began to see what kind of heavenly Father we have, and what kind of ungodly father I had been. I repented!

There is an amazing verse in the Psalms that underscores the idea of truthfulness in our relationship with God. It is Psalm 137:9 "How blessed will be the one who seizes and dashes your little ones against the rock." And that is the end of the chapter. No explanation comes after it.

What in the world are we to gather from such a quotation?

Let me tell you the context in which we find this verse. Psalm 137 is the expression of a Jewish captive in Babylon. One of his captors had tauntingly asked him to sing a song of Zion, his homeland. Not surprisingly, the captive not only had lost his song, but was feeling bitter and resentful. Out of these emotions came his angry thoughts toward his captors: "I wish someone would take your children and throw them against the rocks!"

Why did God allow these words to be recorded in the holy Scriptures? *Because He wants us to know it is all right to tell Him how we are feeling.* He will never reject or condemn us for sharing what is in our hearts. When we tell Him our feelings, He is able to help us work through them.

We read in the New Testament that we are to "come boldly unto the throne of grace, that we may obtain mercy, and find grace to help in time of need" (Hebrews 4:16, KJV). This is God's invitation to those of us who have "blown it," who have sinned and behaved badly. We can get all the help we need to repent of and recover from the things we have done.

What a gracious God we serve! Oh, that I had been this kind of father to my own children!

Breaking the Cycle

The destructive cycle of stifling people, not allowing them to express their thoughts and feelings, must be broken somewhere. I am seeking to do it in my family line, and I pray God will help me be successful.

The Monday morning after God spoke to me so clearly about the importance of being a listening parent, I wrote a letter to my children, repenting for this failure and asking their forgiveness. After describing my revelation from God, I continued with these thoughts:

> I realize I have not given you the same freedom [God] has given us all. It has become clear to me that my responses to you have more often made it easier for you not to share with me what you were really feeling. I realize that I put you down, I condemned you. . . . Much of this came out of wrong thinking

and attitudes on my part—my impatience, my gruffness and hard way of speaking, my lack of understanding that you were children and were acting like children, my strong convictions and wrong ideas about parent-child relationships . . . the "children should be seen and not heard" philosophy of my childhood. [All these] kept me from being the kind of father I could have and should have been.

For this I repent and ask your forgiveness. I ask you to share with me anything and everything that might be in your heart out of the past—no matter what—so we can have clear communication and thus communion and a deeper love. I understand you might have some very unpleasant things to share and say—I am prepared for this and accept it as part of the price I must pay for my failure to be a godly father.

Thank God the "ballgame is not over." I desire to finish well, to be the best for you and for God. In the future please feel free to express to me anything and everything you feel or think. I will listen and respond by the grace of God as I should. This does not mean I will agree, but I will listen and respect your point of view. . . .

In all probability I will fail at times. When I do, please remind me of this letter. Pray I will make all the inner adjustments that will make me the kind of father God is.

I urge you in the light of all this to do two things. First, always tell your Father God how you think and feel. Hide nothing. Be totally open to Him. He will hear with sympathy and understanding. Then listen to Him, give Him a chance to respond to You. Yield in faith and trust to Him . . . remembering it is really impossible for a child to understand all a father does or says.

Second, pray you can create an atmosphere with your children that will enable them to tell you everything, failures as well as successes. In this way you can be God's full agent to them.

I have shared my heart . . . and ask forgiveness. God is good and I am sure you will be. Whatever there is between us let's get rid of it for His sake and for ours and our children's.

The children have responded to me since then. My two sons were able to express in a good way how they felt in their hearts. At my request, one of them gave me a list of the things I had failed in from his point of view.

One daughter, the child most like me, explained she had already told me in the past how she felt, and she had, when we had some very hurtful arguments.

I am grateful to God that at this point in our lives our relationships are good and getting better.

Perhaps the hypothetical situations I described at the beginning of this chapter were more real in your life than not. Perhaps your children used to come to you and talk, but don't anymore. A parent's reactions to a child's failures at an early age set the pattern for communication in the later years.

I hope that this chapter has encouraged you as we have talked about the tremendous listening parent we have in our Father God. Knowing what He is like and that through the indwelling Holy Spirit He can give us the power to be like Him should steer us away from guilt over our past failures with our children.

First John 1:9 says that if we confess our sins, He is faithful and just to forgive us our sins, and to cleanse us from all unrighteousness. What a loving heavenly Father we have! And how He longs for us to share His kind of listening, fatherly love with our children.

12

Giving Glory

One of the greatest errors of my life in dealing with people in general and with my children in particular has been my failure to give them glory, the glory due them as individuals created by God with unique talents, abilities and personalities. One result was that at least one of my children hung around with "the wrong crowd" because those people gave him glory: They appreciated him verbally and non-verbally when I had failed to do so.

The need for glory—another way of describing self-worth, significance or value in one's own eyes—is a soul need. Even as the human body has certain needs and desires that must be met for growth and health, so the soul, the real inner person, has basic cravings that must be fed.

We are aware of physical needs but not quite as conscious of our soul needs. The mother who would never think of letting her baby go unfed in body may well be starving the same child's soul.

It is important for parents to realize that God has designed a healthy and proper way to meet every legitimate need an individual has. If that need is not met in the right, God-ordained way, the individual will be driven to seek fulfillment somewhere else.

Have you ever seen a person eating out of a garbage can and been revolted? How in the world could he or she do that? Remember: A starving person will eat *anything*. The devil knows how to use our driving needs to our destruction, tempting us to satisfy our needs in God-forbidden ways. Starving souls are easy prey and targets for the enemy.

The dictionary defines glory as exalted praise, honor or distinction bestowed by common consent. Glory makes a person feel honored, illustrious or significant.

As I mentioned earlier, glory is another word for self-worth or self-love. And we all need proper self-worth as food for the soul. After all, we live with ourselves; if we do not like ourselves we are in trouble, for we have no way to escape. But if we really love ourselves as Jesus commanded us to do (Mark 12:31), we are secure enough to love other people and deal fairly and kindly even with those who dislike us.

You see, the Christian life is walked out on two "legs": one is a proper self-image and the other is a proper image of God, knowing God as He really is, not as the caricature we so often see of Him. Each is basic and essential to satisfactory, and satisfying, Christian living.

The vast majority of Christians I know have at least one severely damaged leg, if not two. If either leg is faulty, a Christian will limp through life, despite all other advantages or privileges.

One of our parental responsibilities, which we have already discussed, is to educate our children properly in the things of God, giving them accurate pictures of who He is. But we also need to impart the truth about ourselves as children of God—that we were created in His image, are of vast worth in His sight and, no matter what we have done, can be restored to a full and intimate relationship with Him.

I want to make one important distinction here: There is a difference between a *damaged* self-image and an *immature* one. An immature understanding of oneself is natural, and is matured through the processes of life. Proper care of any living thing will result in proper growth. A damaged self-image must be healed and restored.

Two Types of Damaged Self-Images

A person manifests a damaged self-image in one of two ways: by thinking too much of himself or by thinking too little of himself.

Those who think too much of themselves are called

"proud," and pride is an abomination to God. He knows, of course, when pride is caused by a damaged self-image. He longs to work with us to heal it and remove the false partitions that block our hunger for His righteousness.

Many Christians have interpreted the fact that they think too little of themselves as humility. It is not: It is inverted pride. A person with this problem seeks to call attention to himself or herself because of perceived deficiencies. While inverted pride is not as objectionable to others as is thinking too much of oneself, it is just as damaging, and makes a wholesome life impossible.

From my experience I would say that there are at least twenty people who think too little of themselves for every one who thinks too much of himself. The Scriptures teach us to strive for balance in our self-images: "I say to every man among you not to think more highly of himself than he ought to think; but to think so as to have sound judgment, as God has allotted to each a measure of faith" (Romans 12:3). Or, as the Phillips translation puts it, "Don't cherish exaggerated ideas of yourself or your importance, but try to have *a sane estimate of your capabilities by* the light of the faith that God has given to you all" (italics mine).

God's Design for Healthy Self-Images

Parents: God's design for the nurture and growth of healthy self-images in our children involves us! We are to be the source from which our children fill their inner soul needs for glory, value, self-worth. If children do not get glory from us, they will get it somewhere else.

Why do I say this is God's design? Because Jesus, God's own Son, received His glory from His Father. "It is My Father who glorifies Me," Jesus told a group of people on one occasion (see John 16:14). And we all remember the Father saying from heaven, "This is My beloved Son, in whom I am well-pleased" (Matthew 3:17). What His Father thought of Him was what Jesus prized most.

Just so, the glory our children receive from us seems to matter more to them than any other glory, even if they won't admit it. That is why self-images damaged in the home by neglect and ignorant parenting are so difficult to heal. When tender life forms are hurt by the grower, the damage is painful. One angry young adult woman, whose father had sexually molested her and whose mother had rejected her, still slept with her teddy bear—a gift from parents who never gave her the glory she so desperately needed.

We give glory to our children in at least three ways: by the spoken word, by rewards and by increased responsibilities.

Words, Words, Words

In the entire realm of spiritual health nothing is more important than words. What money is to commerce, words are to the inner person. Words are literally soul food.

Parents, then, can most easily and often feed their children's soul needs for glory with words—words of praise, affirmation, commendation, approval and applause. Watch a small child's face light up when his mom or dad exclaims over a picture or school paper he has done. Watch a child of any age brighten when a parent expresses approval of an attitude or action. And fathers, watch your teenage daughter's reaction when you compliment her appearance or treat her with gentlemanly courtesy. This kind of glory-giving may do more than you'll ever know to reinforce her in her search for healthy male-female relationships.

Words of affirmation are particularly important. Tell your child you appreciate who he or she *is*: "I like you for yourself, for all the qualities and traits that make you you." Make sure your children receive not only performance-based appreciation, but affirmation of their worth as human beings.

Rewards

Another way of giving glory is by rewards. Dinner out with Dad or Mom, a party in honor of an achievement, a birthday celebration, a new dress, a special privilege, a little extra spending money—all may say, "You've done well." Rewards tend to affirm performance, so be careful to balance them with affirmation for the inner person, as well.

Responsibility

Increasing a child's responsibilities may also give him or her glory. By this I don't mean loading on chores. I mean things like allowing a teenage son to run errands with the family car, to care for a younger brother or sister occasionally or to help out in the family business. This may be a way of saying, "We trust you and believe you are capable of doing this important task."

One family we knew had a lovely daughter, Janie, their youngest child, whose low sense of self-worth finally manifested itself in a suicide attempt. The girl's therapists suggested to her parents that they give Janie some absolutely necessary, vital chore to help her feel indispensable.

Janie's mother told me, "Reflecting on what the therapist said, I remembered that before assigning household chores to the older children we asked each one to tell us which job he or she disliked the most and which one he or she disliked the least. Then each was allowed to choose his or her task and taught how to do it properly. As the children began to receive praise for their specialties the work always, without fail, improved drastically.

"We realized that in raising Janie we had drifted away from this practice. During a family work assignment time we encouraged her to select more difficult work. She picked cleaning the kitchen and became the best ever at it. Her face still lights up when I ask, 'Would you please get the kitchen in shape? When you do it I know it will be perfect.' "

God's Glory and the World's

In this matter of giving glory, just as in any parenting task, we need the guidance and wisdom of the Holy Spirit to help us give His kind of glory, not the world's.

The world's glory is often superficial, insincere and manipulative. It may be overdone or driven by selfishness or ulterior motives. Unless we are giving glory out of the resources of God's love and wisdom, our children will sense that it is false. False glory, the world's glory, will not satisfy our children's soul needs.

Another thing about the world's glory: It can change in a fraction of a second. I remember hearing a runner in one of the Olympic competitions tell how reporters gathered around him when they thought he had won a race. But when the officials announced he had really been beaten by one one-hundredth of a second, the flock left him in an instant to crowd around the newly announced winner.

The world recognizes with glory only those who are better than others, thus enabling only a few persons to receive its praise.

But God's kind of glory is real, lasting and available for all to receive. If we parents are working with God and listening to His directions as we deal with our children we will give glory on His behalf—the right amounts to the right child at the right time. It can be a vital link in the work of faith God is doing in their lives.

13

Money in the Bank

How many times I have been frustrated with my children because they would not receive what I was giving them—good stuff in the way of Christian education or guidance! It was even more frustrating to know that they were eager to receive from their friends advice and information that I knew was detrimental to their spiritual and emotional growth.

Why won't our children listen to us and benefit from what we want to offer them? After all, look at all we have done for them!

The answer, often, is that we do not have "money" in their "banks," and their friends do.

Think of it like this. Suppose I get a notice from my bank that says: "Your account is overdrawn. We have returned your check in the amount of $191.89 to the Alligator Plumbing Company. Your account has been charged an overdraft fee of $20.00."

This would indicate that my transactions in this matter were deficient. And if I choose to make such transactions a regular practice it will not be long before the bank breaks off its relationship with me.

The same is true in our personal relationships. How often have you said, as I have, "After all I've done for that child I don't understand why we don't have a good relationship. Why isn't he or she willing to accept my good advice?"

An honest mental review reveals the truth. You and I may have put much into our children's lives, providing not only the basic necessities but luxuries, too. We may have given them all kinds of things—*except what they wanted or counted as valuable.*

The Laws of Banking

We can understand an important dynamic of developing good relationships by looking at two basic laws of banking.

One, deposits must exceed withdrawals. This is fairly simple: We must put in more money than we take out. It is not enough to keep deposits and withdrawals equal because the bank may keep some of our money for handling our accounts.

Two, deposits must be made in a currency accepted by the bank. An item may be of great value to you or me, yet be totally unacceptable to the bank. A product considered valuable for bartering by the members of a remote tribe in Africa—cows, for example—may not be useful as currency in New York City.

How These Laws Work in Relationships

All relationships, especially those between parents and children, are best established by keeping the proper balance between deposits and withdrawals.

What are deposits? Deposits are anything and everything we do for someone else that has value in his eyes. Deposits communicate, "You are important to me; I care for you. I love you. You count as far as I'm concerned." Topics we have discussed like nourishing and cherishing, using indicatives, listening and giving glory can all be deposits.

The parent-child relationship begins when the parent makes a deposit in the child's life. Parents certainly feel that the acts of giving birth to and nurturing a baby are deposits, though they may be thrown in our faces later: "I never asked to be born!"

While deposits at first may seem to be all on the parent's part, once the child begins to cuddle and smile the relationship is grounded, for no relationship can be established or maintained by one person. The more deposits each makes in the other's life, the stronger the relationship.

I once asked one hundred men to tell me the most memorable thing they had ever done with their fathers. The number one answer was "The time we went fishing together." Another top one was "The time I went to work with Dad." Few other events even registered. Fishing together and going to work together counted as deposits for those boys They were activities that really communicated fatherly love and concern.

What are withdrawals? Imperatives—commands—will count as withdrawals. In our home we expected everyone to participate in the household duties necessary to maintaining our life together as a family: "Ruth Ann, please wash the dishes; John, please mow the lawn."

Other requests for help, which are a necessity in the give and take of all relationships, are usually withdrawals, too. This is especially true when the requests all come from the parent or all come from the child, making for a one-sided relationship. If properly balanced, however, our requests for help can make the other party feel needed and appreciated, thus giving glory—a deposit.

Negative encounters that put strain on our parent-child relationships are also withdrawals. When John and I had an argument over his failure to wash the car one day, as he had promised he would, I lost my temper with him and strained our relationship. I once promised Ruth Ann I would take her shopping but had to renege because of a last-minute church meeting. As she was disappointed, my broken promise was a withdrawal.

Just as a bank account can stand only so many withdrawals, so it is with our parent-child relationships. We need to make sure there have been enough deposits to cover them.

Jim was a freshman in college when he came to live in

our home, and ever since then we have considered him one of our family, a precious son. He had been on his own ever since his parents died, and told us he needed and wanted a family, especially the input of a godly man in his life.

Being part of a family seemed to give Jimmy real joy. It was a deposit, as far as he was concerned. But was it enough to counteract the withdrawals we were making, particularly when I disagreed with this independent young man's decisions on occasion, and asked him to consider my advice?

Johnnie has shared with me that one morning Jim came into the room where she was having her quiet time. He was beginning to wonder if he had made the right choice in moving in with us. He had not realized, he said, that having the input of a godly man in his life might mean some of his opinions and decisions would be up for discussion!

Asking the Lord to give her wisdom and guide her words, Johnnie reassured Jimmy that I would always advise him out of a caring heart, even if he sometimes misunderstood me.

Years later Jimmy wrote me that he knew we loved him when we advised him, at one point, not to quit college to go on the road for a year with a Christian singing group. Apparently the deposits the Lord helped us to make in Jim's life did exceed the withdrawals!

Back to Basics

Here we return to the basic building blocks for this book: Christian parents need to be relating intimately to

God and cooperating with Him if they want to know which deposits and withdrawals are acceptable in the life of each individual child. This matter of deposits and withdrawals may become glaringly evident when a child leaves God. At a time like that, we parents are often made uncomfortably aware—sometimes by the wandering child—that we have taken out too much.

Here are three general principles to keep in mind as you seek God's guidance about making deposits in the lives of your children.

1. Give of yourself. Giving of yourself is vital and always means giving quality time—quality time, that is, as considered acceptable by the child.

In trying to express love to John once when he was quite young, I promised to take him to Disney World. Personally I have an intense dislike for that kind of amusement; I get bored. So, seeking to fulfill this obligation and still please myself, I decided to get another dad to come and take his child so the two children could play on the rides together while the fathers kept each other company.

I ended up calling several persons. Each one, in turn, agreed to go but then called back to say something had come up.

One day as I was thinking about the situation I said out loud, "I wonder what the Lord is trying to say to me?" Immediately Ruth Ann, who was in the same room, answered, "Maybe He is telling you to go and have a good time with John yourself."

Either I never heard her, or I turned her comment off because it did not meet my need. The trip fell through; we didn't go at that time because I had set conditions on it, conditions for meeting *my* need, not John's.

One day some time later when I was questioning the Lord about this, He said quite clearly, *I spoke to you through Ruth Ann. I wanted you to go alone with John, because that is what he needs.*

Wow! I never thought God would speak to me through a teenager. What a mistake! I sought immediately to remedy the situation. John and I went to Disney World by ourselves, and I learned a lesson: I was more interested in my happiness than in giving of myself to John, and that attitude could not put money in his bank.

2. Give gifts and activities of genuine interest to the child and not just you. This will differ with children's sexes, ages and interests. Jimmy and I may listen to some music he has written. If I go to a movie with John it should be one of his choice. If Ruth Ann wants to play checkers I shouldn't insist we play gin rummy.

You may want to introduce your child to the classics by reading *Treasure Island* together, but if that is not his or her idea of a good time, he or she will consider it a withdrawal. I'm not saying parents can't carry out such activities; just be sure that they are balanced with deposits that the *children* consider deposits. Many times in our relationships with our children Johnnie and I thought we were doing things they would be happy about, only to discover later we had made unacceptable deposits; they had not registered or been received. And some of the deposits they would have received, we did not give.

3. When you see a need in your child's life, make a deposit. Here again we must pay attention to the most fundamental principle of all: walking in the Spirit according to His wisdom and directions. He alone can help us connect certain behaviors as our children's ways of expressing their needs. And He can help us know what deposits will fill those needs.

"Mommy, I don't feel like going to school today."

Johnnie told me she had noticed that Ruthie was beginning to say this quite often. Finding nothing wrong physically, she would send an unhappy little girl off to school, much to her own motherly distress.

So Johnnie went to our heavenly Father for His understanding of the situation. He prompted her to reflect on what day, in particular, Ruthie was feeling "sick." Sure enough, Johnnie realized it was always on Tuesday. The next Tuesday morning, when Ruthie began to complain of feeling ill, Johnnie asked, "Ruthie, what do you do at school on Tuesdays?" Ruthie broke into tears.

"Oh, Mommy, we have art today. I can't stand it! It makes me sick to my stomach. Mine is always the worst in the class. Everybody else loves art."

Johnnie, who had always hated the creative arts, too, because she felt she was not good at them, related to Ruth Ann's frustration. The Holy Spirit prompted her to offer our daughter the comfort He had offered her earlier in life.

"Ruthie, God created each person with his or her own gifts. These gifts are often different, making each person special because they are not like everyone else. You have a sweet spirit and a love for people. These are wonderful gifts from God! You don't have to be the best in art; just relax and do the best you can. That will make your father and me happy."

Johnnie's loving, empathetic words apparently helped Ruthie. And, thanks to the wisdom and understanding given by our loving Father, she knew how to encourage and pray for our daughter on Tuesdays.

Johnnie had made a deposit—giving glory and indicatives—that filled a need in Ruth Ann's life.

Deposits and withdrawals. Nearly all of the verbal and nonverbal exchanges between parent and child fall into one of these two categories. With God's direction we can learn to balance our children's bank accounts so that their needs will be met.

14

Responding to the Gaps

A gap is the space that exists between what is and what ought to be.

Our world is full of gaps. People are full of gaps. Leaders are full of gaps. Institutions are full of gaps. All of these are easy to see—with the exception, of course, of the gaps in our own lives!

We are affected mostly by gaps in those who are close to us—our spouses, our children, members of our extended families, the neighbors, the people we work with, the other Christians at our church. Gaps in people to whom we relate infrequently are not nearly as troublesome.

When we look at parent-child relationships, we find that the hardest gaps to handle are those between our expectations of each other's behavior, and the actual behavior.

Among other behaviors during his rebellious period, John started chewing tobacco and dipping snuff. I cannot tell you how objectionable this was to me personally, not to mention the idea of John's physical well-being and social acceptability.

I saw other gaps in John, as well. Many times he had the wrong kind of friends. His room was untidy. He refused to take his studies seriously.

At the same time, John was seeing gaps in me, his father. I am sure these were as bothersome and annoying to him as his were to me. One time he gave me a list of them, which follows:

> You speak down to me when you are angry . . .
> You go from one extreme to another . . .
> You give destructive criticism . .
> You say one thing and do another . . .
> You do not give me much personal communication . . .
> You give me gifts, rather than affection   .
> You hold things over my head in order to keep me under control.

Right or wrong, he perceived me in this way—filled with gaps. To many of them I could only plead "Guilty." But I put them *all* into my prayer book, so I could pray about them.

Parents and children all have gaps in their lives, big ones and small ones, serious ones and insignificant ones, inherited ones and developed ones, injury-inflicted ones and choice ones, real ones and imaginary ones. Living with each other makes us constantly aware of these gaps, and there is nothing wrong with seeing them. In fact, the Lord often shows them to us.

The big question is: When you see a gap in your child—the wrong type of friend, low or failing grades, bad study habits, sloppy or unconventional dress, drug or alcohol use—how do you respond? We have two choices: intercession or accusation.

Intercession and Accusation

Have you ever had someone "go to bat" for you when the solution to your problem was beyond your ability? Do you remember how you felt toward the person who stepped in on your behalf? Did you feel a deep sense of gratitude? A desire to repay him or her in some way? A closeness?

The person who goes to bat for you is called an intercessor, one who intervenes, mediates, interposes on your behalf, sometimes at great cost to himself.

Now think about it from this angle. Do you have any problem remembering how you felt toward people who, in your time of need, responded with blame, censure, condemnation, criticism, fussing or accusation? Are you drawn to such people? Do you want to be around them? Do you want them as friends?

Of course not. Their reactions leave us feeling

- inferior
  unworthy

- inadequate
- hopeless and
- full of self-pity and guilt.

Someone who responds to a need by blaming, condemning, censuring and criticizing is called an accuser.

The Bible calls the devil an accuser, because he delights in reminding us (and God) of our sins and mistakes. By doing so he discourages us, making us feel all of those bad feelings listed above. The devil has a certain future, however: "The accuser of our brethren has been thrown down, who accuses them before our God day and night" (Revelation 12:10).

When God saw the gaps in our behavior, the big spaces that exist between His rightful expectations of us and our willful actions, what did He do? When He looked at the gap that separated us from Him, cutting off intimate fellowship between us, what was His response?

He could have accused, and been perfectly right and just in doing so, but He did not. He made a plan to fill the big gap of our severed relationship with Him, and the resulting gaps caused by our separation.

He sent Christ into our world, not to accuse or condemn us, but to save us by His death on the cross and through His resurrection. Our God provided all that would be necessary to close the gaps between ourselves and Him. And now Jesus sits in heavenly places interceding for us with perfect compassion and understanding.

As Romans 8:34 puts it, "Christ Jesus is He who died,

yes, rather who was raised, who is at the right hand of God, who also intercedes for us." And Hebrews 7:25 says, "He [Jesus] is able to save forever those who draw near to God through Him, since He always lives to make intercession for them."

Jesus can speak on our behalf because He lived on earth in a body like ours. He experienced firsthand the stress that the evil one brings against all people. He knows how difficult it is, and He knows all we go through. He was "in all points tempted like as we are, yet without sin" (Hebrews 4:15, KJV).

When we are in union with Christ Jesus, the gap between God and us is completely filled. We are complete in Him, and as far as God is concerned a gap no longer exists.

We evangelicals need to learn this truth: We have been justified, made righteous, in Jesus—as righteous as Jesus is righteous. We each have a perfect relationship with God.

We can, of course, draw closer to Him in fellowship. But He can never draw closer to us than He already has. Our relationship with Him is made complete in Christ. It is a gift, a privilege, an opportunity.

Now we must take advantage of the fact that God is our Father. If we are truly seeking to pattern our parenting after that of our heavenly Father, and if we are in union with Jesus, we will respond to gaps in our children in the way He would.

Does accusing our children help them change?

Does it give them hope?

Does it encourage them?

Of course not. Accusation discourages and leads to destruction of the fellowship that could exist between us. All of our fussing, accusing and blaming John for his dipping and chewing did not help one little bit. We learned a big lesson from this: He is still our son, regardless of what he does, but he will not hang around us if all we do is criticize. If he does not hang around us, we will have no input in his life. Since he is a social animal, as we all are, he will then run around with the people who do accept him, people who do not care about or criticize him for his faults and gaps.

Accusation only destroys relationships.

Intercession releases God to be God in all the situations of life. For some reason He chose to allow Himself and His actions to be limited by the extent of our prayers.

"You do not have because you do not ask," James reminds us (4:2). Often we do not have those things we desire for others simply because we did not ask God to provide them. When we ask Him, He acts—in His own way and time, but He acts.

Many times I have suddenly become aware that a change has occurred, a gap has been filled in one of our children. Then I realize I shouldn't be surprised: It is what I have been interceding for, asking God for. And often, as I intercede before Him on behalf of one of my children, He instructs me how to cooperate with Him in responding to or filling a gap. This is part of the work of faith.

During his high school years Richard read one book, and that, as best we can remember, was under duress! He was not what you would call a student. We tried not to criticize or make unhelpful remarks about this gap. Instead we interceded, asking God to change Richard so he would be able to handle university courses and learn to love all the riches books can offer.

Amazingly (although not in God's eyes) Richard became a lover of history. To love history, you must be an avid reader. He was changed, and has stayed that way ever since. As he is now a minister, a profession that requires him to do much reading, we are very grateful.

We had much the same experience with John, except the miracle is greater. John ceased any serious study when he was a sophomore in high school. He barely made it through and then in his first year of college was placed on probation. Here was a gap that needed to be filled!

Through intercession, and obedience to the direction of the Holy Spirit for dealing with John, the gap *was* filled: In junior college John made the dean's list!

Remember: God is the Creator, the Changer. He alone can create a new life, a new heart, a new man or woman. Our part is to intercede, releasing God to do in others what He knows needs to be done, and not what we think needs to be done.

Whatever we are, we are because of the intercession of Christ and of others in His Body. Whatever our children are, they are because of the intercession of Christ, ourselves and others who care deeply enough to pray for them. If this is not true, what would be the point of prayer?

Mistakes We Make in Gap-Filling

It is easy for us as sincere, earnest Christian parents who want the best for our children to jump in without the Holy Spirit's leading, and thus make mistakes. Here are three mistakes we make often.

1. We seek to fill gaps that are filled only by the maturing process.   Many behaviors we perceive as gaps in our children are due to immaturity—literally, to childishness. Some changes will simply come in the natural course of the God-ordained maturing process. Perhaps you have heard parents criticize a small child for refusing to sit still through a long, late evening church service. How unfair! Small children need many hours of sleep, and to accuse them of naughtiness when they are simply too tired to cooperate is to misunderstand normal patterns of child development.

Through intercession, intimate relationship with our heavenly Father and openness to resources He brings along (books, speakers and so on) we can find out how to cooperate with Him to provide an environment where children can mature emotionally, mentally and spiritually, as well as physically.

2. We have unrealistic expectations of performance. I often got angry at John because he was not enthusiastic about yard work early on Saturday mornings. I thought this showed a gap of laziness and indifference. I was determined to fill that gap—not only to make him perform, but to make him perform with the right attitude, as well!

You can guess how much success I had. It was unrealistic for me to expect a teenager to *want* to cut lawns on Saturday morning. This is not to say I was wrong in giving him chores and responsibilities; I simply needed to make sure my expectations took his age and humanity into account.

3. We seek to fill the spiritual gap. We have mentioned already this passion on the part of Christian parents to get our children to make decisions for Christ as quickly as possible. Much of our motivation is out of fear, which can be alleviated by getting a word of faith for our wandering children, and then acting on it in the walk and work of faith.

Yes, children can and do accept Christ at early ages, but let's let God do it in His time and way. Manley Beasly, a choice servant of Christ who is now with his Lord, used to tell me he did not go by what his children said about their relationships with God. He looked, instead, for changed lives. This is scriptural.

If we push children too far and too fast in filling spiritual gaps they will react in one of two negative ways. First, they may rebel, outwardly or inwardly. Outward rebellion may manifest itself as stubbornness, hostility and disobedience. Inward rebellion, far more subtle and terribly dangerous, causes children to conform because it is expedient to do so. But as soon as they leave home they drop out of everything spiritual.

Second, children who are pushed into early "decisions" for Christ can become little Pharisees. In my opinion this is worse than rebellion. These children know and say all the right words and do all the right things. But their hearts are not changed. The Christian Church is full of such people, plastic Christians performing evangelical rituals. Rituals are not wrong if they come out of a changed heart. But without changed hearts to motivate them, such performances are spiritually empty and dead.

How to Respond

Yes, our children have gaps, many of them. Some may never go away. How should Christian parents respond?

1. Stay in union with Christ.   This will help you become an intercessor. See accusation as none of your business. When you do fall into accusation, confess it as sin before God and ask your children to forgive you. Having to ask anyone for forgiveness is strong motivation for not doing something again!

2. Seek His voice.   As you intercede before God for your children, ask Him how you can cooperate with Him in the work of faith.

3. Remember that many gaps are perceived gaps. Some gaps are due only to the culture or the age or gifting of your child. They may also be projections of your own gaps Ask God to give you discernment about this.

Intercession, not accusation, is God's way of responding to gaps. In the next chapter we will explore some principles God has taught Johnnie and me as we have interceded for our children's gaps. They involve cooperating with Him in drawing the lines that govern our children's behavior.

15

Knowing Where to Draw the Lines

"Take that damn earring off, or get out of this house," exploded Gene, a deacon and dedicated member of my church, when he saw an earring dangling from his son's ear.

Sitting in my office relating this story, Gene looked at me with a sheepish smile and continued, "As soon as those words came out of my mouth the Holy Spirit said, *What about your tattoo?*

"I remember clearly the day I came home from the Army and walked into the kitchen, peeling off my shirt," Gene explained. "The moment my mother saw the dagger I'd had tattooed on my arm, she burst into tears. My father, hearing her sobs, rushed in to investigate. He saw the tattoo, understood her tears and blurted out, 'I wonder what in hell he'll do next!' ''

"Gene," I said, as we both broke into loud laughter, "I think it's wonderful you've grown so much as a Christian that right in the middle of all that emotional conflict and anger you heard God speaking so clearly!"

To Fight or Not to Fight

Why was Gene asking for my help and advice about his son's behavior? Because he knew I had gone through an "earring crisis" myself. Such concerns about cultural conformity, behavior and apparel seem to consume lots of parental energy and attention, especially during our children's adolescent stages.

John was about eighteen when he told us he was going to get his ear pierced. I reacted just as Gene did, except I do not think I said *damn* out loud. But I did put my foot down. No son of mine would be caught dead wearing an earring!

Since we were already having trouble with John on many other fronts, this just intensified the battle. One of our other children, who had observed several of our verbal skirmishes, called me and said, "Dad, don't draw the line here. This isn't a serious matter, and it's not worth fighting over."

Usually I am not a very good listener, especially during emotional stress. But this time I was. After thinking (and, I believe, praying) it over, I yielded reluctantly to the good advice and stopped objecting to John's getting his ear pierced.

Two incidents that happened within a short period of time cured me not only of "anti-earringism," but of a lot of other personal "anti's," and gave me much-needed insight from the Holy Spirit in this matter of drawing lines and determining acceptable boundaries for our children's behavior.

Incident Number 1. Mike was a young man in our church who wore an earring and had long hair. To call him unconventional would be to put it mildly. Yet he was the only young man in our church who really reached out to John in a consistent way, a way John would accept, when he was in the worst stages of rebellion. Here in our church, mostly full of "straights," one of the few "non-straights" reached out effectively to John. How could I feel judgmental toward him?

Incident Number 2. After John's initial turnaround toward a relationship with Jesus he headed off to college. His earring, long hair and chewing tobacco went, too.

At the small college he was going to attend we waited in the lobby while he registered. There, playing a pinball machine, was a young man who had on every symbol that people of my generation associate with rebellion and the drug culture. I learned later that he was from Colorado.

By the grace of God I kept from criticizing him to my wife, or even in my mind. Two or three times I was tempted to pray, "Lord, please don't let John get mixed up with the likes of him!" But I didn't.

Three months later the college's student leadership invited me to speak during a chapel service. As part of the program that day, the student body had chosen a boy and a girl to give their testimonies because of their outstanding Christian witnesses on campus.

Can you guess who the boy was? The free spirit from Colorado. Sitting on the platform listening to his testimony I was grateful I did not have to repent of false judgment.

Both of these incidents have helped me quit judging others by their outer appearances. Wearing an earring or long hair has little or nothing to do with the inner state of the spirit.

What did I advise Gene to do about *his* son's earring?

"Go home and tell your son what you just told me about your tattoo," I suggested. "And ask his forgiveness for your anger. Forget the earring."

Drawing Lines for the Wrong Reasons

Our experiences with our children gave us lots of opportunities to make mistakes in the area of drawing lines. Fear of what was going on in our world and of how it would affect them, and advice from too many books and seminars on how to raise godly children, caused us to draw too-tight boundary lines for behavior, dress and moral matters. We tried to guard them from evil with fences, forgetting that unless the Lord guards a home, we labor in vain who guard it (to paraphrase Psalm 127:1). I needed to learn that our responsibility is not to raise godly children, but to be godly parents.

Sure, as parents we have the "right" to draw lines wherever we want to: "This is our house and we are paying the bills!" Sound familiar?

Two cautions are in order, here. First, lines drawn too tightly and for superficial reasons like "What will our friends at church think?" often backfire, driving our children away from us, our values and, often, from God.

Remember, our children get their pictures of God from us. Quite frankly, they do not want a God like the frowning, disapproving spoilsport we have often projected! God sees a child's heart and knows that when it is committed to Him, all these peripheral issues will eventually fall into place.

Second, we must be careful not to judge others, especially for behaviors we consider "un-Christian," which, in reality, have little to do with a person's relationship to God. The Bible says, "Do not judge, lest you be judged yourselves. For in the way you judge, you will be judged; and by your standard of measure, it shall be measured to you" (Matthew 7:1–2). Children have an amazing ability to see right through us to all the hypocrisies and inconsistencies in our own lives, such as:

- preaching at them about bad movies while we watch questionable television programs at home;
- preaching about morals while we practice little deceits over the phone and with people who come to our doors;
- acting and talking one way in public and another way in private.

I know you are thinking, *What are Christian parents supposed to do? We have to have rules.*

You are right. We have to have rules, lines drawn to help us train the children God has given us. But we need to make sure we draw them in the right places and over the issues that count.

Understanding Root Causes

It helps to understand the root causes for the kinds of behaviors that are important to young people and bothersome to adults.

Why, for example, did John choose to wear an earring? I do not know for sure, but I would not hesitate to suggest that, since many young men are now wearing earrings, the root cause was peer pressure.

I remember why I started smoking in high school. Smoking was a symbol of manhood, a means of acceptance. In my mind smoking was something I had to do to be accepted by my peers.

It is easy to forget, as we deal with our children and other young people, what we were like and what we did when we were young. Styles and trends may change from generation to generation, but peer pressure remains the same.

We need to remember what the pull of peer pressure felt like. In fact, we need to recognize the pull it has on us now. Such recollections will help us be more sympathetic and understanding with our children, and will help us to draw lines in the right places and over meaningful, not superficial, issues.

Another root cause of what we might consider outrageous behavior or dress may indeed be a child's need to assert his or her independence by choosing to do something forbidden. Dr. Floyd MacCallum, whose psychology lectures influenced hundreds of students at Christian colleges during the '60s and '70s, used to discuss this need, and how he and his wife allowed for it in their children's lives.

Noting that a prime symbol of rebellion during his son's teenage years was hair length and style, and knowing that his son was needing a "cause" over which to "rebel," Dr. MacCallum explained that he gave the boy the privilege of choosing his own hairstyle when he reached the age of thirteen. Now, while Dr. MacCallum didn't *like* the long, somewhat unkempt look so popular at the time, he was wise enough to know that hairstyle had nothing to do with his son's inner state. It was also a fairly harmless mode of rebellion, posing no dangers to the child or to anyone else. So when his son came home with "the look," Dr. MacCallum and his wife gave him just enough static so the boy knew he was not pleasing his parents (and therefore was asserting his independence), but not enough to drive him away or provoke him: "Well, we're not crazy about it, but if that's the way you want to look, I guess you're old enough to make that decision."

What a wise father! He allowed the boy to let off some of the pressure for personal expression that builds up in adolescence, but contained the behavior within bounds he, as a parent, knew were safe and tolerable.

When we ceased to draw lines with John over things like earrings and tobacco we had a much easier time relating to him. We could accept him and not reject him. We could trust God to deal with John in His own time and His own way. This is exactly what has happened.

Where and How to Draw Lines

Yes, we have to draw lines. But God alone can show us where, and even more importantly, how to do so. He can also give us the right attitudes with which to draw them.

Here are some suggestions.

1. Always, always ask God for guidance on where to draw the lines. He knows which issues "count" for which child, and which don't. He cares about your children and will gladly give you His wisdom.

2. Never make rules with the premise "This is what good Christians do." In the first place, if your children are not walking with God they have no reason to act like Christians anyway, so such reasoning will not motivate them. In fact, it will probably turn them off by promoting an inaccurate and unattractive picture of God.

In the second place, in most of the behavioral issues about which we are talking, the premise is simply not true. The Bible offers clear moral guidelines, but on issues of cultural customs, apparel and conformity we need God's specific directions.

3. Avoid accusations about the motives for your children's behavior.   My friend Gene made the mistake of accusing his son of piercing his ear out of rebellion. He was judging his son's motives. Judging is wrong; judging *motives* is worse. We can't discern motives without the guidance of the Holy Spirit, and even then we are not to use our knowledge to accuse or condemn, but to intercede for our children before the Father.

4. Never draw a line out of fear.   Fear causes us to react, not to respond out of our Christian value system. Draw lines regarding a particular issue only after going to God for guidance and acting in cooperation with Him. If we have received a word of faith for a child, we can trust Him to protect that child from irreparable damage.

5. Never draw a line out of pride.   Forget what other people might say about you. Otherwise, you will be guilty of caving in to the same peer pressure you warn your children about. Your child's life and spiritual well-being are much more important than the approval of others.

6. Never draw a line when you are angry.   The anger of man does not achieve the righteousness of God (James 1:20). It is possible to draw the right line in the wrong way, and "blow" the whole issue. Go to God *first*, for guidance and an attitude adjustment. Drawing a line for the right reason and in the right spirit can in the long run communicate love, not confrontation.

7. Draw the lines as far apart, as wide as you can.
Don't drive your child away over issues that do not
matter. The enemy will delight to use our rules, drawn
according to our own understanding, not God's (Proverbs 3:5–6), to make our children see Christianity as a
set of do's and don't's.

**8. Remember that as your children get older you will
in all probability need to expand the lines.** Again,
only the Holy Spirit can give you specific direction in
this area.

To conclude, we must operate constantly in faith if we
are going to draw fair and clear lines. And faith comes
from hearing a word from God. He may use a friend or
writer or speaker to give us wisdom, but we need first
to be open to hearing from Him about each of our parenting situations. When we have His word, then we can
draw lines with the confidence that He will help us
uphold them.

16

Letting Them Go— and Letting God Take Over

The process—receiving the word of faith, learning through the walk of faith, cooperating with God in the work of faith, enduring the wait of faith and rejoicing in the fulfillment of faith—may take one year for one child, and thirty years for another. But praise God! "Faithful is He who calls you, and He also will bring it to pass" (1 Thessalonians 5:24). God always makes good on His promissory notes, and when He does, He adds exorbitant interest: blessings beyond our wildest dreams.

"Letting go" is not only a godly pattern for parenting; it also should be a hallmark of the entire process. By letting go I mean relinquishing our children to God and His purposes. Oh, we may say piously, "Our children are only 'on loan' from God." But do we mean it? Or do we clutch them to ourselves like possessions? Are we really willing to relate so intimately to our loving Father God that we can release our children to His work in their lives, and hold tight *only to Him* as we cooperate in the process?

God was willing to let His Child leave the glory of heaven, which was His by rights, to enter our sinful world and accomplish God's work in our lives. And if we think it didn't hurt God to watch Jesus go through all the pains and sorrows of human maturing and then to suffer Calvary, we know little of the depths of His Fatherhood.

But He's God! you say. He is all-powerful and, besides, He knew everything that was going to happen.

This is certainly true. He *is* God, He *is* all-powerful and He *does* know the end from the beginning. But this offers all the more reason why we should entrust Him with our cherished offspring. Just as He let go of His Son for the fulfillment of His perfect purposes, so godly parents must learn to relinquish their children into the loving arms of their heavenly Father.

God spoke to Johnnie along these lines even before Richard left Him. Her experience is so applicable to our needs that I have asked her to share it in her own words.

Johnnie Speaks

There was a big lump in my throat one summer day in 1970 as we waved goodbye to Richard and his friend Joe. They had just been graduated from high school. Now they were headed to California with their surfboards strapped atop Richard's old car. Their destination was Campus Crusade's six-week Intensive Bible Study, but we all knew that was just the ticket to get them to California where things were "happening."

The next morning as I prayed for Richard I felt like an old mother hen wanting to cover him with my wings for protection from all danger. I sat in my room and thought about every bad thing that could possibly happen as he and Joe traveled, and I asked God to protect them from each one.

Then I stretched my imagination further to include protection from all the evils we were hearing about surfers on the beaches in California in those early days of the drug scene. I tucked him under my wings a little tighter as I continued this procedure.

Finally I exhausted my list of bad things from which Richard (and Joe) needed protection. As I strained my mind to be sure there was nothing else, our dear Father said, *Johnnie, if I do all you want Me to do for Richard, I'll never be able to do what I want to do for him.*

What a shock! Didn't God want to be sure my son never had any problems? That's what I wanted.

Yet I knew God well enough to understand in my heart that God loved him even more than I did. Perplexed, I realized I had to decide if I could really entrust my precious son to God's hands if His thinking was so different from mine.

Slowly I began to recount how, time after time, God's loving way had proved to be so much better than anything we could ever have figured for ourselves. When we had stepped out on His Word, He had faithfully gone beyond our limited thoughts on a matter. But could He be trusted to know better than my mother's heart?

I remembered how we had given Richard to the Lord before he was even born. During his years in the home I had felt a keen sense of responsibility to be a good steward for the Lord in caring for our son. Somehow God was letting me know that from now on things were going to be different. I saw that as our children entered new stages of life our "giving them to the Lord" had to be extended to include that stage, too.

After all, I could see the alternatives God was showing me. I could either release my child totally into His all-wise care and His loving hands, or try desperately to figure with my finite mind what was best, and then ask God to do it!

Not without apprehension I hesitantly but deliberately went around Richard's life and clipped each string, releasing him in a brand-new way to our heavenly Father, so He could work as He needed to accomplish His plan. When the transaction was completed, God's wonderful peace began to move into my heart. There had been no room for it as long as my heart was full of fear!

Only God Himself knew how important that encounter with Him would be for me in the days to come. He knew Richard was going to be making some bad decisions in the near future, but He also knew He was free, now, to work them for good in our son's life.

Since then, it has been a deliberate, definite choice to let each of our children go. I could never have done it if I had not seen it as releasing them into God's hands, realizing that the direction of their lives was up to God from that point on. I continue to have to remind myself that my part now is to trust God and them. This requires a new thought pattern regarding our relationships, a pattern that must unfold on a choice-by-choice, situation-by-situation basis.

Praise God for His faithfulness! Four out of five of our children have found God's slots for their lives, and we believe the youngest, now in college, will do the same. Four out of five of our children have found God's special partner for life. Each one is perfect: I could never have chosen as well as our heavenly Father did. And what wonderful grandchildren they have produced!

Truly, we can trust Him to know best for our children.

The process of rearing each of our children may be short and it may be long—but God is faithful. The patterns He gives us to use in the parenting process are reliable and workable. And seeking to conform to His parenting image not only draws us closer to Him, but fits us to serve Him better in other realms of life, as well.

How we need to grasp both the greatness and the practicality of God's Fatherhood! When he "setteth the solitary in families" (Psalm 68:6, KJV), He knew what He was doing.

Peter Lord is the author of many books including *Hearing God*, *Soul Care*, and *The 2959 Prayer Plan*. A former pastor, he is now a popular conference speaker and prayer seminar leader.